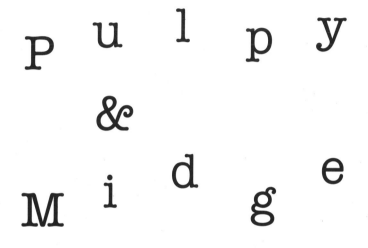

pulpy & Midge

a novel by
Jessica Westhead

Coach House Books, Toronto

Canada Council   Conseil des Arts   ONTARIO ARTS COUNCIL   Canadä
for the Arts   du Canada   CONSEIL DES ARTS DE L'ONTARIO

Published with the generous assistance of the Canada Council for
the Arts and the Ontario Arts Council. Coach House also acknowl-
edges the support of the Government of Ontario through the
Ontario Book Publishing Tax Credit Program and the Government
of Canada through the Book Publishing Industry Development
Program.

LIBRARY AND ARCHIVES CANADA

Westhead, Jessica, 1974-
    Pulpy and Midge / Jessica Westhead.

ISBN 978-1-55245-185-4

    I. Title.

PS8645.E85P84 2007   C813'.6   C2007-905510-9

for Derek

ONE

On the day of his boss's retirement party, Pulpy Lembeck took a taxi to work.

When he got out he thanked the driver and gave him a two-dollar tip, well over the one-dollar tip he and Midge usually gave taxi drivers, which wasn't very often because normally they took the bus.

'Cheers, bud,' said the driver, who seemed like the kind of man Pulpy would've gone out with for a beer if he went out for beer with men, which he didn't. He and Midge mostly stayed in, just the two of them.

Pulpy walked into the welcome area of his office and said 'Good morning' to the receptionist.

'Uh huh.' She nodded without looking at him.

'Cold out there.' He stamped his boots on the bristly welcome mat.

She glanced up from the stack of paper she was hole-punching. 'It's winter.'

'You're right about *that*!' Pulpy opened the closet to hang up his coat, and frowned a little when he saw that it was full.

There was a new coat in there, a shearling one that was taking up a lot of room.

'Did you sign Al's card yet?' said the receptionist. 'There's a card going around that I picked out. It's got a mountain on it, with sunlight. It says "Happy Retirement."'

'I have to think of something to write.' Pulpy folded his own coat in half and laid it on the floor of the closet, near the back. 'It's a great card.'

'Yeah, I'm good at picking them. The trick is finding the balance between thoughtful and sentimental. It's like when you're doing a cake.' She fitted another sheaf of documents into the punch and banged her fist down. 'There's a fine line between sweet and too sweet.'

He shut the closet door and smiled at her. 'How was your weekend?'

'It's Friday.'

'Right! You're right. I just couldn't remember if I asked you what you did – did I ask you?'

'I went to the winter fair. Does that sound familiar?'

'No.' He squinted and rubbed his chin. 'No. I don't think you told me about that. So I guess I didn't ask you.'

'I guess not.'

'Sounds like fun. The winter fair. My wife and I are going there this weekend.'

'I went with my boyfriend and he played the fish game but he lost, so I didn't get a fish.'

'Those fish games can be hard.'

She twisted her mouth at him. 'What do you know about fish games?'

Pulpy shrugged. 'Not much. Just that they're hard. It's all about luck.'

'It's not about luck, it's about skill. He spent a bunch of money on a bunch of tries but he didn't win. He lost. He's a loser.' She brushed some stray hole-punch confetti onto the floor.

Pulpy watched her fingers flutter over the shower of small paper dots. 'Where'd you get the retirement cake?'

'There is no cake.' She reached for a box of elastic bands. 'Al hasn't asked me to get one yet. He's cutting it close if he wants something good – if I don't go soon all they'll have left is the remainder cakes. And you have to give advance notice if you want a personal message iced on. People don't think about these things.'

'Cutting it close, ha,' said Pulpy. The receptionist looked at him, and he cleared his throat. 'What do you know about the new guy who's coming in – anything?'

'Just that he's somebody from a big building.' She pulled out an elastic band and started stretching it. 'That's all I can tell you.'

He puffed out his cheeks and slowly let the air go. 'I guess it's going to be different.'

'Al's leaving, I'm staying. That's about it. And it's about time he retired. The other day he's standing here, waiting for me to do something for him, and he looks at my international garden calendar. And he looks at this month's garden and says, "Is that your garden?" And I say to him, "No, that's a calendar with pictures of gardens in it." And he says, "Oh. Well, it's a really nice garden." And I say, "That's why it's in the calendar." But he still kept on about how much he liked my garden.'

Pulpy blinked at the bright rows of flowers for February, growing someplace warm in the world. 'I'm sure he was just trying to be polite.'

'Do you really think that?' She snapped the elastic band across the room. 'I don't know.'

On the way to his cubicle, Pulpy stopped outside his boss's office and peeked in.

Al was at his desk playing with his animal figurines, which had come from his garden at home. 'The wife wondered where all her nature statuettes went to, so I had to go out and buy her new ones,' he'd said to Pulpy when he first brought them in. 'I like them. They give my office a fresh, outdoorsy feel.'

Pulpy liked them too. He stood there in what he hoped was a casual way, watching while Al pranced his miniature deer up and over his in-tray.

Finally, Al looked up. 'Pulpy! There you are. Can I see you a minute?'

Pulpy smiled and said, 'You certainly can!'

He walked into Al's office thinking about taking Midge out for dinner that night to celebrate. They could go to that fancy surf-and-turf under the hotel. Neither of them ate fish but it was the most expensive restaurant in the area. They could get steak. Or chicken stuffed with something.

'Have a seat.' Al nodded at the old couch in front of his desk. 'You coming to my thing?'

Pulpy sat. 'Yes.'

'Good.' Al put down his deer and picked up his camel, and toyed with its hump. 'Will Midge be there?'

Pulpy made an apologetic face. Weeks ago, on their way home from Couples Ice Dance Expression, he'd asked Midge if she wanted to come.

'Oh, Pulpy,' she'd said, flushed from the laps they'd done around the rink, 'I wish I could. But I think I'd see Mrs. Wings everywhere, and that would just be too much for me.'

'I miss her too,' he'd said, and she'd kissed him.

'I don't think Midge can make it,' Pulpy told his boss.

'Well, that's understandable.' Al was wearing a shirt with little acorns all over it.

'Those are nice acorns,' said Pulpy.

'Huh?' he said and looked down. 'Oh, yeah. The wife picked it out. You know wives.' Al pointed the camel at him. 'Keep up the good work, Pulpy. Because good work is what you do, and I want you to know I recognize that. As a matter of fact, it's high time I showed you that recognition.'

Pulpy leaned forward. 'It is?'

'Anybody home?' A large, rectangular head poked around the doorway then, grinning big teeth at them.

'Dan!' said Al. 'Come on in!'

Pulpy looked up at the tall man who'd just stepped into his boss's office, with his broad shoulders and expensive suit.

'Pulpy, this is Dan.' Al spread his arms wide, and then romped the camel across his desk. 'All of this will be his on Monday.'

'All of what?' Dan extended his huge hand to Pulpy. 'I told him, he better take that couch when he goes! I'm bringing in chairs. I've got chairs that will put that couch to shame.'

Pulpy moved his own, less impressive hand up to be shaken. 'Nice to meet you, Dan.' He winced as the other man compressed the soft meat of his fingers.

'Pulpy, eh?' said Dan. 'What is that, a nickname?'

'He drank a lot of orange juice in college,' said Al.

'Ho-ho!' said Dan. He winked at Pulpy. 'Didn't we all!'

Pulpy didn't know what to say to that.

'Dan and his wife are new in town,' said Al. 'They just moved in.'

'Fresh on the scene!' said Dan.

'Well, then, Dan and I have a few things to talk about, Pulpy, so if you'll excuse us –'

'Oh. Sure.' Pulpy stood up, and Dan sat down.

Dan shifted around on the couch. 'How do people *sit* on this thing? Nice meeting you, Pulpy!'

'Thanks,' said Pulpy. 'You too.'

'Orange juice, ha!'

'Ha.' Pulpy's knuckles still hurt from the handshake, but he waited until he reached his cubicle to massage them.

Pulpy sat at his desk and spread his hands out on his blotter. 'Blot,' he said in a quiet voice.

He looked at the few fair hairs on his fingers and wished there were more of them. He pulled out his keyboard tray and felt the bottom of it graze the tops of his thighs. He decided again to call Building Maintenance to ask them to fix that.

Pulpy pushed the keyboard tray back in, a little harder than he needed to.

Pulpy Lembeck had once been Brian Lembeck. He'd gotten the nickname in college, during lunch in the cafeteria. As he brought a glass of orange juice to his lips, some smart aleck said loudly, 'So you like orange juice, hey, Pulpy?'

The rest of the table looked at Brian, and he shrugged. His silence apparently signalled his agreement, and the name Pulpy stuck fast. Pulpy didn't mind – it gave him a story to tell.

The receptionist's workstation was in the middle of the welcome area, with the white spiral staircase to her right. To her left were the communal photocopier and paper shredder, and the hall to the staff washrooms and then the staff kitchen, which contained a fridge, a microwave, a toaster, a bulletin board, and a table and two chairs.

The receptionist scrutinized Pulpy through her glasses as he came down the steps at lunchtime. 'Going to lunch?'

He nodded.

'What's the weather like out now?'

'I'm not sure,' he said.

'You're not *sure*?'

'I just came from upstairs.'

'You have windows up there, don't you?'

Pulpy glanced at the big window by the front door. 'You're right,' he said. 'We do.'

She wheeled her chair backward, gripping the edge of her desk with one hand. 'I'm going to take a course.'

'What kind of course?' He opened the closet door and peered inside. There were other coats on top of his coat now, so he was going to have to dig.

'It's a performance-improvement seminar. The flyer came over the fax, with the registration form on it. I can sign up any time – it says spaces aren't limited. Al said I could go. But not because I need to improve my performance. Just to expand my knowledge base.'

'That makes sense.' He crouched down to sift through the heavy pile of leather and wool. 'When is it?'

'It's in two weeks. It's called "Be An Exceptional Reception-ist." The flyer says, "Receptionists today must be eager envoys for their workplace." And that's very true. "Front-line staff" is what they call people like me, who deal with the public. I am the face of this company.'

He stood up with his wrinkled coat and nodded. The recep-tionist had told him her name a few years ago but he'd forgot-ten it, and he couldn't bring himself to ask her again. The small, brass nameplate on her desk said 'Secretary.' But she didn't like that term.

'See here.' She showed him the flyer, a smudgy fax page full of bullet points.

Pulpy's eyes went to the registration part at the bottom, but she hadn't filled in her personal information yet.

'It talks about creating a "Samaritan pretense" that wins people over as soon as you meet them, and it says the course will emphasize the potency of positive diction, or how to say "no way" with an "okay."' She folded the paper neatly and tucked it into one of her drawers.

Pulpy watched the receptionist's hair while she did this; it didn't move. He liked the bushiness of it. She'd secured it at the top with a sharp-toothed metal clip. 'Sounds good,' he said, and headed for the door.

'It certainly does.' The receptionist crossed her arms. 'Two weeks.'

'How was the cab ride?' said Midge when Pulpy called her from the food court.

'It was okay, but I don't think it did any good.' His fingers skimmed over the number pad on the pay phone. 'Al didn't even mention the promotion this morning.'

'He didn't? Well, there's still the whole afternoon, isn't there?'

'There is. He's got his thing this afternoon, though.' Pulpy expelled a long breath. 'I think maybe he forgot.'

'Oh, Pulpy,' said Midge. 'How could he forget?'

'I don't know, he was busy. He was meeting with the new boss. I met him too – I shook his hand.'

'Did you shake it hard? Powerful men like a firm hand-shake.'

'I think so, but he shook mine harder. Anyway, I'm going to pick up doughnuts for the thing. Maybe when Al sees the doughnuts he'll remember about the promotion.'

'Maybe Al will tell the new boss to give it to you.'

'Hmm,' said Pulpy. 'He *was* telling him something.'

'See, there you go!'

He relaxed a little. 'How far did you get on your route?'

'I did about fifty leaflets, and that's with Jean's selective targeting method. She calls it looking for the best *candle-date*, ha! Like candidate, but with candles! She's a funny one, that Jean.' She paused. 'You know what would be fun?'

'Tell me,' he said.

'A hobby! One that we could do together.'

Pulpy had the metal pay-phone cord in his hand, and he bent part of it into a U-shape. He held it like that and squeezed it together a few times. 'We've got ice dancing.'

'Ice dancing isn't a hobby, it's exercise. I was thinking something musical, because you used to like music so much.'

'That was then,' he said.

'Oh, hush. I want to see more of that side of you. Your creative side.'

'I don't have a creative side.'

She giggled. 'Tell that to the bedsheets!'

'Midge!' But he smiled.

'Then I got thinking about those keyboards that already have music programmed in. They're very smart, the keyboards today. They're very intuitive machines. We could play backup to a song!'

'Keyboards cost a lot of money, Midge.'

'Not when they're on sale! I've been scanning the flyers and I found one that's very reasonably priced. I picked it up because they said supplies were limited. Listen!'

Pulpy pressed the hard circle of the receiver against his ear and heard *Plink! Plink! Plink!*

'Hold on,' she said. 'It gets better.'

When he got back to the office, the receptionist said to him, 'You notice anything missing from my desk?'

'Um ...' Pulpy looked at her mug, her eraser dish, her magnetized paperclip holder, her tape dispenser, her pen-and-pencil cage, her hole punch and her stapler.

'Water,' she said.

He glanced from side to side. 'You don't have any.'

'That's right. Receptionists can't drink water because do you know why? Because we can't leave our desks, that's why!' She leaned forward. 'The flyer for my performance-improvement seminar says, "A little hydration goes the distance." Think about that when you think about all of us dehydrated receptionists.'

'All right,' he said.

'Tea doesn't count, though,' she said, and took a loud slurp from her mug, which showed a cartoon duck dressed like a secretary. It had drops of sweat flying from its head and was wearing glasses that were comically askew. In its wings the duck held a pencil, a phone off the hook and several loose documents in disarray. The caption underneath read 'Not another crisis ... my schedule's full!!!' She wielded the mug at him. 'I can relate. When it comes down to it, it's just me and the duck,' she said, 'against the office. How was your lunch?'

'It was nice, thanks.'

'Well, mine wasn't. I was sitting reading my book at the kitchen table, and then Cheryl from Active Recovery comes over and says, "Do you mind if I sit here? Don't let me interrupt you." And she *sat down*.'

'Cheryl's nice.'

'Nice. She put me on the spot. "Don't let me interrupt you," she says. What does she think I'm going to do, sit there and read while she eats her lunch? I hate that there's two chairs. If there was only one chair there would be no problem.'

'It's a big table.'

'Not big enough,' she said.

'So that ought to do it,' said the man from Building Maintenance that afternoon. He stood up and put his hands on his thick hips.

Pulpy sat in his chair and pulled himself toward his desk. He slid out the newly adjusted keyboard tray. 'It's still doing it,' he said. 'The bottom of the tray. I can still feel it on my legs.'

'Huh.' The man pulled the front of his shirt away from the roll on top of his jeans.

'That's why I called Building Maintenance. That's why I placed the call.'

'Relax, fellow, relax. Let's see what we're dealing with here.' The man got on his knees again and crawled under the desk to examine the tray-docking device. 'Oh yeah, I see it. Now I see it.'

'They let you wear jeans?' said Pulpy.

'Uh huh. At the start we had to wear suit pants, but then I said to Al – I was the one who said it – "I'm not getting down under desks and wearing suit pants because do you know what it's like under there? It's dusty as hell down there. Unless," I said, "you want to buy the suit pants *for* me." That shut him up like a clam. So now we wear jeans.'

The man's rear end wiggled as he worked. Pulpy looked away.

'That ought to do it.' The man stood up again. 'Give her a go.'

Pulpy got back into his chair, and something on the man beeped. Pulpy jumped a little.

The man from Building Maintenance glanced down at his pager, then back at Pulpy. 'That's me. Mind if I use your phone?'

'Go ahead.' Pulpy pulled out the keyboard tray and the man picked up his phone. Pulpy frowned. The tray was lower now.

'Yeah?' said the man into the receiver. 'It's Davis here.'

He pushed his knees up and the tray rattled and clicked. He put his knees down and felt the edges of the tray pressing hard against his thighs.

'It's Davis, I said. Yeah.'

'Um,' said Pulpy.

'So what's the call? Who's calling?'

Pulpy tried to get his hands in between his legs and the keyboard but there wasn't enough room.

'Over there? What's their problem? Do you even know who you paged? You paged me, and I'm Davis.'

'You did it the wrong way,' said Pulpy.

Davis didn't acknowledge this. 'Okay,' he said into the phone, 'so you do have the right guy, because that's me. There's also Richards, but he's off today. I'm the one who's on, and I'm Davis.'

Pulpy sighed and sat there with the tray on his legs.

'Yeah. Yeah. I'm on my way.' Davis put the phone down. 'So you're all set here, then?'

'Well, actually –'

'Do you know what they said on the other end there? They didn't even know –' Davis shook his head. 'People are ignorant. They don't even know who they're calling when they call. I had to tell them, can you beat that?' He hitched up his jeans and headed for the door.

'So –' said Pulpy.

'It was good meeting you, fellow,' said Davis. 'You need that tray looked at again, you just give me a buzz. You know where I live.' And he winked.

'I guess I do, yes.'

Davis gave Pulpy a quick salute, and then he was gone.

Pulpy looked at the empty space where the man from Building Maintenance had been standing, and he pushed the tray back in again.

Pulpy went to the Coffee Island on his break.

'Hi,' he said to the girl behind the counter. 'Roco-Coco, please, and a dozen doughnuts.'

'Sorry, we're all out of the R-C.' She shoved aside the leaves of the inflatable palm tree by the cash register. 'That's always the first kind to go. Every morning. I told my boss, "Buy more Roco-Coco. They all like that kind." But he keeps on buying the same stock every month. He doesn't listen to me.'

'But you're the one dealing with the public,' said Pulpy. 'You're the front-line staff.'

'Exactly! *You* know what I'm talking about.' She shook her head and her ponytail flew. 'I can do you a Bongo Berry, how does that sound?'

'Sounds good.' He watched her manoeuvre around the palm tree to pour his coffee and pack his doughnuts. 'Why don't you move that tree somewhere else?'

'I tried. He moved it back. Bosses – what can you do? That'll be six-seventy, please.'

'You said it.' Pulpy handed her the money. 'Bosses.'

'What about them?' said a voice behind Pulpy.

'Uh-oh,' said the counter girl.

Pulpy turned to see Dan waving at him from the cream and sugar.

There was the cream-and-sugar side, or the milk-and-sweetener side, which was where you ended up if you weren't fast enough. Pulpy was never fast enough.

He watched Dan wielding the carton of half-and-half amid the throng of clerical staff that always encircled the coffee fixings, their shoulders working as they stirred.

Dan emerged with his mug held high. He was wearing the bulky shearling coat Pulpy had seen in the closet earlier. 'Whew! You gotta be a bull in there!' he said, jerking his rectangle head back at the circle.

Pulpy gave a half-shrug and looked down at the dark liquid in his Styrofoam cup, already turning cold.

'You should get yourself a proper mug,' said Dan. 'Bulls need real mugs.'

'I guess they do.' Pulpy found himself nodding.

Dan's mug was red with white lettering. 'Back off – it's early,' the mug said. Pulpy wondered if he drank out of that mug all day. 'The mug makes the man,' said Dan. 'Think about that.'

'I'll bring one from home one of these days,' said Pulpy.

'Just take one from the staff cupboard. Make it your own.'

'But what if it's somebody else's?'

'Whoa now. Bulls don't think that way, do they?' Dan took a sip of coffee and swallowed hard. 'The secretary even has her own mug. If *she* has a mug, *you* should have a mug.'

Pulpy noticed the single crease down the front of each of Dan's pant legs, how crisp that was. He looked down at his own pleats. Not so crisp.

'I'm bringing in my wife, Beatrice, to keep an eye on that secretary. See how she does things. I want you to meet her, my wife. She'll be there this afternoon.'

'She sounds nice.'

'Oh, she's nice all right.' Dan nodded at Pulpy's dough-nuts. 'Those for the thing?'

'Yes.'

'Nice. You married?'

'Yes.'

'You bringing her?'

Pulpy swirled his black coffee. 'She's not feeling well.'

'That's too bad.' Dan took a slow sip from his mug. 'I'll see you back at the office.' He nodded at the coffee fixings on his way out the door. 'Now get in there!'

'So I have to tell you that, oh boy yes, this has certainly been a really good experience for me, being in this place with all of you.' Al smiled at Pulpy and his fellow employees from the podium at the far end of the boardroom.

A few paces to Al's right, Dan smoothed the arms of his suit.

Pulpy was standing at the back, near the doors and the food table. His box of doughnuts had been placed next to the vast expanse of 'Happy Retirement Al!' cake and a large bowl containing bottles of water and juice.

'But heck, that doesn't mean I should have to *work* here, does it? Ha!'

Everyone in the room laughed, except for Dan. Then he gave a belated 'Ho-ho!' that reverberated after the other laughs had died away.

'The way I see it, everyone's too focused on business and spending these days,' said Al. 'And all these people are watching this reality TV, but I'm at the point where I'm ready for my *own* reality, you know?' He blinked at the assembled workers.

Someone near the back shouted, 'We love you, Al!'

'Well.' Al's smile widened. 'I'm going to miss all of you, very much.'

There were a few scattered 'Awws,' and then Al had to raise his voice as the room burst into applause. 'But business and spending are still the reality at *this* office, and now with Dan here at the helm there's no telling how far you'll go!'

'We're going to pick up where you left off, Al, that's what we're going to do!' Dan stepped over and put an arm around Al's shoulders, and the room fell silent. 'Hello, everyone, I'm Dan. And let me be the first to reassure you all that although I may be new in town, I am certainly not new as far as knowing what my responsibilities are, and where they lie.'

'Psst, Pulpy, over here.'

Pulpy turned his head, and Roy from Customer Service handed him a piece of cake on a small paper plate. Pulpy mouthed 'Thank you' and took it before he realized that the usual time for cake cutting and distributing was after the speeches, and that Roy probably wasn't supposed to be doing this now.

'I also like to help,' said Dan. 'I did a lot of helping at my previous job, and as a result I made some really good friends there and we still communicate. Workplace camaraderie is key. It's key to everything.'

Pulpy's piece of cake appeared to be chocolate with some type of nuts in it. He'd gotten the exclamation mark on his frosting.

Roy was handing out forks now. Pulpy debated accepting his.

'I used to work in a building that had mirrored glass. Mirrored glass, and a lot of floors. And windows everywhere.' Dan was alone at the podium now – Al had moved away.

'Pulpy?' said Roy.

'Oh,' Pulpy whispered. 'Thanks.' He took the fork.

'I would look out those windows and think, "There's a whole world out there." And then I'd think, "Hey, there's a whole world *in here*." And that is what we're all about.'

All around him, Pulpy's co-workers were eating. He speared a hunk of cake and brought it to his lips.

'Just a side note – I'm sure you've all seen the refreshments on the back table,' said Dan, and Pulpy raised a hand to cover his bulging cheeks. 'There will be cake, and drinks, and doughnuts, after we're done up here. But first I'd like to say a little something about teamwork and mutual respect.'

Pulpy ducked behind the crowd to finish chewing.

Dan's speech went on for another half-hour, and when it was over Pulpy headed for the men's room. On his way there he passed the receptionist at her desk, stapling.

'Why aren't you in the boardroom?' he asked her. 'There's cake.'

'Hold on,' she said. 'I'm collating here.'

He waited while she stapled two sets of papers together, and then she looked up at him. 'I wasn't invited. That was my first introduction to the new boss. "Hi, I'm Dan, your new supervisor. Oh, and by the way, we need you to cover the desk during the retirement function." Yeah, thanks. Plus I'm supposed to know when they're doing a cake, because I always pick them out. What kind is it? Is there any filling?'

'It's a chocolate one,' he said. 'I think it has hazelnuts in it.'

'Nuts aren't a filling.'

'Well, they're inside somewhere. I heard.'

'A filling is like cream. Or jelly. Is there jelly?'

Pulpy shook his head. 'No one said anything about jelly.'

The receptionist frowned. 'I'm supposed to know when they do a cake.'

'I'm sure it was some kind of oversight.'

'Yeah.' The receptionist resumed her stapling. 'I'm sure it was.'

Pulpy nodded and hurried down the hall, his tongue digging at a bit of hazelnut in one of his molars.

'Pulpy, this is my wife, Beatrice,' said Dan at the party that followed the speeches. The party was also in the boardroom, except there were balloons now.

'Hi, Beatrice.' Pulpy shook Dan's wife's hand and her long fingernails jabbed into his palm. She was wearing a sleeveless top covered in buckles that seemed to have no practical purpose.

'Hi ... Pulpy?' Beatrice had dark, chin-length hair that was mostly straight, with a few strands jutting out in various directions. The effect unsettled him.

'It's a nickname,' said Dan. 'Isn't it great?'

'What does it mean?' she said, and at the same time she looked Pulpy up and down, starting at his feet.

Pulpy's hands flattened out and he pressed them to his sides. No one had ever looked him up and down like that before. 'It's to do with orange juice.'

'Ah.' Beatrice nodded, still looking.

'How'd you like my speech, Pulpy?' said Dan.

'Oh, fine. It was a fine speech.'

'People were already eating the cake, can you believe that? They'd eaten half of it before Al walked over with the special knife.' Dan frowned. 'I said they'd get cake. I said they'd get it at the end.'

'It was a delicious cake,' said Pulpy. 'I heard.'

'Beatrice picked it out. She knows how to pick a winner, ha!'

Beatrice rolled her eyes. She pointed her doughnut at Pulpy. 'These are *really* good. Dan says you brought them?'

'Oh, well, it's nothing. They're just doughnuts.'

'Mmm. Well, they are *yummy*.' She licked some powdered sugar off her bottom lip and popped the last bite into her mouth.

Pulpy's eyes widened a little and he quickly turned to admire the shiny red 'You Made It!!' balloons taped up in the corners of the boardroom. Then he took a deep breath and looked back at Dan. 'I don't think the receptionist got an invitation to this.'

'That's the way it goes,' said Dan. 'Somebody has to cover the desk.'

'Maybe she didn't want to come,' said Beatrice.

'But she should've been invited,' said Pulpy.

'Must've been an oversight.' Dan shrugged. 'I told you I'm bringing Beatrice in, didn't I?'

'We'll get things sorted out,' said Beatrice.

'We're doing an overhaul,' said Dan. 'I like the way that sounds.'

Pulpy noticed that one of Dan's big square hands was clamped around a plastic water bottle and his other hand was just opening and closing around nothing. 'Overhaul?'

Beatrice made a face for him, squishing out her lips and shaking her head.

Dan chuckled. 'Beatrice is calling it a makeover but I'm going with overhaul. Overhaul says everything we need to say.'

'What, uh –' Pulpy's voice hitched, and he swallowed. 'What do you need to say?'

'Hey, there's the man of the hour!' Dan waved across the room to Al, who was kissing his wife under some of the balloons and a banner that read 'Congratulations Al! Relax, Enjoy, Celebrate!'

'Oh, will you look at that,' said Beatrice. 'Old and still in love.'

'Pulpy has a wife,' said Dan.

'Do you now?' Beatrice said to Pulpy. 'Well, just look at you – how could you not?'

'Um,' said Pulpy.

'So what do you say, Pulpy?' said Dan. 'Are you excited about the regime change? Out with the old and all that?'

Pulpy looked at his old boss frolicking under his decorations. He'd written 'Spread your wings and fly!' in Al's retirement card, hoping it would jog his memory, but Al hadn't opened the envelope yet and by the time he did, he wouldn't be in charge anymore. 'In with the new,' he said, and blinked in the glare of Dan and Beatrice's white grins.

When Pulpy got home, Midge had the fireplace video going.

He stood in front of their small TV set and watched the flames dance across the screen, and then Midge was behind him.

'I pulled the space heater up,' she said. 'For added effect.'

Pulpy looked down at their little square heater pushing orange warmth out of its criss-crossed wires.

'It's a new video. I had to buy a new one because the last one was wearing out. Even with the head cleaner.'

'It looks the same,' he said.

'That's the best part! You can't tell.'

'It's a good video.'

Midge took a step back. 'Don't say video.'

'What? But *you* said video.'

'Not once we get into it. Once you get into it you have to pretend.'

He nodded.

'Did you eat? Because I bought this new product – it's a way to make a whole meal all in foil. And then you just throw the foil away afterwards with no fuss and no scrubbing!'

'Sounds good,' said Pulpy, 'but I had a bunch of doughnuts.'

'Sit on the rug with me,' she said. 'I'll play you something.'

They sat on their rug and Midge pulled their new electronic keyboard out from under the coffee table. She frowned down at the array of buttons along the top, then pressed one. A mournful string of notes drifted out of the tinny speaker.

'That's not a very happy song,' he said. 'I usually think of keyboard music as more uplifting.'

'That must be the dirigible. The man at the store said there was one in there. Dirigibles aren't supposed to be happy.'

'I think you mean a dirge,' he said.

'Yes, yes, a dirge. What did I say?'

He smiled. 'You said a dirigible. A dirigible is a boat.'

She flung her hand at him. 'Oh, you music people with your music knowledge.'

'I'm not a music person,' he said. 'I work in an office.'

'If you make music and you're a person, then you're a music person. Here, let me find you something more tinkly.' She ran her thumbs over the keys. 'It played the prettiest ballad earlier.'

'That's okay,' he said. 'I believe you.'

'Look at me, I'm hogging it!' She lifted the keyboard and put it in his lap. 'Go ahead – experiment!'

Pulpy felt the weight of the keyboard on his legs, and thought of Dan, and Dan's wife, who along with Dan was going to do an overhaul. He put the keyboard on the floor. 'I guess I'm just not feeling very musical right now, Midge, I'm sorry.'

'Oh.' She slid the keyboard back under the coffee table. 'Well, that's okay.'

They watched the fire on TV together for a while and then he said, 'Al never said anything.'

Midge moved closer to him. 'Oh, Pulpy.'

Pulpy stared at the embers. He felt tired and soft. 'How could he forget?'

'And the new boss didn't say anything?'

'He said some things, but not about the promotion.'

'Well,' said Midge, 'I bet it's only a matter of time.'

He looked at her hopeful face and imagined he could see the yellow glow reflected there. 'You're warm,' he said, touching her arm.

'It's because of the fire,' she said, and her hands rose up and flickered in the light.

'Hmm,' said Pulpy at the winter fair the next day, 'those fish games look pretty hard.'

Midge put a hand on his back. 'You can do it, Pulpy.'

'I don't want to disappoint you.'

'You won't.'

So Pulpy lined up and paid for his ping-pong balls, and lobbed them.

The first two missed, but the second two landed with tiny splashes in two small fishbowls with rainbow-coloured gravel and startled goldfish inside.

And Midge said, 'You did it, twice!'

Pulpy smiled. 'I did, didn't I?'

She hugged him. 'You can take one to work and I'll keep the other one at home with me. I'm going to call our home fish Mr. Fins.'

They went home after that and when they got in the door Midge said, 'It'll be nice for you to have a fish at your desk. He'll keep you company.' Then she said, 'Now let's make out like banshees.'

'What does that mean?' said Pulpy. And he stood there holding the two fishbowls until Midge took them from him, one by one, and placed them gently on the coffee table.

'It means,' she said, 'that you do things to me and I scream.'

'Well,' he said, 'let's get started, then.'

The next morning Midge said, 'I think you should take my Candle-Brations catalogue to the office with you today.'

'You do?' said Pulpy.

The alarm hadn't gone off yet and they were still lying under the covers, staring at the ceiling. Mr. Fins and Pulpy's fish were side by side in their bowls on Midge's night table, swimming.

'I got thinking last night that this new boss of yours could be a great new opportunity. All you have to do is show him the catalogue, and then he'll tell his wife about it – does he have a wife?'

Pulpy nodded, thinking of the up-and-down look Beatrice had given him.

'So he'll tell his wife about the candles and the wife will get excited about all the candle deals I can offer her and then she'll tell her husband to give you the raise!'

Midge's eyes were all lit up, and Pulpy imagined she had a couple of her candles in there, the Cinnamon Dreams maybe, or the Towers of Mint. 'Hmm,' he said, 'I don't know how to sell candles, though.'

'You don't have to *sell* them, you just have to *show* them. Then it's my job to burn it and earn it!'

'But I'm just not sure –'

Midge kissed his forehead. 'And you should wrap a blanket or a towel around your fishbowl on the way to work, so it doesn't freeze.'

'Okay,' he said, and the alarm went off.

'What's that you got there?' asked the bus driver when Pulpy stepped onto the bus. He was hugging the fishbowl to his chest and squeezing Midge's catalogue under one armpit.

'A fish.' He looked at the crowd ahead of him. All the seats were taken.

'Who carries a fish around in weather like this?'

'That's why I wrapped his bowl in a towel. So he doesn't freeze.'

'You better hope it doesn't. Move up the bus, please.'

He took a few steps and stopped when the bowl nudged someone's back.

'Keep going. I need you on the other side of the line.'

Pulpy looked down. 'What line?'

The driver sighed. 'I need you on the other side of that line or else this bus doesn't leave the station.'

'Get on the other side of the line!' one of the seated passengers shouted.

Pulpy shuffled another step along and the swaddled fishbowl pushed into a teenager's backpack. 'Sorry,' he said.

The teenager sneered at him.

'Here we go!' said the driver, and started the engine.

The bus lurched forward and Pulpy stumbled backward, dropping the catalogue onto the floor of the bus and spilling water from the fishbowl. The bus stopped.

A rumble of discontent rose from the other riders.

The driver looked at Pulpy. 'Once more and you're off. I cannot abide fish water on my vehicle.'

'I tripped,' he said.

'I will not repeat myself. One more time and you are off this bus.'

Pulpy nodded and braced himself.

The receptionist turned to look at the clock when Pulpy walked in. 'I think the clock is dirty. See it?' She pointed.

The time was 8:39. As far as he could tell, there was no dirt.

'I think I'll have to clean it,' she said. 'I should make a note.' And she looked at the clock again, eyeballed Pulpy and reached for a pen and paper.

Pulpy stood on the welcome mat with the towel-wrapped fishbowl. 'How was your weekend?'

She put her pen down and clicked her pink nails on the desk. 'Over too fast.'

'Start of the week,' he said.

'Uh huh. Under new management too. I didn't think I'd say this, but I miss Al already. At least he included me in things.'

Pulpy stood there while she stuck and unstuck paper-clips to the magnetic top of their container. 'I told Dan you should've been invited to the party,' he said.

She paused with a paperclip at her lips like a tiny silver trombone. 'You told him that?' She put the paperclip down. 'What are you doing with that towel?'

'Oh, this.' The towel was soaked and so was his coat. He unwrapped the bowl and set it on the ground. 'It's for my fish.'

'Well, don't leave the bowl on the floor like that. Here, put it on my desk.'

The fish was orange. It swam in a circle one way, then the other. He set the bowl gently on her desk.

She peered at it. 'It's moving pretty slow.'

'He's probably cold,' he said. 'He'll warm up.'

The receptionist nudged the little bowl and the water sloshed. 'Where'd you get it?'

'The winter fair.' He cleared his throat. 'I won him at the fish game.'

'Good for you.' She dipped her finger in the water and swirled it around.

He puffed up a little. 'It wasn't as hard as I thought it would be.'

'This is a nice fish. The gravel's nice.'

'Rainbow.' He watched the ripples she was making, then shook off his coat.

The closet was full again but there was room on the floor. He deposited his coat and then reached for the fish. 'Well, I guess we should be getting upstairs.'

She pulled the bowl toward her. 'I think it likes it here.'

'Hmm,' he said. 'Actually, I was going to put him on my desk.'

'But it's so nice and bright here, with the window. I think it wants to stay with me.'

'Well,' said Pulpy.

'Besides, you have to get to the boardroom. It's the new boss's first meeting so you better hurry up. It's an *all-staff* meeting, except I have to cover the desk. So now I'm not included in parties *or* meetings.'

'There's a meeting?' He rushed for the stairs, but the receptionist kept talking.

'Am *I* not staff? You would think when there's an all-staff meeting, *all* staff would be invited. But I guess that's not the way it works anymore.' She looked at him standing there. 'Well, what are you waiting for?'

He took the steps two at a time, certain that the fish was watching him go.

'We need a vision statement,' Dan was saying when Pulpy tiptoed into the boardroom. 'And we need it now.'

Nobody said anything. There were about thirty staff members sitting in a semi-circle around the big boardroom table, with Dan at the head of it. One of Al's red retirement balloons, now partially deflated, still adorned one corner of the room.

Pulpy looked for an empty seat.

Dan folded his hands in front of him. 'So we are going to sit here and write a vision statement, and nobody leaves until it's done.'

There were a few murmurs at this.

'Are there any questions?' Dan noticed Pulpy and nodded at him.

Pulpy nodded back and sat down quickly between Roy from Customer Service and Carmelita from the Parts Department.

Carmelita raised her hand.

'Yes?' said Dan. 'And what's your name?'

'Carmelita,' said Carmelita. "From the Parts Department."

'Yes, Carmelita?' Dan smiled at her. 'Stand up so we can get a look at you.'

She turned her head from side to side and then stood, slowly.

Dan continued to smile.

Carmelita crossed her arms over her chest. 'What's a vision statement?'

Dan was silent. Then he put his elbows on the table and put his hands together and said, 'Ah.'

Carmelita sat down.

'I'm glad you asked, actually, because you all need to know the answer.' Dan leaned forward. 'A vision statement is the statement of a company's vision, put into words. It's about how the company sees itself. That's the vision part. The statement part is the words themselves.' He sat back, looking pleased with himself.

Roy elbowed Pulpy. Pulpy didn't know how to respond to that. Then Roy's hand went up.

'Yes?' said Dan.

'Roy here.' Roy stood. 'From Customer Service. Why, exactly, do we need a vision statement?'

'Why?' said Dan. 'I think that's obvious.'

'Not really,' said Roy. 'Al never thought we needed one.'

Pulpy sunk lower in his chair and there was some laughter around the semi-circle, but Dan wasn't smiling.

'Al ran his show his way, and I'm running my show my way.' Dan leaned forward a little further, and his broad shoulders cast a shadow over the table in front of him. 'So like I said, we need a vision statement.'

Roy sat down. 'What do you think of him?' he whispered to Pulpy.

'Oh, well,' said Pulpy, sensing Dan looking their way, 'I think he'll do a good job.'

Another hand went up. This time it was Vince from Archiving.

Dan frowned. 'Yes?'

Vince stood up. 'Hi, I'm Vince from Archiving. The thing is, Al didn't –'

'Excuse me,' said Dan, 'do you have a job here?'

'Yes?' Vince looked confused. 'I'm in Archiving.'

'Actually, the answer to that question I just posed would be no.'

'Sorry?' Vince half-smiled and half-frowned, like he wasn't getting a joke.

'Don't be sorry. Just go.' Dan stood up. 'Now.'

Vince blinked and then slowly made his way out of the room. There were a few more murmurs, but they were quieter now.

'All right.' Dan sat back down and cracked his large knuckles. 'If nobody has any more questions, I'll start taking your vision-statement suggestions.'

When the meeting was ending and Dan had the vision statement tucked into a folder under his arm, he pulled Pulpy aside. 'Pulpy, I'd like to ask you something.'

Pulpy's shoulders stiffened. 'I'm sorry I was late,' he said in a rush. 'I lost track of time this morning, I don't know how it happens. My wife and I, we always set the alarm, so I don't know how the delay happens there, and then there's the bus ...'

Dan shook his head. 'Forget about that. How would you and your wife like to go to the Ice Follies with me and Beatrice?'

Pulpy stared at him.

'We have a pair of extra tickets with your name on them.' Dan chuckled. 'Well, not really. I don't even know what your wife's name is! Ha! What is her name, anyway?'

'Midge.'

'Midge.' Dan rolled her name around his mouth like he was savouring it.

Pulpy looked from Dan's neat pant creases to his own baggy pleats. 'When's the show?'

'Tonight. Does that work for you?'

Pulpy pressed a thumb between his eyebrows. 'I think so. I'll call Midge. I mean, I'm sure it works.'

'On your lunch break, right?' said Dan. 'You'll call her on your lunch break.'

'My lunch break. Yes.' Pulpy nodded. 'Thank you.'

Dan winked at him. 'You're welcome.'

'Tonight?' said Midge.

'He's got the tickets,' said Pulpy.

'What if I can't go tonight? What if I had plans?'

'But you don't. And it's the Ice Follies, Midge – it's your thing.' The food court was busy. He eyed all the lineups forming. He still needed to eat.

'It's not my thing, it's *our* thing. We signed up to take Couples Ice Dance Expression together, remember? So what row are we?'

'He didn't say.'

'Hmm. But the tickets are free.'

'He didn't say that, either.'

'How could he possibly offer you tickets to an event and then charge you for them? What kind of a person would do that?' She sighed. 'Did you show him the catalogue, at least?'

'The catalogue.' Pulpy tightened his grip on the receiver. The damp edge of his coat collar scratched his neck.

'Just bring it tonight, then. We'll show it to his wife. The wife is the key.'

'Right.' He cleared his throat and thought about the square lump of mush that Midge's catalogue must be now, on the floor of the bus.

'What should I wear? Because I have a skirt, but I can't wear nice shoes with it because of the weather.'

'What about those dress pants you bought?'

'I can't wear them anymore. I took them to get altered and the woman at the tailor's said, "Waist in or out?" And I said, "In."'

'Why don't you just take them back and have her fix them?'

'But she's put so much effort into them already. I wouldn't want to bother her. I couldn't go back and ask her to reverse all that work. To *reverse* it, Pulpy! No, I'll have to pick up some more dress pants at the mall. Do you need anything?'

'I really don't think we should be spending money willy-nilly like this, Midge.'

'It's not willy-nilly, it's important. Besides, you're getting a promotion and I'm going to sell lots of candles. And if we're going to succeed we need to look good.'

Pulpy's hands went to his pleats. 'Then I think,' he said, 'that I'd like pants with creases.'

'You mean the same as the ones you have?'

'No, those are pleated. Where there are a lot of creases it's pleats. I'm just looking for a single crease, down the front of each leg.'

'There you go,' she said. 'That wasn't so hard, was it?'

'She said she'd love to come,' Pulpy told Dan after lunch.

'Great!' Dan clapped his big hands, once. 'So it's ten-fifty each. Usually they're twelve but I got a deal. You can pay me later if you don't have exact change. I don't have any cash on me right now. Take a load off!' Dan pointed at the two buttery leather chairs by his door.

Pulpy sat in one and was engulfed.

'That's nice, isn't it? Did I or did I not say I was going to bring in chairs? These ones over here, they're not quite as comfy but they're just as expensive.' Dan indicated the two hard-backed chairs in front of his desk, where Al's couch had been.

'Looks like quality wood,' said Pulpy.

'That they are. That they are indeed.' Dan leaned back. 'So, about your lateness this morning – the secretary tells me this is a chronic problem with you. What was it you were saying about the bus earlier?'

Pulpy nodded fast. 'The bus driver wouldn't leave the station until I stepped over the line.'

'Those buses will be the death of us all,' said Dan. 'And that secretary is a snoop. She should mind her own business.' He looked at his watch. 'Well, back to work.'

'Yes.' Pulpy blinked, and heaved himself out of the chair. 'Back to it.'

'Do you have any food for this fish?' asked the receptionist when Pulpy walked past her desk at the end of the day.

'I do. I guess I forgot to give it to you.' He found his coat in the closet and dug the small shaker of fish food out of his pocket.

'I'm practising positive self-talk.' She tapped a fingernail on the fishbowl without looking at it. 'It says here you can only put eight ounces into an eight-ounce glass.' She smoothed out the seminar flyer. 'What that means is, you can't fill it higher, so don't even try.'

He handed her the fish food. 'Dan said, um, he said you told him I was late all the time.'

She pushed open the dispenser and sniffed inside. 'Well, you are, aren't you?'

'I'm not saying I'm not. It's just that –'

'All I'm hoping to communicate to you is that there is a new boss now, and you should try to make a good impression. I'm trying to help you. It's all about reframing, that's what the flyer talks about.'

'I suppose that's one way to see it, but I still don't think –'

She set the shaker down and rolled it across her desk. 'I could use a little reframing myself these days.'

'You could?' He slid his arms into his coat sleeves and was relieved that they were finally dry.

'Work and home,' she said. 'That's all there is. I get up, I go to work, I go home. Repeat.'

'We all do the same thing.' Pulpy put his hands in his pockets.

'That's exactly it. Eight ounces. *But.*' She wagged her finger at him, cutting a pink streak through the air. 'It all comes down to how you envision yourself, the flyer says. You can dramatically alter your view of your situation with a few simple exercises.'

'How?' He flattened his hands inside the scratchy hollows of his coat. 'What does it say to do?'

She shrugged. 'That's what they teach you at the seminar.'

When Pulpy got home, Midge was waiting for him in the bedroom. She held the men's store bag upside down over their bed and three pairs of pants slid out: one brown, one grey and one black.

'I found three for you and none for me,' she said. 'How do you like that?'

'I thought you were only getting me one pair.'

'I thought you could try them on and see which one you like best.'

'But we have to meet Dan and Beatrice soon.'

'They can wait.' She pushed the pants toward him. 'Try them on.'

'Okay.' He took the pants into the bathroom and closed the door. A minute or so later he opened it again and came out wearing the grey ones.

'Ooh,' said Midge. 'Those are *nice*.'

Pulpy smiled a little and stood straight, then lifted one leg. 'I like them.'

'They fit really well.'

'Let me try on another pair.' He modelled the brown ones for her next.

'Well now,' she said, and sat down on the bed. 'I have to sit down for this!'

'Last pair!' he said, and walked back into the bathroom. He emerged wearing the black pants.

She threw one hand across her forehead and fell back on the bed. Midge had a forehead you could get lost in. 'I want you to make love to me wearing only those pants and nothing else.'

'All right,' he said, 'but then we really have to go.'

'There they are,' said Pulpy. 'That's them. Over there, by the blow-up elephant.'

'That's a nice elephant.'

'It is. I guess it's one of the characters.'

Midge was taking baby steps. 'Oh, Pulpy, it's slippery. Would you –'

He took her arm, and then they were in front of Dan and Beatrice.

'Hi, Dan. Hi, Beatrice,' said Pulpy. 'This is my wife, Midge.'

'Ah-ha!' said Dan. 'So you're the little lady who's been distracting our boy in the mornings.'

'Pardon?' said Midge.

'Actually, Dan,' said Pulpy, 'it's not Midge who makes me late.' He glanced between his wife and his boss. 'It's not her fault, it's the buses, like I was telling you.'

'I know how it is.' Dan winked at them and slapped the nylon flank of the inflatable elephant behind him. 'Beatrice and I used to get up to all sorts of things before leaving for work. Didn't we, honey?'

Beatrice rolled her eyes. 'Notice how he says "used to."'

'Ho-ho!' said Dan.

Midge gaped at them.

'When we first got together people said we acted like we were the only two people in the world,' said Beatrice.

'And now she says I don't even know she exists!' said Dan. 'Har!'

'There's something different about you, Pulpy.' Beatrice pursed her lips. 'I can't put my finger on it.'

'He's wearing new pants,' said Midge.

Beatrice put her hands on her hips and ogled Pulpy's lower half. 'Oh my, yes, those are *sharp*. They're a bit like Dan's, aren't they?'

Pulpy shuffled in place. 'Shall we go in?'

'Yes, let's,' said Beatrice, and turned to Midge. 'Your man here is full of good ideas, do you know that?'

'Hmm,' said Midge.

They walked into the arena, and Midge grabbed Pulpy's arm and started to breathe faster.

'Is she all right?' said Dan.

'Ice has an effect on her,' said Pulpy.

'Well, ice has an effect on me too!' Beatrice said, and hugged herself in a dramatic way. 'Brrr! Let's get to our seats and share some body warmth!'

Dan clapped his big hands together. 'Sounds good to me!'

The four of them made their way to their seats, which were in the front row.

'These are nice seats,' said Pulpy.

'The best,' said Dan. 'They're company seats.'

Pulpy looked over at him, and Dan grinned.

'Al never got company seats,' said Pulpy.

'Not that you knew about, anyway,' said Dan. 'I'll bet he came here all the time. He just didn't like to share *à la* yours truly.'

'No, I don't think so.' Pulpy shook his head. 'Al wasn't really big on events.'

'Then I guess you'd better get used to the new administration, because Beatrice and I love an event. Don't we, Beatrice?'

She smiled at him. 'We love *all* events.' She turned to Pulpy and Midge. 'Now, you two give me your tickets and I'll figure out where everyone's sitting.'

Pulpy and Midge handed her their stubs.

Beatrice squinted at their seat numbers. 'Ooh! You're next to me, Pulpy!'

'And Midge is next to me!' said Dan.

Pulpy and Midge glanced at each other. They all sat down and nobody said anything else for a while.

Then Midge said quietly, mostly to herself, 'The ice is so pristine.'

'Don't you just adore her?' Beatrice said to the men. 'With her skirt and winter boots?'

'She's pretty adorable,' said Dan.

Pulpy reached over and patted Midge's knee. Her boots were black and puffy with Velcro straps, and they made her legs look more delicate than normal.

'It's getting cold,' said Midge.

'Do you want my coat?' said Pulpy.

'Yes, please.'

'Excuse me, Dan.' He took off his coat and reached across Dan to give it to Midge.

'Look at that,' said Beatrice. 'He gives her his jacket when she's cold.'

'Huh,' said Dan.

'*My* husband never gives me his jacket.'

Dan shrugged under his heavy layer of sheepskin. 'You don't get cold.'

'Sometimes I do. Sometimes I get very cold. Sometimes I get chilled right to the bone.'

'Well, next time you do you just let me know,' said Dan.

'I will,' said Beatrice. 'Watch me.'

The rink was spread out below them, with 'Ice Follies' written across it in loopy red.

Pulpy ran his gaze around the big, blue circle once, twice, three times, and then the music started and two of the skaters in their costumes glided into view. One of them was dressed like the model elephant from outside and the other character was a fly, with a fuzzy black body and fast-flapping wings. The fly circled the elephant, and the elephant went down almost immediately.

'Look at that freaky elephant!' Dan said, and laughed. 'Is he ever stupid!'

'They're all stupid,' said Beatrice. 'That's why it's called the Follies.'

'They're not stupid,' said Midge, softly. 'It's all very calculated.'

'That's right,' said Pulpy. 'They're smart enough to *pretend* to be stupid.'

'Well, I don't know about that,' said Dan, 'but boy, that elephant is *funny*!'

'Does anyone want any snacks?' Pulpy asked. 'I'll make a run.'

'No thanks,' said Beatrice.

'Don't worry,' said Dan, 'we'll keep Midge company!'

'We sure will!' said Beatrice, and the two of them smiled wide.

Pulpy looked at Midge in the skirt she'd selected. It was the one with what she said were palm fronds on it, but the skirt was black and the fronds were blue, so Pulpy always thought they looked like knives. 'I'll be right back.'

Midge nodded, not smiling.

When he returned to his seat, he said, 'What did I miss?'

'That elephant does *not* know how to skate,' said Dan. 'He just keeps falling!'

'Midge was telling us about her candle business,' said Beatrice. 'She said you brought something to show us.'

'Oh, um.' Pulpy felt his shoulders go rigid. 'I forgot it at the office.'

'That's a shame.'

Midge looked at him, but he looked away and dug his hand into his bag of treats. 'Does anyone want a salted licorice?'

'Licorice?' said Beatrice. 'With salt on it? Yuck!'

'In it, actually,' he said.

'Always with the specifics,' said Dan, nodding his approval. 'I keep telling everybody you'll go far, Pulpy.'

'Midge?' Pulpy offered her the bag.

She shook her head. 'You and your Dutch sensibilities,' she said, smiling. Then she turned back to the action on the rink.

'Well,' said Pulpy when the Follies were over, 'we should get home.'

'No, no, don't go *home*!' said Beatrice.

Dan shook his head and grinned. 'Beatrice was saying to me earlier that she'd like us all to play charades at our place tonight.'

'Yes!' said Beatrice. 'Charades!'

Midge looked at Pulpy.

'Sounds nice,' he said.

Midge looked away.

'Now, we don't want the husbands and wives being on the same teams,' said Dan. 'Let's mix it up a little. Midge, you be on my team.' He patted the spot next to him on the sectional.

Midge fitted herself into the corner of the suede L-shape and watched Beatrice shimmy across the room to sit next to Pulpy. 'This is a soft couch.'

'It is.' Dan winked at her. 'You sink right in.'

'It's new,' said Beatrice. 'This one here we had at our last place.' She put her hand in the small space between her and Pulpy. 'It's a divan.'

'Hmm,' said Midge.

'Don't mind the boxes, by the way. We're still unpacking.'

'I didn't see any boxes,' said Pulpy.

'Well, we've unpacked most of them, but still, there might be a few. You know what moving's like.' Beatrice stroked the divan.

Midge watched her. 'We've been in the same spot for a while.'

'Okay, charades!' said Dan. 'Who goes first?'

'You have a fireplace,' said Midge.

'We do indeed! It came with the house,' he said. 'Want me to turn it on?'

'Turn it – on?'

'You got it. Watch this!' Dan picked up a remote from the coffee table and pressed a button.

The fire flared to life and Midge's eyes widened. 'Oh my,' she said.

'You like that?' Dan slapped his knee. 'Fire and ice. I love this woman!'

'Let's toss a coin,' Beatrice said to him.

'Good idea,' said Dan. 'Who's got one?'

'I'll bet Pulpy's got a *bunch* of change in his pocket,' said Beatrice. 'I heard it jingling when he sat down.'

'Hmm,' said Midge.

'Let's see ...' Pulpy fished around. 'How about a quarter?'

'That's fine,' said Dan. 'Hand it over.'

'Have some more mini-pizzas.' Beatrice handed Pulpy the snack tray she'd prepared.

'Thanks,' said Pulpy. 'They're really good.'

'The way he's going on about it,' said Beatrice, 'it's like he's never had food cooked for him before!'

'He's had food cooked for him,' said Midge.

'Of course he has. What kinds of things do you make for him, Midge?'

'Oh, simple things.' Midge frowned down at her skirt.

'Simple but good,' said Pulpy.

'We're just so glad to have you two here!' said Beatrice. 'Dan and I haven't had a chance to get the lay of our neighbourhood yet, so we don't know too many people.'

'It's a nice neighbourhood,' said Midge.

'Oh, it's a lot like yours, I'm sure.'

'It's a bit nicer.'

'Is it?' Beatrice smiled.

'Lots of good people in the office, though, hey Pulpy?' said Dan.

'It's a good office.' Pulpy glanced at Midge, who was observing Beatrice.

Beatrice was looking at Pulpy's hands. 'Your fingers are very long,' she said.

'Pulpy has a gift for charades,' said Midge. 'He has magic charade hands.'

'Midge,' Pulpy said, and reddened.

Beatrice giggled.

'You watch,' said Midge. 'He'll draw the thing in the air, just like that. No "sounds like" or "first word, second word," or anything like that. He'll just draw it. It's amazing. Even complex things. You just watch.'

'He is amazing,' Dan agreed, taking the quarter. 'Who's heads?'

'We are!' Beatrice declared, grabbing Pulpy's hand and waving it in the air.

Pulpy smiled at Midge. 'Midge is ambidextrous,' he said. 'She can write my name with both hands. Show them, Midge.' He looked around. 'Is there a pen she can use?'

'Never mind, Pulpy.' Midge was blushing. 'Let's just play the game.'

'Here we go!' Dan let the coin fly.

They all watched it go up and then come down. It landed at their feet, rolled on the gleaming hardwood for a short distance and then was still.

'Heads!' Beatrice squealed. 'We win!'

'Ha, ha,' said Dan. 'You don't win. You just get to go first.'

'Oh, right.' Beatrice smiled slyly. 'I guess I was getting ahead of myself. I have great faith in my partner, that's all.'

'As well you should,' said Dan. 'I can see you becoming a real driving force in the office, Pulpy.'

'You can?' said Pulpy.

'We can,' said Beatrice. 'You're going to be instrumental in our workplace makeover!'

'I am?' he said.

'Do you work there too?' Midge said to Beatrice.

'Beatrice starts tomorrow,' said Dan.

'Probably tomorrow,' said Beatrice. 'I'm not sure yet.'

Dan looked at her, then took two mini-pizzas and ate them quickly.

'Oh,' said Midge. 'I didn't realize you were both working there.'

'Dan's turning things around,' said Beatrice. 'He's going to organize a potluck.'

'That's right.' Dan nodded. 'Staff parties, and potlucks in particular, are proven team builders.'

'We heard about *your* party,' said Beatrice.

'What party?' said Pulpy.

'Your Christmas party!' said Dan. 'Al told me all about it. Ho-ho, sounds like it was quite the shindig!'

Midge made a sound in the back of her throat, and Pulpy said, 'We don't really like to talk about it, actually.'

'Sure.' Beatrice smiled at Midge. 'We had this parakeet once, at our old place, that liked to eat chicken! Can you believe that?'

'Nobody could believe it!' said Dan.

'Nobody could. But all he would eat was chicken. Anyway, one day I was cleaning his cage –'

'She was using the vacuum,' said Dan.

Beatrice gave him a sideways look. 'And I was using the *vacuum*,' she said, 'and I sucked him up! I was cleaning the cage and – whoops – up he went. Trying to get rid of one mess and ending up with another.' She shook her head. 'So we can relate.'

'I miss that chicken-eating bird,' said Dan.

Beatrice nodded. 'We all do.'

Pulpy looked at Midge, who was looking at her skirt again. 'Well,' he said, 'that's quite a story.'

Beatrice nodded, and elbowed him. 'Now let's see those magic charade hands in action!'

A few weeks before last Christmas, Midge had befriended a pigeon that was roosting in their backyard flowerpot. She earned the bird's trust gradually, progressing from breadcrumb-lobbing to offering crusts at arm's length. Pretty soon the pigeon was accepting whole pieces of toast from her palm.

One day Pulpy walked into their small square of backyard, and Midge was sitting on a lawn chair in her winter coat, with the pigeon perched on her head.

'Shh,' she whispered. 'Mrs. Wings is sleeping.'

'Her eyes are open,' said Pulpy.

Midge lifted her arm to check her watch, careful not to startle the bird. 'Well, she hasn't moved for half an hour.'

'That's quite a while.'

She beamed at him. 'Isn't it?'

Pulpy smiled at her and the pigeon, and left them alone.

A few weeks later, Midge hosted a Christmas fondue-and-candle party for Pulpy's office mates.

'It'll increase my sales and your visibility,' she told him. 'If we're going to advance in this world, we need to take the initiative.'

Unfortunately, Al and his wife brought their schnauzer. By the time Midge thought to check on Mrs. Wings after performing her clean-burning-wick demonstration and then cutting a loaf of bread into little cubes, there wasn't much left of her pet pigeon but a few bloody feathers.

Al had promised Pulpy a promotion the next day.

TWO

'Did I tell you they got my underwear stuck in the cash register?' said Midge while Pulpy was getting ready for work.

'No,' he said, and waggled his eyebrows. 'I don't think you did.'

They were sitting on the loveseat. Pulpy was in his shirt and tie and new brown pants, and Midge was in her robe.

'I was in line at the department store buying your pants, and some underwear for myself because I was running low. I bought a few pairs of the shiny kind you like, with the lacy elastic? And somehow the cashier closed the cash drawer on one of them, and then she started yanking on it. Well, at first it was tugging. But it wasn't very long before it was yanking.' She bent her elbow and rammed it sideways to show him.

'Hmm.' He stood up. 'Did she say anything?'

'Not to me. But she said to the woman who was bagging for her, "I can't get these panties out of my cash drawer." Like it was the panties' fault. And the woman who was bagging for her said, "Why don't you ring in the purchases first, and *then* get the panties out when the cash drawer pops open?" It was a spectacle. Shoppers at the back of the line knew what was going on. I don't know how I'm going to show my face when I return your pants today.'

'I think I'll keep them all.' Pulpy took his coat off the coat tree and pushed his hands through the sleeves. 'I think I'll keep all three pairs of pants. Then you don't have to worry about returning them. It's time I gave my wardrobe a makeover. Plus, they're very comfortable.'

'And Beatrice likes them too.' Midge frowned. 'The way they *jingle*,' she said.'

'Beatrice?' His zipper caught on the way up and he struggled with it. 'Midge, she's my boss's wife.'

She crossed her legs. 'I don't think I'd like a thong. Would you like me to wear a thong?'

He blinked at her. 'I'd like it if you liked it. Only if it was comfortable for you. Or it doesn't matter.'

'Then maybe I'll try it.' She looked at the empty space next to her on the couch and cinched her robe tighter.

'That might be nice.' Pulpy reached in and moved some hair off her forehead. The way Midge's hair feathered at the sides of her head was like the scalloped edge of a seashell, and he loved that about her.

'Although I really think it would be uncomfortable. They *look* uncomfortable,' she said. 'Plus nobody I know wears one. At least, nobody's told me they do.'

'Would your friends tell you they were wearing a thong?' The seashell scallops didn't show up in photos, and Pulpy thought that was a shame. 'I think my friends would be embarrassed to tell me.'

'Your friends wouldn't wear a thong.'

He nodded and started putting on his boots. 'I should get to work.'

'Let's have the evening to ourselves tonight,' she said. 'I want it to be just us. I'll show off my new hairdo for you.'

'Okay, that sounds nice. They won't cut too much, though, will they?'

'I'll tell them.' She smiled at him. 'How's your fish? I bet it's fun having him on your desk.'

'Oh, fine.' He lifted his right foot to pull on that boot and nearly lost his balance.

She reached out to steady him. 'Mr. Fins loves it in our bedroom. He just swims and swims.'

'Pulpy!' said Dan's voice as soon as Pulpy sat down.

Pulpy jerked, and Eduardo in the next cubicle leaned back a little to see around their partition.

Dan came up and clapped Pulpy on the back. 'Beatrice and I had a great time with you and Midge last night!'

'Well.' Pulpy watched Eduardo listening. 'Thank you. We did too.'

'A *great* time. And I was thinking – Beatrice and I were saying to each other after you left – that you are exactly the person we need to set things right around here.'

'I am?'

'You are.'

'Is Beatrice here today?'

'She's going to start tomorrow.' Dan focused on Pulpy's computer screen. 'She had some appointments to attend.'

Pulpy moved his cursor, just to do something. 'Midge is getting her hair cut today.'

'There you go.' Dan smiled at him. 'Beatrice was saying she'd love to go shopping with Midge sometime. Do you think Midge would like that?'

'Oh, sure.' He nodded. 'Sure she would.'

'Great. You know, Pulpy, I think we can really do a lot better here. There is definite room for improvement in this office, and as head of the Social Committee you could be a real force for change.'

'Do we have a Social Committee?'

'We do now. You can't organize a potluck without a Social Committee.'

'Hmm,' said Pulpy. 'I never really think of myself as a force.'

'Well, you can start today. Because a force is what you are. A force to be reckoned with.'

Pulpy looked down at his chest and pulled at his shirt to make the buttons align more evenly. 'Maybe you're right.'

'I know I am. And I'm glad to see you're coming around. Now all we need is some forward momentum and there's nothing we can't do.'

He pinched his fingers along the neat fold down the front of his new pants. 'Then I guess it's worth a try.'

'So!' Dan put his hands on his hips. 'What are you and Midge up to this evening?'

'Hmm, well. I'm not sure.'

'Great! We'll come over.'

'Oh, Pulpy, my hair looks awful!'

'What happened?' Pulpy had the pay phone between his cheek and his shoulder and was holding a napkin dispenser from one of the food-court tables. He pulled out a napkin and dabbed it onto the mustard stain on his new pants.

'I said to her, "The front and the sides are good. Don't touch the front or the sides. The top and the back, that's all I need done." But she didn't listen to me!'

'I'm sure it looks fine. But maybe you should try a different hairdresser next time.'

'I couldn't do *that*.' She went quiet for a second. 'I've been with her for so long, Pulpy. We have a history together. And then what if the new hairdresser did a bad job? A *worse* job? Then I'd have to go back to my old hairdresser and she'd know I'd seen someone else and it would be very uncomfortable.'

'You could if you wanted to.' The stain wasn't coming out. He shoved the soiled napkin into the breast pocket of his coat and pulled a fresh one out of the dispenser. 'It's all about reframing.'

'Where did you hear that?'

'The receptionist. She's taking a course.'

'Hmm,' said Midge.

'Did we have a plan for tonight?' he said. 'Were we doing anything?'

'No, we said we were staying in, remember?'

Neither of them said anything for a few seconds and then Pulpy cleared his throat. 'Guess what? Dan made me the head of the Social Committee.'

'He did? That's got to be a good sign. Has he said anything about your promotion yet?'

'Not yet. But I'm organizing a potluck. I have to make a sign-up sheet.' He lost his grip on the napkin and it drifted to the floor. 'Dan also said Beatrice wants to go shopping with you.'

'What? But I don't even know her.'

'But at the Ice Follies. You got to know her then. And she's my boss's wife.'

'I know she's your boss's wife. I just didn't like the way she looked at you. Or me. She has a very judgmental way of looking at other women. She starts at their shoes and then she looks up, like to see what kind of a person would be wearing those shoes.'

'Really? I didn't notice that.'

'Well, you wouldn't. You always give people the benefit of the doubt, Pulpy. That's what gets you in trouble.' Midge sighed. 'Why would she want to go shopping with me?'

'I don't know. Maybe she's lonely.'

'How can she be lonely? She's married.'

'Sometimes married people get lonely,' he said.

'Not us, though, right?'

'No way.' His neck was hurting, so he tried to reposition the phone by squishing his cheek sideways, but the motion dislodged the receiver and it fell and swung in a wide arc on its cord. He grabbed for it, letting go of the napkin dispenser. 'Hello? Midge?' The dispenser banged onto the floor.

'What happened?' she said. 'What was all that noise?'

'Nothing. I just – Nothing.' He toed the dispenser, unsuccessfully trying to right it.

Pulpy sat in front of his computer screen and typed 'Food To Bring To The Potluck.'

He looked at that for a minute and then changed it to 'Food I Will Bring To The Potluck.'

He cursored back. 'Potluck (Food) Contribution.'

That one made him nod. He spaced down and typed 'Employee Name' and made a bunch of lines underneath. Then he hit Print.

When he went downstairs to post the sign-up sheet, the receptionist said to him, 'Do you smell that?'

He sniffed the air. 'Popcorn.'

'That's right. I hate popcorn! I can't stand the smell of it.' She glowered. 'He thinks he's so smart, but he's not. He's stupid.'

'Who?'

'You know who. He comes up to me with a package at the end of the day yesterday. "Would you overnight this for me?"

he says. "Overnight this." Like he's making up some new language. Like he can't be bothered saying, "Would you send this by overnight courier, please?" A "please" would've been nice. But that's not even the point. "Overnight this."' She sucked on her teeth in disgust.

'So did you?'

'Did I what?'

'Over – Send it by overnight courier?'

'Of course I did. He's my boss, isn't he? I have to do what he says, but I don't have to like the way he says it.'

'Have you met his wife yet?'

'No.' She scowled. 'Why?'

'Nothing.' He waved a hand. 'Hey, where do you get your hair cut?'

'What?'

'What stylist do you go to?'

She reached up and touched her hair. 'You wouldn't know him.'

'No, but my wife – she needs a new hairdresser. So I just thought –'

'Hold on, I think I might have one of his cards somewhere.' She picked up her purse, pulled out a business card and gave it to him.

'Thanks.' He looked at the card. '"Artistic Ladies Hair Cut. Dedicated to Your Satisfaction." That sounds nice.'

'Yeah, he's good.' She yanked a pencil out of her pen-and-pencil cage and then fitted it back in. 'I think so, anyway. Just don't ask my boyfriend.' She squeezed the pencil's pink eraser nub. 'He doesn't know anything.'

Pulpy put the card in his pocket and placed the sign-up sheet on her desk. 'I'm organizing a potluck for the office. Do you want to put yourself down for something?'

She glanced at the sheet and then pushed it away. 'I'll probably have to cover the desk.'

'Oh. Hmm. I don't know.' He picked up the paper and looked at the fish. 'Maybe I should change the fish's water.'

'I guess so.' She put a finger into the fishbowl and swirled it. 'Just not right now.'

'Sure,' he said. 'I'll do it later, then.'

'Hey, there he is,' said Eduardo when Pulpy walked into the kitchen. He was eating popcorn with Carmelita from the Parts Department and Jim from Packaging.

'You know, when you microwave popcorn,' said Pulpy, 'the smell fills the entire workplace.'

'Yeah, so?' Eduardo shook the paper bag so it rattled, and Jim stuck his hand in.

'I'm just saying,' said Pulpy, and turned away to pin the sign-up sheet to the bulletin board.

'What's that for?' said Carmelita.

Pulpy wrote his name on the first line of the sign-up sheet, then his pen hovered over the contribution space. 'It's for the company potluck.' He left it blank and took a step back.

'Oh yeah?' She picked a piece of kernel out of her teeth and walked a few steps forward. 'When is it?'

'Next Tuesday.'

The three of them advanced on him and studied the sheet.

'Do we have to make something?' said Jim. 'Or can it be store-bought?'

'Sure, I guess you could buy something.'

'You got a pen?' said Carmelita.

'I have this one but it's from my desk. Maybe I'll put a string up, with a pen attached. In case people don't have one with them. I don't even know what I'm bringing yet. Dan just asked me to make up this list.'

'Ooh, the new boss,' said Eduardo. 'So this is his idea?'

'I'm organizing it, though,' said Pulpy.

'Lucky you.' Eduardo elbowed Carmelita. 'Stand up and let's get a look at you.'

She curtsied, then said in a high voice, 'What's a vision statement?'

Eduardo stuck out his tongue and panted, and the three of them snickered into their buttery fists.

Pulpy stared at them. 'I should get going,' he said, and headed for the door.

'See you later,' said Carmelita.

Jim waved, but Eduardo just kept eating popcorn.

'It doesn't look bad,' said Pulpy. 'It looks pretty.'

Midge's hand went up to poke at her new hairdo. She still had the scallops, but now there were fewer of them on the left side. 'It's lopsided. It leans to the right.'

'I don't think so.' He was sitting at the kitchen table and she was standing by the sink. There were two artichokes on the counter.

She tilted her head at him and the lump of her hair shifted irregularly. Then she pushed one of the scaly green vegetables so it wobbled. 'The worst part was I had to go around on my route afterwards, Pulpy. I had to ring people's doorbells and say hello to everyone with this hair.'

'It does bounce a little differently.'

'What?'

'But that's all. That's nothing. What's bouncing got to do with anything? Here, look at this –' He reached into his pocket and handed her the receptionist's hairdresser's card.

'"Artistic Ladies"?' She looked between him and the card. 'What is this?'

'The receptionist goes to them. She has nice hair.'

Midge handed the card back to him and turned on the tap, hard. 'Thank you.'

'You're welcome.'

'I'm making us artichokes.' She held one under the water. 'I thought we could have a quiet, relaxing night in tonight, just us and our artichokes.'

'Hmm,' said Pulpy. 'Well, Dan and Beatrice are coming over in a bit so I guess it won't be just us.'

'What do you mean? For dinner?'

'No, only for a few drinks,' he said quickly. 'Just to talk.'

Midge sliced the stems off the artichokes. 'I don't really feel like talking, with my hair like this. At least, not to anybody but you. I thought it was going to be you and me alone tonight. I thought we were going to be romantic.'

'I didn't really know this was all going to happen. He sort of invited himself over.'

'So why didn't you say no?'

'Midge, he's my boss.'

'But this is our home,' she said. 'And I'm making artichokes.'

'That's okay. You make your artichokes. I want you to make them.'

'They're for *us*. Not just me.'

The doorbell rang.

'I'll get it,' he said. 'You keep doing what you're doing.'

'Hello, hello, hello,' said Dan when Pulpy let him and Beatrice in. He stepped forward and set a large plastic bag down by the coat tree.

'Hi, Dan. Hi, Beatrice,' said Pulpy.

'Hello there, Midge!' said Dan in a loud voice. 'What are you doing so far away?'

'Hi, Dan. Hi, Beatrice.' Midge nodded from over by the stove. 'I'm making artichokes.'

'Mmm, artichokes!' said Beatrice.

'I only have two,' she said.

'I'm sorry,' Pulpy said to his boss and his boss's wife. 'We haven't eaten dinner yet.'

'That's okay,' said Dan. 'Beatrice and I had some dip. What kind was it again, honey?'

'Greek,' she said.

'That's right, Greek. Delicious.'

'I think Pulpy got dip all over his *pants*!' said Beatrice.

Pulpy looked over at Midge. 'It's a stain from lunch,' he said. 'Please won't you come in?'

'I think we will.' Dan stepped onto the carpet runner. 'Ho-ho! Rolling out the plastic carpet for the VIPs, eh?'

'It's a runner,' said Pulpy. 'Because of the winter.'

'Take off your boots, Dan,' said Beatrice.

'All right, all right.' Dan took off his boots. 'Aren't you going to take off your shoes?'

'My shoes are part of my outfit.' She flexed one of her feet in their sharp-looking high heels. 'Pulpy doesn't mind, do you, Pulpy?'

'No, that's fine. Please make yourselves comfortable.'

'This couch of yours looks very nice indeed,' said Dan, and sat down.

'It does.' Beatrice sat down beside him. 'This whole place is just so cute!'

'Cute indeed,' said Dan, in Midge's direction.

'Won't you join us, Midge?' said Beatrice.

'I have to cook.'

'Oh, that's right. Well, you go right ahead. We'll just sit here and pick your handsome husband's handsome brains.'

Midge rattled the lid on the pot.

'Smells good!' said Dan.

'It's only boiling water,' she said.

Pulpy put his hands on his knees.

'Well,' said Dan, 'Beatrice's boiling water never smells that good!'

Beatrice slapped his arm and smiled at Midge. 'There's something different about you, Midge. Did you get your hair cut?'

'So!' Pulpy clapped his hands. 'I put the sign-up sheet for the potluck on the staff bulletin board today, with a pen on a string. Did you see it?'

'Are we talking shop here?' said Dan. 'Because let's consider the ladies, now.'

'I can talk shop,' said Beatrice. 'I work there too, remember? Starting tomorrow.'

'Then let's consider Midge.' Dan smiled over at her.

'Don't worry about me,' said Midge. 'I'm just here with my artichokes.'

'That you are,' said Dan. 'They look like nice ones too.'

Midge dropped them in the pot.

Dan sat back. 'How long do those things take, anyway?'

'About forty-five minutes,' said Beatrice, 'or until the bottoms get soft enough to slip a fork in. So now Midge has time to sit with us!'

'I have to make a salad,' said Midge.

'Lettuce!' said Dan. 'Don't get me started on lettuce!'

'So,' said Pulpy. 'What are you two up to this evening?'

'This is it,' said Dan. 'This is our night.'

Midge set a head of romaine on the cutting board and chopped it in half.

'Do you need any help?' said Beatrice. 'I'm a whiz with croutons.'

'She is,' said Dan. 'What brand do you use again, honey?'

'I don't use a *brand*. I make them from scratch.'

'I'm fine, thanks anyway,' said Midge.

'Whoa, watch out, Midge – she'll dry out all your bread-crumbs with her powers of dehydration!'

'Why don't you just talk to Pulpy about something unimportant?' said Beatrice. 'Midge and I will get the real work done around here.' She stood up and stomped over to the kitchen. 'Give me a tomato to slice, Midge. Throw me something green.'

Pulpy looked at Midge, but she was bending over to get something from the fridge. Then he saw Dan looking at her too.

'Don't pay attention to my wife,' said his boss. 'She gets like this.'

'Like what, Dan? Why don't you tell them what I'm like?'

'Maybe I will.'

'Here, Beatrice.' Midge thrust a spoon and a white jar at her. 'You can put some of this mayonnaise in a bowl if you like.'

'You know what? Never mind,' said Dan. 'I was going to say something serious but now is not the time for serious. Now is the time for fun, and I think we all know what kind of fun I'm talking about.'

Midge and Pulpy looked at each other.

'Snakes and Ladders!' said Beatrice, and she pointed her spoonful of mayonnaise at Midge hard enough that a dollop landed on the side of her head.

Midge reached up, slowly, and gave the creamy glob a tentative prod.

'Oops,' said Beatrice, and the spoon clattered into the sink.

'Are you all right, Midge?' said Pulpy.

'No, no, it's fine. Excuse me for a minute.' And she rushed down the hall to the bathroom with her hand over her hair.

'So, like I was saying,' said Dan, 'what's more fun than Snakes and Ladders?'

'I believe that's what *I* was saying,' said Beatrice, returning to the living room.

'That sounds great,' said Pulpy, 'but we don't have Snakes and Ladders.'

'Then it's your lucky day,' said Dan, 'because we brought it with us!' He jumped up and reached for the plastic bag.

'Make some room for me, Pulpy,' said Beatrice. 'I don't want to sit beside my *husband*.'

Pulpy moved over and Dan pulled out the board game just as Midge came back from the washroom, one of her asymmetrical half-scallops now gone bristly with the dried grease.

'All clean?' Beatrice asked her from the loveseat. 'Sorry, Midge, that was me getting overexcited.'

'I got it out,' she said.

'Now, tell me,' said Beatrice. 'There's definitely something different about you. Your hair is leaning more to one side, isn't it? What an interesting look.'

Dan opened up the board on the coffee table and started shaking the dice in his big, square fist. 'Sit next to me, Midge,' he said. 'Let's mix it up a little!'

Pulpy woke up the next morning in an empty bed. He looked around, stretched and checked the time. 'Midge?'

No answer.

He yawned and got up, and found Midge in the kitchen. 'Good morning,' he said.

'Good morning,' she said. 'Would you like some toast?'

'Yes, please.' He sat down at the table.

Midge put two slices of bread in the toaster and stood there, waiting.

'Did you have fun last night?' he said.

'Would you like jam on your toast?'

He looked over at her. 'Jam sounds tasty.'

The toast popped up and Midge took the slices out one at a time. She buttered the toast first, then spread on the jam.

'Thank you.' He nodded at it. 'It looks good.'

'It's toast.'

'All the same.' He took a bite. 'Yum!'

'You didn't say that about the artichokes,' she said. 'You didn't say *anything* about the artichokes.'

Pulpy swallowed. The toast was dry. He looked around for something to drink. 'Could I please have some juice?'

'It's in the fridge.'

He stood up and got a glass, and opened the fridge.

'You didn't even finish it,' she said.

'What?' He looked down at the juice he'd just poured.

'The artichoke I made you.' She was standing with her back to the toaster, and her pink robe was reflected in the chrome.

Pulpy sat down. 'It was good.' He drank some juice. 'I just wasn't all that hungry, I guess.'

'You said you wanted me to make them.'

'Yes, I said that. But you made them differently than usual. We usually just eat the hearts. I didn't know how to eat it the way you made it last night. I didn't know what I was supposed to do.'

'You dip the leaves. I showed you. You dip the leaves in the mayonnaise and the lemon butter, and you scrape off the artichoke meat with your teeth.'

'Midge, I didn't know.'

She turned toward the fridge and moved their real-estate-agent magnets around. 'But I showed you.'

'I guess I was nervous around Dan and Beatrice,' he said.

'Then why did you invite them over in the first place?' She peeled off one of the magnets and scowled at the photo of the real estate agent, who was giving the thumbs-up. 'It was supposed to be our night.'

'I told you, he invited himself.' Pulpy felt the acid from the juice rise up in his throat, and he forced it back down.

Midge slapped the magnet back on the fridge. 'Well, next time you can un-invite him.'

'But, Midge –'

'I have to get ready for work,' she said.

There was a man standing at the receptionist's desk when Pulpy arrived.

'I'm telling you,' the man was saying to her.

'I know it,' said the receptionist.

Pulpy walked past them to the closet and realized that the man was Gary, who used to work in Packaging.

'My personal thing is, I don't create unhappiness for other people,' said Gary. 'That's my own thing. I do not go around creating pain. I mean, sometimes it happens, you don't intend it, but it happens. That's fine. I mean, it's not fine – you didn't mean it, but that's the way it goes sometimes. But my own personal agenda is not to deliberately set out and make people miserable. Which is what some people do, and the way I feel is that the people in positions of power are the most insecure people, because they go after that power because they're insecure and they need to control the world around them.'

The receptionist was nodding at everything he was saying.

'It's the people who *don't* care about power, those are the ones who are the most secure in themselves and what they're doing. Because they don't need to assert themselves in that way. They don't need to go around creating misery. And that's me. I make it my policy *not* to create it. And that's what I go by and that's my motto. I feel really strongly about that.'

Pulpy put his coat away and walked over to them. 'Hi, Gary,' he said. 'What are you up to these days?'

'Pulpy! Long time no see.' He flipped a hand palm up and palm down. 'Some of this, some of that – I've gone freelance. I'm a consultant now.'

Pulpy strolled over to the staircase and leaned against it. 'Who do you consult?'

'No, no.' Gary shook his head. '*They* consult *me*.'

'Who's "they"?'

'Whoever I'm working for.'

'You're your own boss,' said the receptionist.

'That's right.' Gary stuck out his chest. 'It's a whole new world when you're working for yourself. And if you ask me, a better world.'

Pulpy looked down at his starchy golf shirt. He didn't play golf. Why was he wearing a golf shirt?

Gary was wearing jeans and a sports jersey. 'Yep. No more watching the old clock for this guy, no sir.'

'Sounds like the life for me,' said the receptionist.

'It is the life,' said Gary. 'It is *the* life. It's a whole new perspective when you're working for a client instead of a boss. And if you ask me, a better perspective.'

Pulpy looked at the receptionist and then back to Gary. 'I bet it's complicated to do your taxes,' he said.

'Oh, I have an accountant for that.'

'You have your own accountant?' said the receptionist.

'Uh huh. We do a trade: I consult for him, he does my taxes.'

'I do my own taxes,' said Pulpy, a little louder than he meant to.

'I used to do my own taxes,' said Gary, 'back when I worked nine to five. But now I have so many different sources of income, I can't keep track of them all. Ha, ha!'

'Ha,' said Pulpy.

The receptionist had her elbows up on her desk and was resting her chin on her hands, staring at Gary. The overhead fluorescents glinted off her glasses.

'Hel-lo there,' said Dan, from the stairs.

They all jumped a little at his voice, and looked up.

Dan hopped down two steps at a time, winking at Pulpy as he passed him. 'Hi. I'm Dan, the new supervisor,' he said to Gary. 'I don't think we've met.'

'This is Gary,' said Pulpy. 'He used to work in Packaging.'

'Packaging, eh?' Dan crossed his arms. 'Well now.'

'But now he's a consultant,' said the receptionist.

Gary cleared his throat. 'I just came by to see if you might need any help around here.'

'Oh, well,' said Dan, 'I think we're doing fine, thanks.' He looked at Pulpy. 'Who's in Packaging now, what's his name?'

'Jim.'

'Well, we've got Jim now,' said Dan. 'So I think we're good.'

'Oh, ah,' said Gary, 'I meant do you need any consulting? I'm a consultant now.'

'A consultant, eh? Hmm. No, I think we're fine. Like I said.' Dan extended his hand. 'But it was nice to meet you, Gary.'

Gary's hand rose to meet Dan's, and he wiped the other one on his jeans. Then he looked around like he didn't know where he was. 'So I guess I should –'

Dan nodded and headed for the stairs. 'Yep, back to work.' He smiled at Pulpy and the receptionist on his way up.

The receptionist glared at Dan and slowly took her elbows off her desk.

'Back to work.' Pulpy watched Gary walk out the door.

The receptionist swivelled in her chair to look at the clock.

'Those buses, you know,' said Pulpy quickly. 'Those bus drivers on those buses. You think you leave the house with plenty of time to spare and then, boom, the bus sits in the station an extra twenty minutes.'

'I always give myself at least twenty extra minutes in the morning to get to work,' she said. 'On top of the time I think it'll take. On *top* of that. That way I'm never late.'

'That sounds like a good system.' Pulpy moved past her and peered down into the fishbowl, at the rainbow-coloured pebbles on the bottom. He was pretty sure the fish looked up at him.

'Pulpy!' Dan called from upstairs. 'Can I see you a minute?'

'Coming!' He smiled at the receptionist. 'I'd better get up there.'

She typed something on her keyboard and kept her eyes on her monitor.

Dan grinned at him at the top. 'What's going on down there?'

Pulpy squeezed the railing. 'What?'

'Keeping tabs on unwanted visitors, I like that. How's the potluck coming along?'

'I posted the sign-up sheet,' he said. 'And I put a string next to it, with a pen tied on. So if people don't have a pen with them they can still sign up.'

Dan strolled into his office. 'Did you tell me this already?'

'I think I mentioned it last night.'

'Ho-ho, last night! Your wife's a real snake charmer, isn't she?' He pointed at Pulpy and leaned back in his chair.

'Ha, yes. You won the game.'

'We did indeed!' Dan handed him a slip of paper. 'I need you to go back downstairs and get this file for me.'

Pulpy looked at the outline where Al's couch had rested on the carpet. 'All right.'

'Just ask the receptionist to find it for you. And watch out for those ladders – they'll get you every time!'

'I will, thanks. Ha.'

'Come over here and look at this,' said the receptionist when Pulpy went back downstairs. She pointed at her screen. 'I'm paying my bills online!'

Pulpy's eyes widened. 'What if you get caught?'

She pushed her mouse around in a tight circle on its pad. 'Who's going to catch me? *He* doesn't know what goes on around here. I run this show, in case you didn't notice.'

'But what if Dan finds out? Maybe he's monitoring things. He could've installed special software and we'd never know. You don't want to lose your job over this.'

She laughed, hard. 'Big deal.'

Pulpy gave her the slip of paper. 'Dan sent me to – I need to get this file for him.'

She frowned at the paper, and then scrunched it up and tossed it into her recycling bin. 'Get the file yourself,' she said. 'You think I'm getting it? I'm not getting it.'

'I'll get it,' he said. 'Let me get it.' He headed for the filing cabinet.

'It's not in there,' she said. 'It's in that pile.'

He nodded and moved toward the tower of files on her desk.

She jerked her head at them. 'They pile up. I used to have someone in here to do the filing, but not anymore.'

He went through the colour-coded folders, careful not to move anything out of place.

'I haven't had time to do my work today,' said the receptionist. 'I've been busy all day doing other people's work and I haven't had time for any of my own.'

'There's never enough time.' Pulpy was halfway down the pile now.

'I mean, I'm only one person. I'm just one person here.' She unscrewed the cap on a bottle of correction fluid and started painting little white streaks on an important-looking document. 'Filing is for temps. I had a temp in here and they took her away. And how do you think that made me feel? I'll tell you how it made me feel, it made me feel like saying, "Fine, then you can go and get your own damn files."' Her hand sped up and the tiny brush zipped across the page, leaving bigger and sloppier streaks in its wake.

'I remember when she was here.' Pulpy found Dan's file and eased it out carefully. 'Aha. This is the one.'

The receptionist frowned and stopped working. 'I used to have peanut shells all over the floor from her. They never got cleaned up. I said to her one time, "Must be a nice job where you can sit and shell peanuts all day." And she said, "I do not shell peanuts all *day*. I have them for my *snack*." So I told Al about it and that was that.'

Pulpy blinked. 'But I thought you said –'

She straightened in her chair. 'They could have brought in someone else. But they didn't.'

Pulpy handed the file to Dan. 'Here you go,' he said, and put his hands in his pockets. There was a bit of fluff in the left one, and he balled it between his fingers.

'Did she get it for you?' said Dan. 'Or did she make you get it yourself?'

'Well.'

'I knew it.' Dan leaned back in his big chair and crossed his arms.

'It's the file you wanted,' said Pulpy.

'That's not the point.'

'She's really busy.'

Dan snorted. 'She's useless, is what she is.'

'They used to have a temp in for the receptionist. She's all by herself out there now.'

'I heard the temp wouldn't stay with her. I heard she ate the temp alive.' Dan lifted the file and gave it a shake. 'She needs supervision. She needs quality control, is really the thing. She's a loafer.' He slapped the file down on his desk.

Pulpy stared at him. 'She has a lot on her plate.'

'Uh huh. Well, Beatrice'll get things sorted out soon enough. She's around here somewhere – she said something about liaising with Building Maintenance. She's doing a few spot checks today and tomorrow she'll start nine-to-fiving proper.'

'Oh.' Pulpy glanced over his shoulder. 'I haven't seen her.'

'Well, she's around, like I said.' Dan coughed, and pulled the file toward him. 'You and Midge have plans for tonight?

Because Beatrice and I don't have any plans, and we thought maybe we could all do something.'

'Well –'

'Great! It's settled. You're coming to our place for dinner.'

Pulpy warmed both quarters in his hand before he dropped them into the pay-phone slot.

'Hello?' said Midge.

'Hi, Midge.'

'Oh. Hi, Pulpy.'

He watched the blue digital message scrolling across the pay phone's little screen, telling him to press the diamond button to start a new call. 'Did anything interesting happen on your route today?'

'Not really.'

He took a breath. 'I'm really sorry about last night.'

She didn't say anything at first, but then she said, 'Well, there was this one woman. She was wearing this horrible top – the kind that shows off your middle. She just answered the door wearing this short top, and without warning she'd move and expose her stomach. Where there was a shirt one moment there was skin the next. I suppose there are people who like that sort of thing. If you like women who show off their stomachs in that way. Myself, I prefer modesty.'

'That sounds pretty interesting,' he said, then cleared his throat. 'Dan and Beatrice want to have us over for dinner tonight.'

'Oh,' she said.

'They want to thank us for last night.' He closed his eyes and rubbed his forehead. 'It'll be fun. We'll bring them a gift.'

Midge sighed. 'What kind of gift?'

'I don't know,' he said. 'We'll think of something.'

'It says on the flyer, "Control what you can control,"' said the receptionist when Pulpy came back from lunch.

'What does that mean?' Pulpy put his coat on the closet floor.

'It means, "Don't look for easy answers to hard questions."'

'Hmm. Have you seen Dan's wife today? I heard she was doing spot checks.'

'Oh, I saw her, all right. Poking around. She kept her distance from my desk, though, which suits me just fine.' She reached for her highlighter. 'Do you think I should mention my seminar to the new management?'

'You mean you haven't told him about it?'

'Al already said I could go.' She shrugged. '"Harness your energy and you will harness your stress." I'll ask him closer to the date, after I register. I'll get all my work done and that way he won't be able to say no.'

Pulpy nodded. 'The fish looks better. He's swimming more.'

'Oh yeah?' She glanced at it, then back at the flyer. 'This is the best one, right here: "Even VCRs know how to pause." That is the best.'

Pulpy didn't like the way the flower man was looking at Midge. He was leaning against the counter by the cash register, just looking.

'Excuse me,' said Midge. 'We'd like to buy a plant.'

'Well, you're in the right place.' The flower man winked at her. 'Would this plant be for you?'

She shook her head and her lopsided scallops bounced. 'It's a gift. For someone else.'

'A gift, hmm? In that case, I would recommend this plant here.' He pointed to a tall, spiky one and pushed his hips away from the counter.

'Ouch,' said Pulpy, 'that looks sharp.'

The flower man nodded. 'The leaves will cut you if you brush against them. But this is a fine gift because these plants live a long time. They're very good on water.'

'I'm never good about watering,' said Midge. 'I just can't tell when they need it.'

The flower man leaned forward, and Pulpy could see a few dark hairs peeking over the collar of his green-and-white-striped shirt. 'I'll tell you a trick. You have to get your thumb right in there, stick it in the dirt, like this –' He burrowed his thumb in the soft, dark soil next to the stem of the plant, and left it there.

'Oh,' said Midge, and smiled at him.

The flower man smiled back. 'And then you pull it out and have a look.' He showed her his thumb. There were bits of earth stuck in the creases of his pink skin, and under the nail. 'See? If there's dirt on it, like this, you don't need to water your plant. But if your thumb comes out clean, it's watering time.'

Pulpy watched Midge watching the flower man and his big, dirty thumb, and he put his arm around her and pointed to a different plant. 'Actually, I think we'll take that one there,' he said. 'The one with the yellow leaves.'

'That one?' The flower man shook his head, but he was still looking at Midge. 'No, no. That one's not a good gift plant.' He stroked one of the long, spiky leaves of the plant he'd had his thumb in. 'See? They can be friendly, if you treat them right.' He looked at Midge some more.

'We'll take this one,' she said.

'Ow,' said Pulpy on the bus to Dan and Beatrice's place. 'Ow, ow, ow.'

'Oh, hush,' said Midge. 'I'm sure Dan and Beatrice will have bandages.'

'I got blood on their plant.'

'The leaves are dark. They won't notice.'

Before they knocked on Dan and Beatrice's door, Midge checked her shadow and tried to make her hair more even on both sides.

Pulpy sucked on his throbbing finger.

Beatrice answered the door. She was wearing a silky top with wide-legged pants that were tight at the waist. A strip of bare skin showed in between.

Pulpy saw Midge's mouth form a tight line, and then the three of them smiled at each other and said their hellos.

'We brought you a plant,' said Midge.

'Ooh, that's a nice one!' Beatrice took it from her. 'It looks artificial!'

'Be careful.' Pulpy held up his finger. 'The leaves are sharp.'

'Oh, poor baby!' Beatrice set the plant down and seized Pulpy's hand. 'You need a Band-Aid! Does it hurt?'

'No, no, I'm fine.'

'But it *looks* like it hurts! Your nice, long finger!' She cocked her head back. 'Dan! Come and take Pulpy and Midge's coats!'

'What's she yelling about?' Dan strolled toward them, wearing a shiny shirt. 'Hi, Pulpy. Hi, Midge. Here, let me get that.' He helped Midge off with her coat, and Beatrice disappeared down the hall. 'What is this, wool? Very nice.'

'It keeps me warm,' said Midge.

'I'll bet it does.' Dan looked over at his wife, who was rushing at them with a first-aid kit. 'What are you doing with that?'

'Pulpy has a wound. Pick up that plant there, will you? They got us that plant.'

'I've got my hands full with the coats here, dear.' He rolled his eyes at Pulpy.

'Where's your bathroom?' said Midge.

'I'll show you,' said Dan.

Beatrice ripped open the Band-Aid with her teeth. She pulled off the non-sticky strips and let them flutter to the floor. 'Give me your finger,' she told Pulpy.

Midge headed down the hallway with Dan, looking back at them over her shoulder.

After dinner they took their glasses of wine into the living room. Pulpy sat next to Midge on the sectional and Dan and Beatrice reclined on separate ends of the divan in front of their large bay window.

'That was delicious,' said Pulpy.

'Thank you,' said Beatrice. 'I apologize for the peas, though. Dan did those.'

'I always do the peas.' Dan made a shooting gun with one hand and blew on his index finger. 'Peas are my specialty.'

'I love peas,' said Midge.

'Who doesn't?' said Dan.

Midge perched on the edge of the couch. 'Dan, would you mind turning the fire on?'

'Ho-ho!' he said, and reached for the remote. 'The lady likes it hot!'

Pulpy looked sideways at her, but she was watching Dan press the button.

Flames roared up in the hearth and Beatrice lifted her glass. 'To us.'

They all raised their glasses.

'Clinky-clink,' said Dan.

'Clinky-clink!' Beatrice giggled into her hand. 'Dan and I always say that when we do a cheers.'

'Well, then,' said Pulpy. 'Clinky-clink from us too.'

Beatrice's eyes locked on him. 'How's your booboo?' she said, and gulped back her wine.

Pulpy inspected the pink circle of his swaddled fingertip. 'A lot better, thanks.'

Midge put a hand on his knee.

Dan leaned back. 'You know, this makes me think. The lack of team spirit at our office is sort of like getting a cut on the end of your finger. It's like a cut on the end of our *collective* finger. So what do you do? You can put a Band-Aid on it, but that's not quite enough. So what then?'

'You could hold on to the Band-Aid,' said Pulpy. 'So it doesn't slip off.'

'You could. You could indeed. But I think there's a better way.'

'Dan,' said Beatrice. 'I thought we weren't going to talk about work in front of Midge.'

'Don't worry about me,' said Midge.

'No, no, she's right.' Dan held up a hand. 'Midge, forgive me.'

Midge pushed herself further into the couch and drank some wine.

'Work talk can make people feel uncomfortable.' Beatrice stood and walked over to pluck the bottle of red from the dining room table. She set it on the coffee table in front of her and sat down again. 'We don't like to exclude anyone.'

Dan uncrossed his legs. 'No, we do not.'

'So, Midge.' Beatrice smiled and reached back to finger the lacy white drapes behind her. 'When are we going to take our shopping trip? How about tomorrow?'

'Our shopping trip,' said Midge.

'Dan *did* tell you about it,' Beatrice said to Pulpy.

'He did.' Pulpy turned to Midge. 'Remember I told you?'

'No, no, yes. The shopping trip.' Midge blinked at him. 'Tomorrow would work, I guess.'

'Perfect!' said Beatrice. 'Oh, we are going to have fun!'

Dan pointed at Pulpy. 'You and me, then. They get a girls' night, we get a boys' night.'

'All right,' he said.

Dan made a fist and hit his leg with it. 'Boys' night!'

The four of them sat there and sipped their wine, and then Midge smiled at their hosts. 'So, how did you two meet?'

Dan picked the fireplace remote off the coffee table and started to play with the settings.

'Tell them, Dan,' said Beatrice.

Pulpy watched Midge gape at the flames as they grew, shrank and grew again.

'We were at a hotel bar,' said Beatrice. 'Sounds easy to remember, but Dan always forgets the story. Isn't that funny?' She filled up her glass.

'Hilarious.' Dan swigged the last of his wine and reached for the bottle.

'I just like to ask,' said Midge in a quiet voice. 'It's always nice to hear people's stories.'

'It *is* nice, isn't it?' said Beatrice.

Midge took a sip of her wine, which was almost gone. 'Pulpy and I met at the mall. We were in a pet store.'

'Commerce,' said Dan. 'Good omen.'

Pulpy smiled at his wife. 'We were both standing in front of the fish tank.'

Beatrice pivoted toward Dan. 'Do you see that? Do you see how they take turns telling the story?' She looked back to Pulpy and Midge. 'Dan got his wedding speech off the Internet.'

Dan banged his glass down so it sloshed, and stood up. 'It wasn't the whole speech. Just part of the speech.'

'Oh, just part of the speech. That's okay, then.' Beatrice glared at him.

'I'm sure it was a very nice speech,' said Midge.

Pulpy finished the few drops left in his glass. 'He gave a fine speech at Al's retirement party.'

'I wrote my wedding speech. I thought of it *myself.*' Beatrice nodded at her husband. 'He used one of those automatic word generators.'

'She goes on and on about her speech,' said Dan. 'It really wasn't that great.'

Beatrice slammed her own glass onto the table, spilling red, and stood to face him. 'I put my *heart* into that speech!'

'Yeah, your heart.' Dan slumped back onto the divan and picked up his wine.

Beatrice did the same.

Pulpy and Midge sat there on the sectional, holding their empty glasses.

'It smells like oranges,' said Pulpy the next morning as he watched Midge's finger paint a line down the middle of his thin chest with blue lotion.

'It smells nice,' she said. 'But wait until it starts working. Then it smells stronger.'

'When does it start working?'

'It's activating right now.' Midge rinsed her finger in the sink and wiped it on her pink robe. 'Just you wait.'

They sat side by side holding hands on the cold rim of their bathtub in their small bathroom in their small apartment, and waited.

Midge checked her watch. 'Now whenever we're apart you can touch the love line on your chest and think about us.'

Pulpy squeezed her hand and peered down at his chest. 'How long does this part take?'

'Ten minutes,' she said. 'So what are you and Dan going to do tonight?'

'I'm not sure. Something. What about you and Beatrice?'

'I don't know.' She sighed. 'She said she'd call me.'

'You don't have to go if you don't want to.'

She rolled her eyes. 'You tell me that *now*.'

'Sorry, Midge. I guess I was just trying to make things go smoothly.'

'Pulpy,' she said, retying the bow on her robe, 'there's being nice and there's being nice.'

He looked at her. 'What do you mean?'

'Never mind. Now pay attention to this next part.'

He could see the hairs sitting there, mixed in with the depilatory cream, and then she wetted a washcloth and dragged it over his skin. The hair came away clean.

'It burns at the roots,' she said. 'It's a chemical burn.'

'I didn't feel it burning. It was just sort of tingly.'

'They designed it that way.' She touched the right side of his chest, under the nipple. 'Now this half is yours.' She touched the left side in the same spot. 'And this half is mine.'

He bent his head for a better look at his pale torso and its new hairless line. His white briefs camouflaged him against the white porcelain. 'You and your ways.'

'Don't worry,' she said. 'It'll grow back.'

'I'm not worried,' he said, 'but I should get ready for work.'

Pulpy walked into the office, dumped his coat in the closet and then suddenly became aware of the sound of woodwinds. He looked around, blinking. 'Where's that music coming from?' he asked the receptionist.

'He's got them piping it in,' she said. 'You can hear it all through the office. It's a semi-live feed. He was all excited about it. There's somebody playing the flute somewhere, I guess. But there's a delay on it. He had a guy in here to hook it up. He put these wires all around my work area and now I'm worried I'll get electrocuted.'

'He wouldn't let you get electrocuted.'

'Oh, wouldn't he?' She shook her head. 'Don't be so sure.'

Pulpy eyed the lumpy nests of black cables around the receptionist's chair, and noticed that the fish was swimming more slowly than usual. 'Have you changed the fish's water yet? It's looking sort of grimy in there.'

She waved a hand. 'Be my guest.'

He picked up the fishbowl, gently. 'I'll be right back.'

Pulpy carried the fishbowl to the men's room and set it on the counter, and then paused when he heard a grunt from one of the stalls.

He looked at the fish and cleared his throat.

The man's voice went silent and there was a shuffling noise.

Pulpy plugged one of the sinks and turned on the tap. When the sink was half full he turned off the tap, rolled up one sleeve and stuck his hand in the fishbowl. The fish swam away from him.

'Uhh,' said the man's voice.

He cupped the fish in his palm and plopped it into the sink. He poked the fish in the belly and it swam away from him.

'Ohhh,' said the man's voice.

He emptied the scummy water into the other sink and rinsed out the bowl. He gave it a scrub with some paper towel and filled it up with fresh water.

'Mmm!'

Pulpy jerked his head around. The voice sounded different that time. Higher.

'Shhh!' said the man's voice.

In a rush, Pulpy scooped the fish out of the sink and dropped it into the bowl. He hurried out of the men's room, down the hall to the welcome area, and deposited the fishbowl on the receptionist's desk.

'If you ever leave a voice mail at a place of business, make sure to include your call-back number in the message,' she said. 'Otherwise your message will get erased.'

He stood there with his hands at his sides. 'I always do that.'

Davis from Building Maintenance came down the hallway from the direction of the men's room, hitching up his jeans. He nodded at Pulpy as he went by.

'That's good,' said the receptionist. She pressed a button on her phone and an automated voice recited the caller's phone number. Then the caller's recorded message played.

'To erase this message press seven,' said the automated voice. The receptionist's index finger descended. 'Message erased.'

Pulpy watched the man from Building Maintenance descend the stairs into the basement, and then shook his head. 'But you had the number for that one.'

'But *the caller* didn't leave it.' She sneered at her handset. 'And he doesn't know that his number was automatically stored. So he should've left a call-back number. One of the messages before was, "I found a pen with your company's name on it. What kind of services do you people provide?" Can you believe that? But he left a call-back number, so I had to call him back and answer his stupid question. That's the way it works.'

'It makes sense, I guess.'

'You guess?' She shook her head. 'There's a system and you follow it. That's all there is. Like somehow I get here on time every day. Somehow I manage to get up when my alarm goes off, instead of just lying there, which is really what I'd rather do when it comes down to it. But somehow I make it in. And I'm never late. I wish I could be late, just once. But I won't let myself.' She raised an eyebrow at him. 'I just can't do it.'

Dan was humming along to the music and tapping his fingers on his desk when Pulpy hurried past his half-open door. He waved him in.

'You've got to love the Winter Flute,' said Dan. 'It's a classic.'

'I don't think I've ever heard of the Winter Flute before,' said Pulpy.

'Then you haven't lived.' Dan grinned and bopped his head to the melody. 'It touches you. I could almost feel good about the world, listening to the Winter Flute.'

Pulpy moved his neck a little. 'The receptionist told me about the semi-live feed. She showed me the speaker system you hooked up.'

'Beatrice is going to do an audit of her processes,' said Dan. 'There needs to be a system in place.'

'I think she has a system already.'

'Still, Beatrice is going to look things over. She's here today. Are you going to get coffee?'

'I usually only get coffee on Fridays.' Pulpy looked at Dan's desk. 'Isn't that the receptionist's mug?'

'I don't see her name on it,' said Dan. He poked the cartoon duck. 'It's funny, isn't it? "My schedule's full." Ha!'

'But she always uses it.'

'Well, there's plenty more where it came from.' He handed the mug to Pulpy. 'Pretend it's a Friday and head over to Coffee Paradise for me, will you? Forget about Coffee Island – they use inferior beans. And I'm having a caffeine fit, so you'd better fill that mug to the top.'

'What kind of coffee do you want?'

'Just get me the house blend with a shitload of cream and sugar.'

'All right.' He left Dan's office, hurried down the stairs and walked back past the receptionist's desk as fast as he could, with the duck turned away from her.

'Hello,' she said.

He looked over, but she was on the phone. He decided not to get his coat.

The decor of Coffee Paradise was similar to the Coffee Island's, but fancier. Instead of one inflatable palm tree, there were real-looking mini-palms in every corner of the room, their broad green fronds waving gently in warm, coconut-scented gusts of forced air.

Pulpy stood in line and took deep breaths through his nose. The smell reminded him of Midge. She used a lotion called Tropical Mist.

Up ahead, the man at the cash appeared clasped together, like he was sucking in his face and holding it there. He had a name tag that read 'Your Barista: Claude.'

The customer in front of Pulpy stepped aside and Claude said, 'Can I help you, sir?' to Pulpy, who was still sniffing.

He stopped. 'Yes, please. I'll have one house blend in this mug.'

'And how will you take that?'

'Oh –' Pulpy swivelled his head and realized there was no help-yourself area for coffee fixings. He relaxed a little. 'Cream and sugar, please. Lots of both.'

Claude nodded. 'Anything else?'

'Yes. Do you have any Roco-Coco here?'

The barista sucked himself in further. 'What's that?'

'It's a kind of coffee. Roco-Coco. They have it at the Coffee Island?'

'Well, this isn't the Coffee Island, is it? This is Coffee Paradise. We have Coca-Loca. It's probably the same thing.' Claude pointed to one of the dispensers, with a sticker showing a wild-eyed coffee bean in a Hawaiian shirt.

'I don't think it's the same,' said Pulpy.

'Well,' said the barista, 'it's your call.'

Pulpy looked around Coffee Paradise, at the tall business-men occupying tall mahogany booths. He turned back and concentrated hard on the blackboard with its prices. 'I'll have a large jalapeno-pumpkin, please,' he said, feeling suddenly bold.

'What?' said Claude.

'The jalapeno-pumpkin. It says right there.'

The barista turned around, slowly. 'That's our lunch menu,' he said. 'That's a soup.'

'Oh.'

Claude smirked at a customer in line behind Pulpy. 'If you want soup, I'll give you soup.'

'I don't,' said Pulpy. 'I want coffee.'

'Well, then,' said the barista. 'Maybe you'd better decide what you want. What kind of coffee, I mean.'

Pulpy heard a few snorts behind him. He shuffled in place. 'Large,' he said.

'Large what?'

'Your house blend again. Or Colombian? Something easy.'

'Nothing is ever easy,' said Claude.

'Aren't you cold?' asked the receptionist when Pulpy walked back in.

He stopped in a pose that shielded the two coffees from her. 'Sorry?'

'You're not wearing your coat. That's not very smart in this weather.'

'Oh, that.' He gave a half shrug and continued walking, his body buffering the coffees.

'Hold on,' she said. 'Let me see something.'

'What?' he said. 'I have to get upstairs.'

She sat back in her chair. 'Fine.'

He passed by her with the scalding mug and his own hot cup pushed against his chest, and started up the steps.

'You really think you know what goes on around here?' she said.

'No.' He paused with his back to her. 'I don't.'

'You don't know anything about the way things work. I see everything that happens. People don't think I notice, but I do. I'm the eyes and ears of this place.'

He nodded and kept going.

'Thanks,' said Dan when Pulpy handed him the mug. 'What did you think of Paradise?'

'It's all right.'

'You're right it's all right. I love that place.' He tilted back his head and poured in coffee. 'Ahh. You still haven't gotten yourself a mug?' He took another long drink and then gave the receptionist's duck a kiss. 'I'm telling you, they're the only way to go.'

Pulpy frowned while Dan wasn't looking. 'Well,' he said, 'I'd better get back to work.'

Dan rubbed his hands together. 'We're still on for tonight, right? You and me, out on the town?'

'Yes. Boys' night.'

'Boys' night!'

'Yes,' said Pulpy. 'What are we going to do?'

'I don't know yet. We'll eat somewhere.' Dan coughed. 'Have a seat, Pulpy.'

Pulpy sat.

'I want to tell you something, and that is this. The way things work around here,' he said, 'is that there is a thing that *you* do, and there are the things that *we* do. It's all connected, and interwoven. But if a stitch slips, then the whole cog is going to fall apart, and it is just not going to roll.'

Pulpy tightened his hold on his Styrofoam cup.

'I think that's pretty straightforward,' said Dan. 'But the way things are going around here, I just don't know. Because typically, people don't have a whole lot to offer an organization. It's up to the organization to take from its people what it sees fit. To impart on them the requirements that they are expected to fulfill, and to follow through on making sure that those requirements are met and that the expectations are delivered.'

Pulpy squeezed his cup some more and the Styrofoam crumpled, spilling hot coffee onto his lap. He yelped and jumped up.

Dan handed him a tissue and then opened one of his drawers. He took out a small black pager and slid it across the desk. 'This is for you.'

Pulpy smacked at his new brown pants with the Kleenex and looked at the pager's shiny silver clip and neat little screen. 'Oh, well –'

'Go ahead, take it.'

'Hmm. It's just that, would you be paging me at home at all? Only because I have a feeling that Midge – she probably wouldn't be too keen on that.'

'Take it.'

'Okay.' Pulpy picked up the pager and slipped it into his coffee-stained pocket.

'Have you been touching your love line?' Midge asked when Pulpy called her at lunch.

He reached up and poked his chest. 'I have.'

'I knew it!' she said. 'I sensed you were thinking about me. Guess what?'

Pulpy smiled. 'What?'

'A lady on my route today had fruit on her shoes. Each shoe had a little bunch of miniature plastic fruit on the toes. A tiny lemon, an orange, a lime and cherries. Or maybe they were apples. I couldn't tell because the size ratio was off. So what are you and Dan doing tonight?'

'I don't know. I think he wants to go to a restaurant or something. Have you heard from Beatrice yet?'

'She wants to meet at the mall at six.' She sighed. 'So when will I see you? I don't plan on being home later than eight. Or nine. Nine at the latest.'

'I'll probably be home around then too.' He cleared his throat and lowered his voice. 'Dan gave me a pager this morning.'

'A pager? Why would he give you one of those?'

'So he can page me, I guess.'

'But why does he need to page you? At home? You better tell him I don't want him paging you at home. Tell him your wife said that. Tell him I do not want any beeping going on during our private time.'

'I'll do what I can, Midge.' He looked down at the coffee stain on his pants – the area was a slightly darker brown than everywhere else. 'That's all I can do.'

When Pulpy came back, Beatrice was sitting next to the receptionist at her desk.

'Hello, Pulpy!' she said. 'Look, I've joined the ranks!' She waggled her ID badge at him and the receptionist glared at her. 'I'm teaching the secretary about ergonomics. But now it's time for my lunch break so I'd better get going!' She stood up. 'I talked to Midge, did she tell you?'

The receptionist reached down to readjust the height of her chair, her gaze moving from Pulpy to Beatrice and back again.

He cleared his throat. 'She did, yes.'

Beatrice clapped her hands. 'I'm *so* excited about our girls' night!' She turned to the receptionist, who was busy with the back of her chair, removing a beaded net that Pulpy hadn't seen before. 'Did you have any questions?'

The receptionist didn't say anything.

'Perfect! So I'll get that survey from you after lunch!' Beatrice smiled at both of them and headed down the hall toward the staff kitchen.

'What was she talking about?' said the receptionist. 'Isn't Midge your wife?'

'I don't know,' he said. 'I mean yes, Midge is my wife, but I don't know what Beatrice is talking about.'

'She gave me this stupid back support but I'm not using it.' She dropped the beads into one of her drawers. They rattled loudly. 'The first thing she does is, she comes over here and she tells me, "You shouldn't cross your legs like that. It's bad for your back and it's bad for your circulation." So I said, "Well, how do *you* cross your legs?" And she said, "I don't." And I said, "I'm comfortable this way." And she said, "I haven't crossed my legs in years." And I thought, maybe *she* wants to sit there with her thighs all spread out over her chair but I sure as hell don't. I almost said that to her too. But I didn't. I just kept on crossing my legs.'

Pulpy's eyes went to her legs as she spoke. The thigh underneath was distributed across the seat of her chair, and the one overtop appeared smaller. They were both fleshy triangles, starting narrow at her knees and widening further up.

'What are you looking at?' she said.

'Nothing.' His face went hot. 'I was just –'

She ignored him. 'The thing is, you trade one evil for another. You either have your thighs all squashed out on the seat or you get varicose veins. You pick your poison. Then she tells me I'm supposed to have my arms in the neutral position when I type. I don't know what she's talking about – my arms are just fine, thank you very much.' She blew out a long breath and put her hands on her desk. 'And my mug is missing. Have you seen it anywhere?'

Pulpy took a small step back. 'What mug do you mean?'

'My duck mug. You haven't seen it?'

He creased his forehead and pretended to think for a moment. 'A duck? Like a nature scene?'

'No! The duck with the glasses on.'

'Sunglasses?'

'No! Glasses like mine. It's on my desk every day.'

'Ah.' Pulpy put a finger on his nose. 'Yes, okay, yes, now I know which one you mean.' He looked at the floor. 'I'll keep an eye out for you.'

'Thanks.' She smiled at him. 'You know something? You're the only one around here who gives a damn about me.'

'Oh, I'm sure that's not the case.' Pulpy reached over and gave her shoulder a tentative pat. She closed her eyes and leaned into him, and he pulled away quickly and put his hand in his pocket. 'I should get upstairs.'

Pulpy sat at his desk and lifted his knees. His keyboard tray rattled.

'Stupid tray,' he said.

'Did you say something?' said Eduardo.

'No.'

Lift. Rattle.

'Stupid,' he whispered.

'Now, before you go looking at the menu,' said Dan, 'I think I should tell you that the wings here are killer.'

'Killer?' said Pulpy.

'You can't go wrong with the wings at this place.'

'All right.' Pulpy put down the menu, which had sketches of sports equipment on it. 'You've convinced me.'

'You'll get the wings?'

'I'll get the wings.'

'Yes!' Dan smacked his palm on the table.

Pulpy jumped a little in his chair, which had domed pleather padding on the seat and the arms.

Their waitress appeared and smiled at them. Her T-shirt was tight. 'Are you ready to order?'

'You bet we are!' said Dan. 'We'll each get a three-pounder of wings, volcano-style.'

The waitress started to write on her order pad. She had long nails with a fleur-de-lis pattern on them.

'Volcano?' said Pulpy.

'They're hot.' She stopped writing.

Pulpy looked at Dan.

'Anything less than volcano and you don't get the whole experience,' he said.

'I'm fine with volcano.' Pulpy smiled at the waitress, and her pen descended again.

'You want another pitcher here?' she said.

Pulpy looked at the half-full one already on the table.

'Just keep 'em coming, sweetheart!' Dan winked at her.

'I'll be right back.' She tucked her order pad into her apron and walked away.

Dan watched her. 'Now that,' he said, 'is something.'

'What?' said Pulpy.

Dan grinned at him. 'Come on.'

Pulpy focused on a small rip in the red plastic tablecloth.

The waitress returned with their pitcher and set it down between them. 'Anything else?'

Pulpy couldn't look at her.

'No thanks, sweetheart,' said Dan. 'I think we're perfect.'

She nodded and left them again.

Dan leaned forward, putting his arms on the table. His suit jacket was hanging over the back of his chair and he'd loosened his tie. 'So, Pulpy, what kind of trouble do you think our women are getting into tonight?'

'Trouble?'

'You know.' Dan reached for the half-finished pitcher. 'Spending our hard-earned money and all that.'

'Oh, well. Midge earns her own money.' Pulpy watched the level rise in his glass as Dan filled it up.

'You know what I mean.' Dan took a long drink of his beer. 'Damn, this is good beer.'

Pulpy took a small sip. 'It's pretty good.'

'What makes you tick, Pulpy?'

'Pardon?'

Dan emptied his glass and poured another. 'What goes on, you know –' He tapped his own forehead. 'Up here?'

'Oh, I don't know.' Pulpy drank more beer.

'Well, we're all enigmas, I guess.' Dan topped him up and raised his own full glass in a toast. 'Clinky-clink,' he said. They were onto the next pitcher now.

'Clinky-clink,' said Pulpy. He was starting to feel a bit unsteady.

A while later Dan said, 'You all right?'

Pulpy wiped his forehead and looked at the dark design his blotted sweat made on the napkin, which had a cartoon of a basketball player slam-dunking a chicken into a vat of sauce. 'I'm fine, thanks.'

'You didn't eat that many wings. Look at your bone pile compared to mine.'

'Yours is bigger.'

'I'll say it is.' Dan swallowed some beer and then belched softly into his hand.

Pulpy picked up his glass and pushed his finger through the ring of moisture underneath. 'This beer stays cold,' he said.

'It's a new pitcher.'

'Oh, I forgot.'

'Ha! But who's counting, right?' Dan slapped Pulpy's shoulder, hard enough that Pulpy worried he might spill his beer. He put his glass back down, firmly, and faced his boss across the table. 'Dan, about the pager, I've been thinking about it, and –'

'Pulpy, I need to say something to you. And I'm not saying this to come down on you in any way.'

Pulpy leaned back a little. 'Okay.'

'I'm just saying it to get at something else I want to tell you.'

'Sure.' Pulpy drank some beer.

'Your punctuality is not the best, Pulpy.'

His stomach made an unruly sound. The wings had been very hot. 'Yes, you're right, I'm sorry. Yes, I know that.'

'And most employers would frown upon that. Most employers would, in fact, not condone it.'

'Al did,' said Pulpy in a quiet voice.

'What was that?'

He cleared his throat. 'Al didn't really mind so much, as long as I made up the time at the end of the day.'

'Uh huh. Well, like I was saying, *most* employers wouldn't condone it.' Dan poured more beer for both of them. 'But I am not most employers, as I'm sure you've figured out by now.'

'I have, yes.'

'And I like you, as I've said. As I've said many times. And when you get right down to it, punctuality doesn't matter.'

'It doesn't?'

'No. What matters is that you and I are men of action, and men of action make their own schedules. Pulpy, as of now, you've got flex hours.' Dan selected a mostly eaten wing from his bone pile and put it in his mouth. 'As of right now.'

Pulpy watched his boss remove the wing, cleaned of meat, and replace it on the mound. 'Flex hours?'

'Flex. As in you get to flex your muscle of judgment when it comes to when you arrive at and leave work.'

'Thank you, Dan.'

'Within reason, of course. I mean, we're still talking eight hours here. As long as you get the job done, and work your full eight hours, I have absolutely no qualms. Think of it as my gift to your marriage.'

'Sorry?'

'You know. This way, you and Midge in the morning ...' Dan winked. 'Now you can have more time together.'

Pulpy frowned a little. 'I don't think that's really any of your –'

'Let's do a toast to marriage!' Dan hefted his glass. 'Clinky-clink!'

'Clinky-clink.' Pulpy lifted his own glass and touched it to his boss's. 'To marriage.'

Dan tipped his head back and drank.

Pulpy filled his mouth with beer and slowly let it all go down. The dark room went out of focus for a moment and he put both hands on the table to stabilize himself.

'You okay there, Pulpy? You're looking a little –' Dan made a teeter-totter motion with his sauce-spotted hand.

'Well, I'm just – I'm okay.'

'Great.' Dan poured him another. 'So, tell me more about Midge. Fill me in on that wife of yours.'

Pulpy felt his mouth moving in a number of different directions and he concentrated on making it form a straight line. 'Midge is my wife.'

'That she is.'

'I love her very much.'

'I know you do.' Dan reached for another wing bone. 'She's a lovely woman.'

'She is. She is lovely.'

Dan nodded. 'She's lucky to have you. Beatrice and me, we don't have the same rapport you two do. But that's fine. I mean, that's the way we like it. She goes her way, I go mine. And we like other people's company.' He leaned forward. 'We like you and Midge.'

'We like you too,' said Pulpy.

'That's good. That's really good.' Dan nodded, and drained his glass. 'There was something else I wanted to ask you,' he said. 'It's about our secretary.'

Pulpy looked past him to the television set mounted over the bar. There was a game on, but he couldn't tell what type.

'What do you think of her?' said Dan.

People in the stands started cheering. 'She does a good job.'

'I don't know about that, Pulpy. I don't think I agree with you there. Her methods, her processes, they're outdated and inefficient. Beatrice and I are doing an overhaul, as you know, and Beatrice has been trying to introduce her to new and improved ways of doing things. But she refuses to adopt them.'

'She already has a system in place. I guess it works for her.'

Dan laid his palm flat on the table and spread his fingers wide apart. 'Do you see this? This is the hand of a man who knows what he's talking about.'

Pulpy stared at it, and then Dan curled it into a fist.

'Everything we're trying to do for the good of the office, she obstructs. She sits there, and sits there, and Pulpy, just one time –' He looked directly at Pulpy, unwavering. 'I see her sitting there, and I want to corner her.'

Suddenly Pulpy could hear the blood rushing in his ears, louder than the cheers from the TV, louder than the conversation sounds around them, louder than the loud music that was playing over everything else. 'She does a good job,' he said again, quietly.

Dan's eyes had contracted into angry pinpricks and he looked like he was going to say something else, but then he swerved around and focused on the game behind him. When he turned back a minute or so later he was grinning. 'What the hell, huh? Let's have some more beer.'

Pulpy watched him pour, and felt dizzy, and then an alarm went off inside him and he sat up in his chair. 'What time is it?'

Dan checked his watch. 'It's only ten. Huh. Can you beat that? Time really does fly, doesn't it?'

'I have to go now,' said Pulpy. 'I have to go home.'

The apartment was dark and quiet when Pulpy got in. He took off his coat and boots and tiptoed into the bedroom. The bed was empty.

He looked at the fishbowl on Midge's dresser. 'Hi, Mr. Fins. Where's Mrs. Pulpy?'

The fish swam to the surface, dove back down and darted from side to side in a happy zigzag.

Pulpy went back to the living room and sat down on the loveseat. He crossed his legs.

He felt something on his neck and realized he was still wearing his ID badge. He reached up and undid the safety clip on the lanyard. He took it off and refastened it in front of his face. The click it made was louder than he expected.

Then his thigh started beeping. 'What –' He looked down. It was buzzing too. The pager. He took it out of his pants pocket and held it in front of his face, trying to focus on the numbers on the glowing screen.

He got to his feet and went to the phone and dialled.

Dan picked up on the first ring. 'Pulpy!'

'Oh, hi.'

'Tonight was fun, wasn't it?' Dan was slurring his words a little.

'Sure.'

'We gotta have boys' night more often, I say.'

'Okay. But I should probably get off the phone, Dan, in case Midge is trying to reach me.'

'Beatrice left a message and said she'll be home late, so I wouldn't wait up.'

'Oh.' Pulpy sat back in the loveseat.

'The thing about us men is, we have to stick together. A wife is all well and good, but a man needs the company of other men.'

'Hmm. It's just strange I haven't heard from Midge, that's all.'

'She probably figured I'd get Beatrice's message and tell you. I wouldn't worry about it.'

'You're right.'

'You're right I'm right. Damn, those wings were good, weren't they?'

'They were really hot.'

'The hotter the better, if you get my drift. Now, like I was saying about that secretary.'

Pulpy rubbed his forehead. 'What were you saying, Dan?'

'She sits there, and sits there, and sits there. Doesn't she?'

'I'm not really sure what you're talking about. She sits at her desk all day. That's her job.'

'Her job. I keep hearing those words. I don't like them.'

'I'm pretty tired, Dan. I should probably get some sleep.'

'Sleep, yes. Shut-eye. And don't forget about those flex hours! You go ahead and doze away with your wife tomorrow morning, on me.'

'Yes, thank you. Goodnight, Dan.'

'Goodnight, Pulpy.'

The first time Pulpy met Midge, they were both standing in front of a tropical fish aquarium at the pet store in the mall.

He noticed her scalloped hair and wide-set brown eyes, and the way she stood perfectly still with her hands folded in front of her. Her face was blue-green and ripply from the tanks all around them.

There was a plastic mermaid in the one they were watching, alone beside a treasure chest. The chest would open and close, letting loose a curl of bubbles that jiggled the little bodies on the surface.

'Congo Tetra, Yoyo Loach,' he said, pointing.

She shook her head. 'I think that one's actually a Neon Tetra.'

'Oh.'

'They should get rid of the dead ones,' she said. 'How do they think the live ones feel, looking up at all those floaters?'

'Which one do you want?' he asked her.

She looked at him. 'I don't want a dead fish.'

'No, no, pick one of the swimming ones,' he said. 'I'll buy it for you.'

'But you don't even know me.'

'I'd like to.'

She smiled a blue-green smile.

'I'm Pulpy,' he said.

'I'm Midge.'

He waited for her to wonder aloud about his name, but she didn't. She just asked him for a Fancy Guppy, and he asked her out to dinner.

THREE

'Pulpy,' said Midge over breakfast the next morning, 'if you were unhappy you'd tell me, right?'

He stopped eating his cereal. 'What do you mean?'

'With us. If something about us was making you unhappy.'

'Nothing about us makes me unhappy.' He looked past the beautiful disarray of his wife's hair to the fridge, where Midge had affixed a 'To Buy' list with a real-estate magnet.

'But you'd tell me.'

'Sure I would.' There were practical things on there, like 'soap' and 'foil food,' but there were also a lot of other things, like 'mojito pitcher,' whatever that was, and 'more shoes.'

'Okay.' She bowed her head. 'It's just that we used to have ESP.'

'We did?'

'That's the way I thought of us, anyway. Like we could read each other's minds.' She sighed. 'These days I don't know. I just feel disconnected sometimes. Don't you, every so often?'

'Not really,' said Pulpy. 'I just go along.'

'I wish I could do that.'

'There are plenty of better things to wish for,' he said.

'I suppose there are.' She perked up a little. 'Did you have fun last night?'

He shrugged. 'It was all right. What about you?'

'Beatrice and I talked about candles.'

'Wax is a good icebreaker.'

'It is! Beatrice is the one who brought it up, though. She wanted to know about the business, I guess. Or else she just likes candles a lot. We had that in common, anyway. Plus, I bought these clamdiggers!' She lifted a leg to show him the pants she was wearing, which went to just below her knees.

'Those are nice,' he said. 'They're kind of short, though. Won't you be cold?'

'They're for the summer. I like what they do to my calves, see?' Midge stood up and posed on tiptoes for him so he could see her leg muscles flex.

'I *really* like those clamdiggers.' He reached for her.

She backed away. 'I don't want you to be late because of me.'

'That's the best part. I won't be, because Dan gave me flex hours last night. That means I'm allowed to be late.'

'Well, then,' she said, and sat on his lap. 'I let Beatrice browse through my route catalogue – I brought it with me just in case. I told her, "When you light a pillar candle for the very first time, you have to let it burn an hour for every inch of its diameter. This permits the wax pool to spread to the outer rim and stops your candle from hollowing out in the middle." I love telling people that. Nobody knows that stuff.'

He stroked her back.

'And then I said, "I have to be up front with you, Beatrice. It's worth keeping in mind that scented candles are smokier than unscented candles."' She brought her face close to his. 'She was really listening, Pulpy!'

'That's great.' He touched his nose to the expanse of her forehead.

'I'm sorry I was so late. But you were such a handsome sleeper when I got home I didn't want to wake you.'

'I wouldn't have minded.'

'I know. But now you're all rested and ready for the day. *And* you have flex hours.' She kissed him.

He kissed her back. 'Let's get you out of those clamdiggers,' he said.

'Good morning, Pulpy!' said Beatrice when he walked in at nine-thirty.

The receptionist, sitting beside her, turned and peered up at the clock.

'Good morning,' he said to both of them, and sniffed the air. 'What's that smell?'

The receptionist sneezed.

'It's air freshener,' said Beatrice. 'I picked it up last night, when Midge and I were out. Oh, we had *fun*, Pulpy!'

The receptionist looked between them with red-ringed eyes. She sneezed again.

'That's good,' he said quickly. 'But why do we need air freshener?'

'I said to myself yesterday, "It really stinks around here,"' said Beatrice. 'I said to myself, "I am going to buy some air freshener and really have a go at this place." Don't you think that was a good idea? It's orange spice.'

Pulpy looked at the receptionist, who was scratching at her throat. 'Well –'

Dan threw open the door then and planted his feet wide. 'Morning, Pulpy. Morning, Beatrice.' He took a deep, approving breath. 'It smells great in here!'

'How do you feel, darling?' said Beatrice. She winked at Pulpy. 'Dan needed a few extra zzz's this morning.'

'I guess we both did, hey, Pulpy?' said Dan, huffing the air. 'What is that, citrus?'

'It's orange spice,' said Beatrice.

Dan clapped Pulpy on the back. 'Sounds like just the ticket for our nine-thirty man over here!'

Pulpy held out his arms to keep his balance. 'You said I had flex hours.'

'He did?' said the receptionist.

Dan ignored her. 'I guess I did say that, Pulpy, you're right. And the moral of the story is, don't put stock in anything I tell you after five pitchers of beer, ha!'

'Oh.' His bottom teeth moved up over his top lip.

'But I meant it, though. I'm just kidding you, Pulpy.'

The receptionist sneezed, twice.

Dan blinked at her, and then strode forward and kissed his wife hard on the cheek. 'Today is going to be fantastic!' he said. 'I can feel it.'

'Are you all right?' Pulpy asked the receptionist when Dan and Beatrice had gone upstairs.

She shook her head and wheezed. 'Allergies. She sprayed that stuff right in front of me.'

'Don't worry.' Pulpy unzipped his coat. 'It's aerosol. It'll dissipate.'

'Until she sprays it again.' She sighed and scratched her puffy face.

He looked at the fish. 'Hey, I was thinking maybe I should keep the fish upstairs, on my desk. There's a draft every time the door opens here. The cold's probably not good for him.'

'No, I don't think so.'

He paused with his coat halfway off. 'It might be the best thing for him.'

'Well, it wouldn't be the best thing for me. I like having it here. It's a conversation piece. People come in, they comment on the fish. They'll say, "Nice fish," or "Where'd you get that fish?"'

His coat slipped from around his waist and he jerked out an arm, but the fabric hit the wet floor before he could catch it. 'What do you say when people ask you the second question?'

'Why?' she said. 'Is it a *secret* you gave it to me?'

'No, no, it's not. Ha. I was just thinking of the fish's best interests, that's all.'

She smiled at him. 'Because it's kind of our thing, the fish. Isn't it?'

He was bending to pick up his coat but he paused, folded into an awkward angle. 'What do you mean, "our thing"?'

'If you want to know what I say when people ask me where I got the fish, I tell them my boyfriend gave it to me. That way he comes off as less of a loser.'

He straightened up and cleared his throat. 'Did you tell your boyfriend you got a fish from me?'

'He doesn't care about those kinds of things. Fish. What about your wife? Does *she* know?' Her smile widened. 'She thinks it's on your desk, doesn't she? You didn't tell her you gave it to me.'

'I didn't give him to you, you took him.' He tossed his coat into the closet and shut the door.

'How is that any different?'

'I love my wife,' Pulpy said quickly.

'And I love my boyfriend,' said the receptionist. 'Sort of.'

'I'll see what I can do about the air freshener,' he said, and headed for the stairs.

'What do you mean, she's allergic?' said Dan.

'Just what I said,' said Pulpy.

'Well, I don't buy it.' Dan stretched and yawned.

'Did you see her out there?' said Pulpy. 'She looks terrible.'

Dan made an eye-rolling monster face, letting his tongue loll out of his mouth.

'That's not really –' Pulpy crossed and uncrossed his legs on the hard-backed chair. 'I mean, she's really sick out there.'

'So what do you want me to do about it, Pulpy?'

'You could ask Beatrice not to spray any more air freshener.'

'How can I tell her that?' Dan picked up a pen and signed his name on a piece of paper lying in front of him. 'You know how women are about the way things smell. And how come you're so concerned, anyway? What's that secretary ever done for you?'

'Nothing. I'm just advocating for her, that's all. She works hard. She's a hard worker.'

Dan squinted at him and grinned a lopsided grin. 'Huh.'

Pulpy reddened. 'What?'

'You know something, Pulpy?' Dan put his head down, then brought it up again and rocked it back and forth. 'I have a hangover the size of the planet Earth. Of the whole *Earth*, Pulpy! My God, my head feels like it's going to go supernova. Dammit to hell, my head hurts! How do you feel?'

'Not so good.' Pulpy stood up. 'I guess I've got a headache too.'

All of the pay phones were occupied when Pulpy went to them at lunch. He sat down at a nearby table and waited.

There were three phones: one was being used by a tall man with big teeth, one by a short woman with long hair and one by a teenage boy wearing suspenders. Pulpy did a double take. Teenagers were wearing suspenders now?

He looked at the two quarters in his hand. He flipped one of them end over end between his fingers.

The short woman hung up, and Pulpy headed for her phone. But then the teen with the suspenders reached for that receiver too and took it off the cradle.

Pulpy stopped, and then kept going. 'Hi,' he said to the teenager.

'Yeah?'

'Um, I was going to use that phone.'

'So?'

'So, you're already using one.'

The teen shrugged. 'I need two.'

The suspenders, Pulpy could see now, had red pinstripes on them. 'Why do you need two pay phones?'

'I'm doing a conference call.'

'What?'

The teenager showed Pulpy the back of one of his hands in a dismissive way, which was hard to do while he was holding the receiver, and turned away from him.

'Excuse me,' said Pulpy. 'I need to contact my wife.'

'Whatever.' The teen put two quarters into the second phone. 'Hey.'

The teenager dialled. 'Hi, is Bruce there?' he said into the phone Pulpy wanted to use. 'Yeah, I'll hold.' Then he spoke into the other receiver. 'Jaybird, you still there? I'm holding for Bruce, that cocksucker.'

Pulpy opened and closed his mouth, then stopped himself.

The teenager glanced at him over his shoulder. 'You still here?' He went back to the receiver. 'No, not you. There's some weird businessman standing behind me. Yeah, he's a cocksucker too.'

'Excuse me,' said Pulpy, 'I really do not think –'

'Bruce!' said the teen into Pulpy's phone. 'I got Jaybird on the other line!'

Pulpy looked at his watch.

'Yeah, hold on.' The teenager switched phones again. 'Jaybird, you still there?'

Pulpy sighed and walked away.

When Pulpy returned from lunch the receptionist was screaming in short, high bursts.

'What?' He rushed in. 'What's wrong?'

She was bent over the paper shredder, gesturing wildly. 'I'm stuck!'

He ran to her. Her ID badge, still on the lanyard around her neck, was in the shredder's sharp-toothed mouth.

'Where's the Off button?' he shouted.

'Right there! Push it!' She flailed an arm at the machine.

'I can't see where you're pointing! Where is it?'

'*Push it!*'

'I can't see it!' Then he remembered the safety clip and gave her lanyard a yank. The badge came loose and the reception-ist collapsed into Pulpy's arms.

'Thank you,' she said. 'You saved me.'

He blushed and helped her right herself. 'I just undid the clip.'

'You're the only one who came. A woman screams in an office and people do nothing.'

'Maybe they thought you were frustrated about something.'

'A scream of frustration is not the same as a scream of fear. People can tell the difference.' She brushed at her sleeves and tugged at the bottom of her ruffled blouse. 'I almost strangled to death here!'

'You wouldn't have strangled. The safety clip would have snapped apart.'

'Well, what if it hadn't?'

'But it's a safety clip. That's what it's designed for.' He demonstrated with his own badge.

She glared at him. 'I need you to be on my side here.'

'I am on your side.'

She sat in her chair and pulled herself in tight to her desk. 'Then why are you friends with them?'

'Who?'

'You know who.'

He glanced around, and lowered his voice. 'I'm not *friends* with them.'

'I told you before, I'm the eyes and ears of this place. So, what do they say about me?'

He paused. 'They don't say anything about you.'

'Oh, don't they?'

'What's going on here?' said Dan from the top of the stairs. 'Someone said they heard screaming.'

Pulpy's breathing quickened. 'The receptionist got her ID badge caught in the shredder,' he said. 'But she's all right now.'

'Is it jammed?'

'What? I said she's all right.'

'Did she jam the shredder?'

'I don't know.' Pulpy leaned over the shredder, which was still chewing on the plastic card. 'It looks fine to me.'

'Well, you'd better get that badge out of there before it breaks the machine. And then come up to my office.'

Pulpy looked up at his boss.

Dan stared back at him, hard, and then walked away.

Pulpy walked over to Dan's office and stood in the doorway.

'Come on in,' said Dan. 'Sit down.'

Pulpy sat on a hard-backed chair in front of Dan's desk.

'Nah, sit in a comfy seat.'

'Okay.' Pulpy switched to one of the lounge chairs further away.

'That's better, isn't it?'

'It is comfy.' Pulpy patted the leather arm. 'Soft.'

'Soft is right!' Dan nodded. 'Soft indeed.'

They sat there for a moment and looked at each other.

Pulpy felt a stiffness feathering up and down his neck. 'Is everything okay?'

'Everything is dandy,' said Dan. He grinned wide. 'Couldn't be better. You?'

'Well, I guess things are good. I guess.'

'Great!' Dan stopped grinning and leaned toward him. 'We need to have a powwow, Pulpy, about the potluck. It's on Tuesday. Are we prepared?'

'I guess so,' said Pulpy. 'I still have to think of something to make.'

'How many people are coming?'

'I'm not sure. I could check the sign-up sheet. I haven't checked it since I put it up.'

'I already did,' said Dan.

'Oh.' Pulpy blinked. 'How many names?'

'There are *two*, Pulpy. Mine and yours.'

Pulpy furrowed his brow. 'Only two? Really? Because I was sure that Jim from Packaging and Carmelita from the Parts Department and Eduardo –'

'It's just you and me.'

'What about Beatrice?'

'Forget about Beatrice.' Dan's voice got louder. 'We're still married, what the hell, so my name can count for both of us. Did you hear what I just said?'

'Yes. Two.'

Dan pounded his desk with the flat of his palm, and Pulpy jumped. 'This is unacceptable! Where are the rest of the names? Why haven't people been signing up?'

'I don't know.' Pulpy started to sweat across his hairline.

'This is why we need a powwow.' Dan loosened his tie with an impatient tug. 'This is why I gave you that pager, if you really want to get down to it, because emergencies can and do arise, and make no mistake, this is an emergency. This is an urgent Social Committee situation.'

'Yes, well, about the pager, Dan, that was something I –'

Dan cut him off. 'What are you and Midge up to tonight?'

'Tonight? Oh. Well –'

'Great, then tonight it is. Powwow.'

Pulpy nodded slowly. 'Powwow.'

Pulpy sat at his desk and made a few entries on his screen. He scrolled down and made a few more. Then he turned and knocked on his partition. 'Eduardo?'

'Yeah?' Eduardo stuck his head around.

Pulpy cleared his throat. 'Um, I heard you didn't put your name down on the sign-up sheet for the potluck?'

Eduardo squinted at him. 'Yeah, that's right.'

'It's just, I was just wondering. Because I thought you and Jim and Carmelita were going to. Put your names down.'

'We were until you told us it was Dan's idea.'

'I'm not sure what you mean.'

'Let me spell it out for you, Pulpy.' Eduardo leaned forward. 'We don't like Dan.'

Pulpy's eyes widened, and he lowered his voice. 'You don't?'

'Now Beatrice, Beatrice is a different story.' Eduardo wiggled his eyebrows. 'The guys think so, anyway.'

'Just the guys?'

'Oh, that's right.' Eduardo snorted. 'You're *married*.'

Pulpy frowned. 'What does that have to do with anything?'

'Nothing. Forget about it. Anyway, we don't like Dan, so we're not doing the potluck. But you go and have fun kissing up at your little tea time with the boss-man.'

'I'm not kissing up,' said Pulpy.

'Whatever,' said Eduardo. 'I gotta get back to work.'

Pulpy returned to his screen and made another entry, pressing hard on the keys. Then he scrolled down too far and had to go back up again.

When Pulpy got home, Midge's hair was different. The scallops were gone and it was all in a jumble.

'What happened?' He touched her head. 'Did you get it cut again? Did you go to the stylist the receptionist goes to? You didn't tell me you had another appointment.'

'I did it myself.' She sat primly on the loveseat. 'I went into the bathroom and I cut my hair. It fell into the sink and I rinsed it away.' She patted her hair. 'I think I did a pretty good job.'

Pulpy nodded. 'It's ... nice. What kind of scissors did you use?'

'Nail ones. They were all I could find.'

He pictured her in their tiny bathroom, concentrating hard and wielding the tiny scissors. 'It looks really nice.'

Midge bit her lip. 'You didn't call me today.'

'I know, I'm sorry. I tried, but all the pay phones were busy.'

She nodded and clapped her hands together. 'Let's get drunk, Pulpy. I feel like getting drunk.'

'That sounds like an idea, Midge,' he said. 'But we can't.'

'Why can't we?'

'Dan and Beatrice are coming over. We can get drunk tomorrow.'

'I might not feel like it tomorrow. And why are they always coming over here? We're not even friends with them.'

'I told you, I'm on the Social Committee.'

'For work, Pulpy,' she said. 'For *work*.'

The doorbell rang.

'You sit there and relax,' he said. 'I'll get it.'

Midge stood up and walked to the fridge.

He glanced at her, and then answered the door. 'Hi, Dan,' he said to his boss, who was standing there alone. 'Where's Beatrice?'

'She's in the shop,' said Dan. 'The beauty shop, that is!' He slapped his thigh in a comical way.

Pulpy smiled.

'She went and booked some spa retreat for the weekend – said she needs to refresh her soul. I said, "Refresh away, but make sure you don't come back to me with crystals glued on down there." You know how that's the big thing these days, that or shaving the bikini hair into funny shapes.' He stuck his head into the room. 'Where's Midge?'

'Well,' said Pulpy, and looked back toward the fridge.

Midge had lined up the sugar bowl, a bottle of club soda, a few wobbly limes, a clump of green leaves and a twenty-sixer of rum on the kitchen counter.

'Hello, Midge!' said Dan. 'What are you doing over there?'

'Making a mojito,' she said. 'Would you like one?'

'I sure would!' said Dan.

'I'll make a pitcher, then.'

Pulpy stepped back and gestured at the couch. 'Why don't you come in?'

Dan strode into the living room. 'I think your wife's trying to get me drunk!'

'Hmm,' said Pulpy. 'Let's sit down, shall we?'

'That is one of my favourite things to do.' Dan sat on the couch and lolled across it, his limbs dangling.

Pulpy sat across from him on the loveseat with his feet flat on the floor and his knees together. 'So,' he said.

'Better make mine a double, Midge!' Dan called, undoing his tie and sliding it out from under his collar. 'It's been a rough day at the office for your hard-working men over here! Ha!'

Midge was stirring the greenish contents of a tall glass pitcher with a long wooden spoon. 'I'm one step ahead of you, Dan!' she called back.

Dan grinned and sprawled out even more. 'You'd better hold on to that one,' he said to Pulpy.

'I will, thanks, Dan.' Pulpy sat up a bit straighter.

Midge walked over with three drinks. 'Here we are, gentlemen.'

'Here we are indeed! Midge, you're one in a million.' Dan accepted his mojito from her. 'Wait a minute. Did you do something different with your hair?'

'I cut it myself,' she said. 'Earlier today.'

'I think you missed your calling,' he said. 'It looks fantastic.'

'Oh, well.' She reached up and burrowed a hand in the jumble, then smiled.

Dan smiled back at her.

'Sit next to me, Midge,' said Pulpy, patting the loveseat.

'Okay.' She walked backward until her calves connected with the cushions and then she plunked herself down.

Pulpy took a tentative sip of the pale liquid his wife had given him, and the torn leaves floated up to his lips. 'You've never made this before,' he said. 'Have you?'

'I found a recipe,' she said.

'I love a good mojito,' said Dan.

'How did you get here, Dan?' said Pulpy, a bit loudly. 'Did you drive?'

'Uh huh. I'm parked on the street.'

Pulpy nodded. 'You're good until midnight.'

'Midnight, eh? Well, I guess I can afford a ticket if I get one.'

'Well.' Pulpy shuffled closer to Midge. 'Until midnight you're good.'

Midge looked at him. 'You have mint in your teeth.'

Pulpy stood up, walked through the kitchen, and grimaced into the hall mirror.

'Damn, that's a good mojito!' said Dan.

'Thank you,' said Midge.

Pulpy picked out the mint and walked back in. 'So,' he said, and looked from his wife to his boss. 'Should we have that Social Committee powwow now?'

Dan raised his drink. 'This is enough social for me, right here.'

Midge nodded and drained her glass.

Pulpy wound his fingers more securely around his almost-full mojito. The glass was cold and slippery.

'There is just the right amount of booze in this,' said Dan. 'Tasty.'

'Thank you,' Midge said again. 'Let me pour you another.'

'Don't mind if I do!'

She took their empty glasses to the kitchen.

Pulpy sat down on the loveseat and looked at his watch. 'Maybe we should pace ourselves.'

But they didn't seem to hear him.

'Tell me something about candles, Midge,' said Dan. 'Beatrice says you know all about them.'

'Oh, well, I wouldn't say I know *all* about them.' Midge handed Dan his fresh drink and took a gulp from her own. 'I'm learning as I go along.'

'You know more than most people, I'll bet. Beatrice says you showed her a catalogue?'

'I did, but it's the same one Pulpy brought to work so I'm sure you've seen it by now.'

Pulpy stiffened.

Dan looked at him. 'No, I don't think I have.'

Midge sat down next to Pulpy and took another drink. 'Pulpy, you didn't show Dan the catalogue?'

'I've been meaning to,' he said quickly. 'Dan's just been really busy lately, so I haven't wanted to disturb him.'

'My door is always open for you, Pulpy, you know that,' said Dan. '*And* for your lovely wife.' He winked at Midge.

Midge giggled mid-sip.

'Hmm,' said Pulpy. 'Well, Midge, why don't you show Dan your copy now? That way he doesn't have to worry about the one at work.'

'I'm not worried, who's worried?' said Dan.

'I'm not worried!' said Midge.

Dan held his glass out to her. 'That's the spirit, Midge. Clinky-clink!'

'Clinky-clink!' she said, and threw her head back and laughed.

Dan caught Pulpy's eye and shifted his hips on the couch.

Pulpy frowned and stood up. 'I'm getting a glass of water. Does anyone else want one?'

Midge waggled her empty glass at him. 'Can you mix us another pitcher of mojitos?'

'I don't know what's in them,' he said.

'Oh, what good are you, then?' said Midge, and then she put a hand over her mouth and her eyes widened above her fingers.

Pulpy's shoulders sagged.

Dan leapt up. 'I know what's in them!'

Midge dropped her hand to her lap and looked down at it.

Pulpy opened his mouth to say something but then closed it again.

'Do you have any more limes, Midge?' Dan called from the counter. He'd rolled up his shirt sleeves to expose his thick, hairy forearms.

'Hold on, I'll get them for you.' She got off the loveseat and hurried past Pulpy to the kitchen.

Pulpy sat down by himself and watched the two of them hand ingredients to each other. They were both laughing, and Midge wasn't paying any attention to him at all.

'Pulpy? Pulpy, wake up.'

Pulpy opened his eyes the next morning to see Midge standing over him with an urgent look on her face. He patted the spot beside him and closed his eyes again. 'Come back in.'

'Pulpy, I made pancakes.'

'Yum!' he said with his eyes shut.

'I made pancakes so we can feed him and then ask him to leave.'

He opened one eye. 'Ask who to leave?'

'Dan.'

He sat up and rubbed his face. 'Dan's still here?'

'I couldn't let him drive home in the state he was in. He's on the couch,' she said. 'But I don't want him staying all morning, and we have Ice Dance.'

He checked the time. 'How long have you been awake?'

'Long enough to make pancakes. Please, Pulpy.'

'I don't remember going to sleep.' He got out of bed. 'Did we give him a blanket?'

'There's a blanket on him.'

Together they walked down the hall and through the kitchen, and stood on the border of tile and carpet peering at their guest.

Dan was turned away from them on the couch with a blanket covering his legs. He was still wearing his clothes from the night before.

'See? He's still sleeping,' she said.

'He looks pretty comfortable. Nobody's ever slept on that couch before.'

Midge shrugged.

Pulpy cleared his throat.

Dan didn't move.

Pulpy leaned in a bit and knocked on the wall. 'Hello?'

Dan shifted a little on the cushions.

'I'm going to take the pancakes out,' said Midge. She headed for the kitchen.

'Pancakes?' Dan said, and rolled over to face Pulpy.

'Hello,' said Pulpy. 'Good morning.'

'Uh. Morning.' Dan sat up slowly. 'What time is it?'

'Eleven.'

'Eleven, eh? What time did we hit the sheets?'

'I can't remember.'

'Ho-ho! That is the sign of a good night!' Dan grinned. 'Damn, those pancakes smell good! You've got a special lady on your hands, my man. That Midge – she's a firecracker!'

'She is,' said Pulpy. 'Bang.'

'Bang is right. Bang is what my head is doing right now. Those mojitos pack a *punch*!'

'They do indeed.' Pulpy stood there. 'Well, I'll let you get up. We're in the kitchen.'

'I'll be right there.'

Pulpy turned around. Midge was setting plates on the table. He sat down. 'Do you want me to help?'

'No, you sit.'

'Okay.' He pulled in his chair.

Dan joined them. 'Good morning, Midge!'

'Good morning, Dan,' she said.

'I said to Pulpy, "Damn, those pancakes smell good!" I told him he's got a special lady on his hands.'

'I heard that. Thank you.'

Pulpy ran his hand along the smooth underside of the table and watched the two of them.

'Do you need any help there?' said Dan.

'No thanks, I'm fine. You have a seat with Pulpy. Would you like some coffee?'

'Yes, please!' Dan sat down. 'Coffee is exactly what I would like!'

'How do you take it?'

'Just dump in a shitload of cream and sugar.'

'Well, I don't know if we have a shitload, Dan,' she said, 'but I'm sure you'll manage.'

'Banter, ha!' said Dan. 'I love banter in the morning. Pulpy, the honey that pours forth from this woman's mouth, you could bottle it and make a fortune.'

'Hmm,' he said.

'Pulpy?' Midge tilted the coffee pot at him.

'Yes, please.' Pulpy faced his boss across the table. 'So, I don't think we ever ended up discussing the Social Committee last night.'

'Ha, ha! No, we did not.'

Pulpy reached for the sugar. The lid was off the bowl from last night. 'So ... should we? Discuss things?'

Dan waved a hand. 'Who needs discussion? Not me, that's for sure.'

Midge set glasses of orange juice in front of them.

'Orange juice! Ha!' Dan said to Pulpy.

Pulpy blinked at him. 'So what do you have planned for the rest of your day, Dan?'

Dan took a long drink from his mug and stretched. 'I was thinking I'd laze around the homestead, seeing as Beatrice is away and all.'

'That sounds nice for a Saturday.' Midge served the pancakes. 'Could you get the syrup out of the fridge, please, Pulpy?'

'A nice, lazy day.' Pulpy opened the fridge and started moving things around.

'Ho-ho, look at all those real estate agents!' said Dan. 'It's like a convention on there! Are you two in the market?'

'We might be,' said Midge. 'We're considering our options.'

'Well, I think you've got yourselves a little piece of heaven right here.' Dan crossed his arms behind his head. 'And I for one am looking forward to spending some more time in it today.'

Pulpy froze with his hand on the ketchup bottle, which had been concealing the syrup. 'Oh, you meant you wanted to laze around *our* homestead.'

'That's right,' said Dan. 'You're sure you don't mind?'

Midge gritted her teeth at Pulpy over the fridge door. 'Well,' she said.

'Actually, Dan,' said Pulpy, straightening up, 'we sort of have a weekend routine.'

'Oh? And what's that?'

'We just have things we like to do.'

Dan opened and closed one of his big hands. 'What kinds of things?'

'Just – things.' Pulpy sat back down at the table. 'Would you like some syrup?'

'No thanks. I just need some of this.' Dan hacked a chunk of butter from the block on the table.

Midge sat down between them. 'I'll have the syrup, please, Pulpy.'

Pulpy eyeballed the distance from himself to Midge and from Midge to Dan. She was closer to Dan. He edged his chair toward his wife and handed her the syrup. 'Sorry we can't invite you to stay, Dan. We would if we could.'

'No, no, it's fine. I understand.' Dan frowned at the pale, unmelted chunk of butter on his stack of pancakes. 'I'll just finish my breakfast and go.'

'Sorry the butter's cold, Dan,' said Midge. 'We like to keep it refrigerated.'

'That's okay, Midge.' Dan smiled at her. 'You're still the hostess with the mostest in my books.'

She focused on her knife and fork. 'Thank you, Dan.'

'But this is nice, though,' Pulpy said to his boss. 'Seeing you in the morning outside of work.'

'Yes, nice.' Dan pressed his thumb down on his pat of butter and stared at Midge. He wasn't smiling anymore.

Midge's fork made a high-pitched scraping sound on her plate. 'Oops. Sorry,' she said.

Dan kept looking at her as he rubbed the softening yellow square across his pancakes. 'See that?' he said, licking melted butter off his thumb. 'Works every time.'

Pulpy tipped the syrup bottle upside down and squeezed. The dark brown liquid oozed out in a long, wavering line.

'What are you thinking about, Midge?' said Pulpy later that day.

'Shh!' She put a mittened hand over his mouth. 'He's talking about the tango.'

The instructor was performing a demonstration, and their classmates were gathered around him. 'When doing an ice tango, every sinew of your body must strain against every other sinew,' he said as he whooshed dramatically from side to side. 'That sensual synergy is intrinsic to an elegant rink routine.'

Midge made a funny little noise. 'Elastic glue.'

'What?'

'Sometimes our marriage feels big and small at the same time,' she said. 'Like pulling apart, and then coming back together. Like glue, but elastic. Like elastic glue – is there such a thing?'

'Sure,' he said. 'There probably is.'

'You think I have these fantastic ideas, but they're not. They're just what I think.'

'You think fantastically. That's okay.'

She stuck her toe pick into the ice. 'Why haven't you shown the catalogue to anyone at work yet?'

'I've been meaning to. I just haven't gotten the chance.' He swallowed. 'Midge, um, about last night. Did anything ... ?'

She jerked her head toward him. The absence of her scallops made his heart lurch.

'I mean, I know *you* wouldn't,' he said quickly, and slid one of his skates back and forth. 'I don't remember very much, that's all. But maybe if I went to bed – did I? And if you and Dan were alone – were you? He might've ... because you know you can tell me if something –'

She closed her eyes, and when she opened them again her lashes were wet. 'I can't remember, Pulpy. All I know is, you went to bed and it was just me and Dan, and he started asking me about candles. And then I woke up and made pancakes.'

'Passion!' yelled the instructor. 'That is what this sport is all about.'

Pulpy gave Midge a small smile. 'It's okay.'

'Is it?'

He squeezed her hand.

Midge smiled back at him. 'Do that again. I like it.'

He gave her mitten another squeeze and waited for her to say something else.

'Come on, let's skate,' she said. 'Skate with me.'

'Okay,' he said, and together they pushed off, resuming their slow progress around the rink.

'The problem with me cutting my hair,' said Midge on Monday morning, 'is that I couldn't get the back. Could you do it for me?'

Pulpy looked at her head. 'I don't know.'

'But you're my husband.'

They were sitting at the kitchen table, and Midge had already tucked a couple of paper towels into the neck of her robe. There was a pair of poultry shears on the placemat in front of her.

'Aren't those scissors for chicken?' he said.

'I found them at the back of the gadget drawer last night.' She picked them up and made them open and close. 'They're better than my nail ones.'

'What if I don't do it right?'

'You can't do it wrong,' she said. 'You just cut and make it shorter.'

'But how much shorter?'

'I don't know. An inch?'

'An inch is a lot,' he said.

She shrugged. 'If you don't want to do it, I'm not going to make you.'

'It's not that I don't want to. It's just that, well, I'm not a barber, Midge.'

'I know you're not a barber, Pulpy. I only need you to cut the *back*.' She took hold of his wrists. 'Use your magic charade hands on me.'

'All right, then,' he said.

'Good.' She let him go and straightened in her chair. 'We'll sweep up afterwards.'

Pulpy tried his best to picture an inch in his head, and then he picked up the scissors.

On the way to work, Pulpy pressed one of his hands against the cold glass of the bus window.

Midge's hair had floated down around him in small brown puffs.

Outside, everything was white. He wished the snow would melt. He wanted it to be spring. He wanted Midge to be able to wear her clamdiggers and not be cold.

Pulpy closed his eyes and pictured sun. He pictured himself and Midge sitting in their backyard, passing the fly swatter back and forth for killing wasps.

Then he felt the chill in the air and pictured Midge last Christmas, showing everyone how to trim a candlewick – you had to leave just enough. Then Midge with a fondue fork and that awful look on her face when she realized Al's dog was in the backyard with Mrs. Wings.

He opened his eyes and looked up. He was sitting near the back doors of the bus and the letters over the exit read 'TO OPE DO R S AND ON ST P.' Pulpy thought about someone standing there scraping off the N and the O and the S and the T and the E. He imagined them starting and then feeling like they just couldn't stop.

Midge's clouds of hair on the floor. She'd been sweeping them up when he kissed her goodbye.

The receptionist was standing outside the building when Pulpy got to work. She was holding a bucket in one hand and a big scoop in the other.

'Hi,' he said. 'What are you doing out here?'

'He's got me salting.' She showed him the bucket, which was full of dull-grey crystals. 'Who asks a woman to salt?'

He chewed on his lip. 'Do you want me to do it?'

The receptionist stabbed the air with her scoop. 'No,' she said. 'I'm almost done.'

Pulpy squinted at the snow and then at her. 'You don't have a coat on.'

'Tell me that again. Tell me I don't have a coat on. Don't you think I know that? Don't you think I'm freezing out here, with this salt, and that I've been freezing since I came outside without my coat? And that was half an hour ago.' Her breath was coming out in big, white plumes.

'Why aren't you wearing your coat?'

'He hands me the bucket and the scoop and says, "Can you salt around the building?" He's holding the door open while he's saying it. What else was I supposed to do?'

'I'm sure he didn't mean for you to go out in the cold like that,' said Pulpy.

'You're sure, are you?'

Her lips were a smear of gooey red against her pale face. Pulpy saw goosebumps on her bare forearms, and he couldn't help but notice that she was wearing a very thin blouse.

'Anyway, since when are you and the boss such bosom buddies?' she said.

Pulpy yanked his gaze back up. 'What do you mean?'

'You know what I mean.'

'He's just being nice to me. I don't know why.'

The receptionist tossed some salt on his shoes. 'Better get inside where it's warm.'

Beatrice was sitting at the receptionist's desk when Pulpy walked in.

'Pulpy!' She waved a file at him and then fanned it under her chin in an exaggerated way. 'Whew! It is *hot* in here!'

'Hi, Beatrice.' He headed for the closet.

'I'm redoing the filing system,' she said. 'It's going to be much better when I'm done with it.'

Pulpy dropped his coat on the closet floor. 'The receptionist is outside.'

'That's right, with the salt.' Beatrice was wearing what appeared to be a tight painter's smock, with various colours splattered across it. 'Is she doing a good job?'

'She's not wearing a coat.'

'She isn't? Well, that's not very smart.' Beatrice swivelled then and looked up at the clock, and turned back to him with her bright pink mouth in a little O. She wagged a finger back and forth. 'Tsk, tsk. You are *late*, mister!'

'Oh.' He shuffled his feet. 'Well, I – the bus – and Dan gave me flex hours ...'

She snorted. '*I* don't care if you're late!'

'Hmm. Well, I should get upstairs.'

'Come over here first. I want to show you something.' Two of her fly-away hair strands twitched at him.

He slowly approached the desk.

'Dan told you I went on that spa retreat, right? On the weekend? He said you and Midge showed him a really good time, by the way. You had mojitos? Mmm! But like I was saying, from the spa, my skin is still really soft. I was feeling it this morning.' She rolled up her sleeve and stroked her arm, then held it out to him.

Pulpy nodded. 'Nice.'

'Go ahead, feel it for yourself. Feel my skin!'

He hesitated, then reached out and prodded her with his fingertip. 'Soft,' he said.

'It smells amazing too. Did you smell it?'

'I think so.'

'No, you'd know it if you did.' She brandished her bare arm at him again. 'Take a whiff, and then you can go.'

'Um.'

'Come on!'

'All right,' he said, and leaned forward.

'Ho-ho! What's going on down *here*?' said Dan from the top of the steps.

Pulpy shot back upright. 'Nothing. I was just –' He looked at Beatrice.

'Don't worry about my *husband*,' she said. 'He doesn't mind you taking a sniff.'

'Come on upstairs, Pulpy,' said Dan. 'I need to discuss something with you.'

'She wanted me to smell her arm,' said Pulpy as soon as he was in Dan's office. 'And touch it, but I only used one finger.'

'I don't care.' Dan waved a hand at him. 'Have a seat.'

Pulpy sat on a hard-backed chair. 'Midge uses Tropical Mist,' he said, 'and she always smells nice.'

'And that's the main thing. Nothing better than a good-smelling woman, no sir.' Dan put his feet up on his desk and crossed them at the ankles. 'Now let's get down to business.

From where I stand the situation is twofold: one, lack of hype, but we'll fix that today with the office-wide potluck-reminder email you'll send out; and two, lack of employee morale, but the whole point of the potluck is to boost team spirit, so there you have the whole chicken-and-egg thing, and there's not much we can do to reverse that process. So, basically, you'll send the email after this meeting, and we'll go from there.' Dan clapped his hands together and stood up.

'Which is the chicken part?' said Pulpy.

'That's the whole point.' Dan came around and sat on his desk directly in front of Pulpy so that their legs were almost touching. 'Because either way you look at it, morale will be hatched from the potluck, and the potluck's success will depend on morale. I can't think of any other reason that would account for a poor turnout.' He lifted one foot to tap the underside of Pulpy's chair. 'Can you?'

Pulpy shook his head slowly. 'I can't think of anything.'

'Well, you let me know if you do.' Dan bent his big head to look at Pulpy eye to eye. 'I'm counting on you.'

'You won't regret it.'

Dan gave him a light, stinging punch on the arm, and walked back to his chair. 'Better get to it, then.'

'Um, just one thing, speaking about employee morale.' Pulpy cleared his throat. 'I saw the receptionist out front this morning with a bucket of salt.'

Dan nodded and pressed Enter a few times on his keyboard.

'She didn't have a coat on.'

'Is that woman crazy?' said Dan. 'She sure acts crazy, from what I've seen. That is one crazy secretary.'

'Receptionist,' said Pulpy.

'Excuse me?' Dan shook his head. 'Hold on.' He pressed Enter one more time and then frowned at his screen. 'Dammit.'

'She likes "receptionist" better than "secretary."' Pulpy rubbed the back of his neck.

Dan punched the Up arrow on his keyboard three times. Then he turned back to Pulpy. 'The tag on her desk says "Secretary."'

'Yes.' The fax machine on Dan's desk let out a series of urgent *bleep*s, and Pulpy jolted at the sound. 'But she doesn't like that word.'

'You have to wonder about people who are so particular about things.'

Pulpy took a big breath and recited, '"For all clients to enjoy a quality product, and for all employees to enjoy quality respect."'

'That's some kind of vision statement, isn't it?' said Dan. He shook his head appreciatively before reaching for the fax.

Pulpy noticed some familiar shapes in Dan's garbage can: Al's animal figurines were in there, heaped on top of each other.

Dan saw Pulpy looking and said, 'Al never came and picked them up.'

Pulpy didn't say anything.

Dan balled up the fax and tossed it into the trash with the animals. 'I had a nice time with you and Midge on the weekend. A *real* nice time.'

'It was,' said Pulpy. 'It was a good time.'

'That wife of yours, ho-ho!'

'What about her?'

Dan pursed his lips and folded his hands in front of him. 'Did you know, Pulpy, that there are so many candle-scent varieties that it would be appropriate to say they are endless? And not only are there the primary scents, but there are all the combinations you can make with them. A creative person would be hard-pressed to ever run out of fusion ideas.'

'She told you that, I guess.'

'She did. She's a whiz with candles, that Midge. If I were you I'd be more concerned about her than about the *receptionist*.'

Pulpy stood up. 'Of course I'm more concerned about Midge. Midge is my wife.' Al's camel was crowning the trash pile beside the crumpled paper.

'Yes, she is.' Dan grinned at him.

'I'd better go and send that email.'

'Yes.' Dan kept grinning. 'You'd better.'

Later that day when Pulpy walked by the receptionist's desk, he noticed that the fish didn't look very good. It was barely moving. 'The fish isn't looking very good,' he said to her.

'What?' She peered into the murky bowl. 'Looks fine to me.'

'Maybe I'll just change his water again.'

'Be my guest.' She refastened the metal clip in her hair. 'I'm telling you, I cannot *wait* to take my seminar. It says in the flyer, "Front-line staff need frequent breaks to keep their stress level in check." Frequent. Not just one, which is what I get. But not *her*, no. She lectures me on ergonomics and then goes gallivanting off to who knows where. Plus, she's in the washroom every time I turn around.'

Pulpy lifted the bowl and brought his face close to the glass. There was scum on the sides. 'Are you feeding him?'

'What do you mean, am I feeding it? What kind of a person do you think I am?'

'Just a sprinkle, right?'

'I don't know, a shake or two every now and then.' The receptionist narrowed her eyes at him. 'Whose fish is it, anyway?'

'He's my fish.'

'Whatever.' She waved a hand at him. 'Enjoy.'

He cradled the bowl with one arm. 'I'll be right back.'

Pulpy set the fishbowl down, gently, on the counter in the men's room.

He plugged one of the sinks and turned on the tap. 'Okay, fish,' he said when the sink was half full. 'Here we go.' He put a hand in to scoop up the fish.

The fish allowed itself to be lifted out.

Pulpy tipped it into the sink water. The fish flicked its fins once and then was still.

'Hey, fish,' he said, and poked it in the belly.

The fish let him.

'You don't like belly pokes! Get mad!' said Pulpy. 'Swim away!'

The fish didn't move.

'Hey, fish.' Pulpy patted the surface of the water, and the fish swayed with the waves he'd made. 'Don't,' he said. 'You're okay.' He emptied the bowl into the other sink and gave it a hard scrub with a length of paper towel. Then he rinsed it out, twice. 'No wonder you're miserable. This bowl is dir-ty!'

He filled the bowl with fresh water and set it back on the counter. 'There we go – your house is clean again.' He picked up the fish and it flopped into his hand. 'Flap your gills! Wiggle your tail!'

But the fish didn't do either.

'Fish,' he said. 'Fish.'

Then the door opened and Roy from Customer Service walked in.

Pulpy dropped the fish into the bowl and started to wash his hands.

'Hey, Pulpy,' said Roy. 'What are you doing over there?'

'I was changing the fish's water for the receptionist.'

Roy walked over and put his hands on his hips. 'Hmm. He doesn't look good, does he?'

'I think –' said Pulpy, horrified to hear his voice catch. 'I think he's dead.'

'Damn,' said Roy.

Pulpy just nodded.

Roy reached over, awkwardly, and patted Pulpy's shoulder. Then he put his hands in his pockets.

The two men stood there together, looking at the fishbowl.

Then Roy glanced at his watch. 'I guess you should take it out to her, huh?'

'I guess I'd better.'

'Poor little guy.' Roy looked at the door.

Pulpy felt tears starting, and he swiped at his eyes. 'He's from the winter fair.'

'The winter fair, eh? How about that.'

There was a knock on the door.

Roy jerked his head around. 'That must be the cleaner!'

'Why are you shouting?' said Pulpy.

'Just so the *cleaner* can hear there's still people in here, so she doesn't come barging in!'

'Oh. Well, I guess we'd better go, then.'

'I'll see you out there, Pulpy.' Roy nodded at the stalls.

'Right. Okay. See you, Roy.' Pulpy hugged the fishbowl to his chest and left the men's room. He passed Beatrice on his way back to the welcome area. 'Hi, Beatrice.'

She was leaning against the wall, and gave him a lazy smile. 'Hi, Pulpy. What's that you've got there?'

'It's my fish.'

'Oh yeah? I thought it was the secretary's fish.'

'He isn't really anybody's fish now. He's dead.'

'Aw, that's too bad.' She smiled again and headed down the hallway.

'See, there she goes again,' the receptionist said, and then noticed the fish. 'What did you do to it?'

Pulpy shook his head. 'Nothing – I. Nothing.' He set the fishbowl down on her desk and stood with his hands folded behind him.

'Here,' she said, and pushed Beatrice's chair around for him. 'Have a seat.'

Pulpy sat.

She held the bowl up to the fluorescent lights. 'You did a good cleaning job, anyway.'

'Thanks.'

'Why didn't you just flush it?' The receptionist gave the bowl a little shake and the dead fish wobbled inside.

'I don't know.'

She put the bowl down. 'It was a cheap fish, anyway.'

'He wasn't cheap,' said Pulpy. 'I won him.'

'You're right.' She nodded. 'I'm sorry.'

They sat there, together, with the fishbowl between them.

The receptionist lowered her head and peered at Pulpy through the glass. She tapped on the bowl. 'At least it won't have to put up with all the crap around here anymore.'

The fishbowl was gone when Pulpy went to get his coat at five o'clock.

'It's in the kitchen,' said the receptionist when she saw him looking for it. 'The bowl, I mean. I flushed the fish.'

'Oh.' He nodded slowly. 'You can keep the bowl if you want.'

'What do I need an empty fishbowl for?' she said.

'You could get another fish.'

She shook her head. 'Too much trouble. Besides, I've got other plans. I'm saving up money. I'm saving up and I'm going to do something big.'

'Good for you,' he said, and found his coat under a poncho and a ski jacket.

She jutted out her chin and scratched the bottom of it. 'Good for me is right. Good for me and screw everybody else.'

'Screw them,' Pulpy said, and then quickly looked around.

'I have a resignation letter started at home,' said the receptionist. 'I could finish it at any time.'

He froze with his coat halfway zipped up. 'What do you mean? You're leaving?'

'Who knows? All I know is, I don't have to be here.'

'You can't leave,' he said. 'That means they win.'

'There are other things I want to do. More important things. I do important things, you know.'

'I know. This place would fall apart without you.'

'Not *here*. When I'm away from here, I mean. On my own time. There are things that I do that are important.'

'Of course there are.' He pulled his zipper the rest of the way up, where he could feel the cold metal against his neck. 'It's good to do those things. My wife is into candles.'

'I didn't plan for this. I didn't think this was where I would end up. I don't even want much, you know. All I want is some recognition. I want somebody to say, "You're doing a good job."'

'You're doing a good job,' he said.

'Not *you*,' she said, but smiled. 'Thanks, though.'

'You're welcome.'

'They just have to keep pushing me,' she said. 'That's all they have to do.'

Pulpy stopped at the grocery store on his way home from work.

He walked up and down the baking aisle, but nothing caught his attention. He stopped a clerk who was passing by. 'Excuse me.'

The young man stopped. 'Yeah?'

'I'm looking for something to make for a potluck.'

'A what?'

'A potluck. You know, like a communal lunch? Everybody brings something.'

The kid scratched his neck, which was red with ingrown hairs. 'What do you usually bring?'

'That's what I need help with.' Pulpy held out his hands. 'I've never been to a potluck before.'

'Well, me neither.'

'Something with flour? That's why I thought the baking aisle.'

'Sure,' said the clerk. 'Flour's good.'

'But what should I make with it?'

'Look, mister, I gotta get back to the meat counter. I'm the only one who knows how to slice. Usually there's two of us, two slicers. But today it's just me. So I gotta get back in case there's something that needs slicing.'

'Give me one idea first,' said Pulpy.

The kid put a thumb on his chin. 'I don't know, why don't you buy something pre-made?'

'But I feel like I should *make* my contribution myself. From scratch.' Pulpy plucked a small container of rainbow sprinkles off the shelf next to him and shook it in a slow, halting rhythm. 'I'm the organizer.'

The deli clerk watched him. 'I gotta go.'

'Yes, okay.' Pulpy put the sprinkles back on the shelf. 'What should I buy that's pre-made, then?'

The clerk scratched his neck again. 'Puff pastry's a big seller – the already puffed-up kind. It's in the bakery section with the pies and stuff.'

Pulpy nodded. 'Thanks.'

'Sure. Have fun at your potluck.'

Pulpy nodded. 'I'll try.'

'Pre-puffed puff pastry?' said Midge when Pulpy showed her his purchase.

She was standing by the stove, where two small pots of water were boiling two individual foil packets.

'The deli clerk recommended it.'

She nudged the plastic-wrapped pastry he was holding. 'So what are you going to put in it?'

'What do you mean?'

'You can't have puff pastry plain. You have to fill it with something. Like whipped cream or soup mix.'

'Midge, those are two very different things.'

'Puff pastry is versatile like that. You can put anything in it.'

'The clerk didn't say anything about putting something inside it.' He leaned toward the boiling water and sniffed.

'He probably didn't know.' She waved him away from the stove. 'You can't smell anything from those – they're sealed.' She put on oven mitts and then used tongs to flip the foil packets over.

Pulpy shrugged. 'He seemed like a smart kid.'

'Well, he doesn't know about puff pastry.' Midge put lids on the two pots. 'Dinner's going to be ready in ten minutes.'

Pulpy tucked the pastry under one arm and started opening the kitchen cabinets. 'Do we have something I can use for a filling?'

Midge thought for a minute. 'We might have some nuts.'

'Nuts aren't a filling,' he said. 'Do we have any jelly?'

'We have Peach Delight jam. Everybody likes peach. You should wait until tomorrow to put it in, though, or else it'll get soggy.' She took the length of flaky pastry from him and held it at arm's length. 'This is for Dan's potluck?'

'I'm the one organizing it.' He took the pastry from her, and then he sucked in a breath. 'Oh, no.'

'What?' said Midge. 'Are you okay?'

He set the pastry on the counter and walked out of the kitchen and across the living room to the coat tree. 'I didn't send the potluck email.' He put on his coat and boots. 'I have to send it before tomorrow.'

'Where are you going? What about dinner?'

'I have to do this, Midge, I'm sorry. I'll be back soon.'

'I don't like this.' Midge crossed her arms. She still had the oven mitts on. 'I don't like this one bit. He's got too much control over you.'

'Midge, he's my boss.'

'And I'm your *wife*.'

'I promise I'll be back soon.'

'I don't like him, Pulpy.'

He paused with his hand on the doorknob. 'You didn't seem to mind telling him all about candles the other night.'

She opened and closed her mouth. 'But I *told* you –'

He shook his head. 'Sorry. Forget I said that.'

'Go and send your email. Mr. Fins will have dinner with me.' She let her arms fall to her sides and the oven mitts fell off, one at a time, and landed with soft *whap*s at her feet. 'You never even talk about your fish at work. You haven't even given him a name.'

He heaved open the door. 'I'll be back soon.'

The welcome area looked lonely without the receptionist. Pulpy kept his coat on and headed upstairs to his desk.

He waited for his computer to warm up and then clicked on his email. He started composing a new message with 'POTLUCK TODAY!' in the subject line. Then he cursored back and changed it to 'Potluck today!', which looked less frantic.

He realized then that he didn't know where Dan planned on holding the party, so he typed underneath, 'Potluck lunch Tuesday. Sign-up sheet in the kitchen. Location of potluck TBA.'

He also didn't know when it was supposed to start. 'Start time TBA.' He finished off with 'All welcome!' Pulpy read the whole thing over, nodded and hit Send.

Then he checked his Inbox. There were two messages waiting for him, one from Dan and one from the receptionist. He opened Dan's first.

'I'm very disappointed you didn't send the email,' it said. Pulpy frowned and pressed Delete. Then he leaned in a little and opened the email from the receptionist.

Back when he'd first met her and then forgotten her name, he figured he'd find it out as soon as she emailed him. But then he'd received a company-wide email from her and her name wasn't in her address – just 'secretary@.' Which she hated as much as her desk nameplate.

This time the email from her was a forward. Pulpy started reading and then stopped and minimized the window. It was a rude forward. And he was the only recipient.

His finger hovered over the Delete key, then pulled back. He took a hasty look around the empty office and returned to the email. It was a list of riddles, each of them using racy language to describe a mystery object. The first one was, 'You put your finger in me and play with me when you're bored. What am I?' Pulpy gaped. He looked left and right, and then took off his coat and hung it over his chair.

The next riddle read, 'I come and stuff your box. What am I?'

I don't know, thought Pulpy, and then he heard a noise.

He jumped and punched Close, harder than he meant to, and swivelled guiltily around in his chair.

'Mmm!'

It was the same noise he'd heard in the bathroom before, but this time it was coming from down the hall. He turned off his computer and pushed his chair back, carefully. Then he stood up and walked quietly toward Dan's office.

'*Mmm*!'

Dan's door was half-open and the sounds were coming from inside. Pulpy held his breath and peeked in.

There were two pairs of feet wiggling on the floor behind Dan's desk.

'Mmm, Eduardo!'

Pulpy shook his head. That Eduardo, he thought, and started to tiptoe away.

'Beatrice, you rock me,' said Eduardo's voice.

Pulpy stopped with one foot in the air, then lost his balance. His arms flailed out and he put a hand on the wall to steady himself.

'Did you hear something?' said Eduardo.

'No, did you?'

Pulpy stood there, his eyes wide.

The feet behind the desk stopped wiggling.

'Maybe I'll go check,' said Eduardo. 'The Building Maintenance guy might still be around.'

'No, he's not – I saw him leave. I'm sure it's nothing.' Beatrice giggled, and there was a light slapping sound. 'Now pay attention to *me*!'

'Ouch!' said Eduardo. 'Now you're going to get it.'

Beatrice squealed, and Pulpy ran for the stairs.

'What was *that*?' said Eduardo. 'That was definitely something.'

Pulpy yanked the front door open, and only when the cold hit him did he realize he'd left his coat on his chair.

The next morning Pulpy and Midge were eating margarine on toast and mango-flavoured peaches from a can.

'I'm sorry I missed dinner,' he said.

She shrugged. 'It tasted like tinfoil, anyway.'

He folded a piece of his triangle-shaped toast in half to make a smaller triangle. 'I thought you might wait up.'

'I was tired. Did you send your email?'

He nodded and made another fold in his toast, then flattened it. 'Are you all right?'

Her forehead creased into a zigzag, and she pushed her chair back. 'I'm going to feed Mr. Fins.'

Pulpy watched her walk out of the kitchen and down the hall. He tasted blood on the roof of his mouth from the toast's rough edges.

'Hello, Mr. Fins,' he heard her say from the bedroom. 'Are you hungry?'

He took a sip of coffee and swished it around in his mouth, then winced when ragged bits of skin flapped in the current.

Midge came back and sat down, and sighed over her peaches. 'He doesn't seem to have any appetite these days.' She slurped up a slick, golden wedge, and the tip of it wriggled between her lips.

'Why do these peaches taste like mangos?' he said.

'They're peaches in mango essence. It says on the label.'

'Why would they cover up the taste like that? Everybody likes peach.' He smiled at her.

She didn't smile back.

'I'd better get my puff pastry ready.'

She retied the bow that held her robe closed. 'I guess you'd better.'

He picked up a knife and sliced the pastry down the middle. Then he opened the fridge and took out their jar of Peach Delight jam and spread it up and down the soft centre.

Midge kept eating.

He stopped spreading and arranged the top half of the pastry over the bottom half. 'I probably won't be able to call you at lunch today,' he said. 'Because of the potluck.'

'I have a life of my own, you know,' she said. 'I don't just wait around for you to call me on your lunch hour. In fact, after I'm done my route today I'm going to have coffee with Jean. What do you think about that?'

'I think that's good.'

'Are you finished?' She pointed to the knife he'd used.

He nodded. 'I can try to call you from my desk later on, though.'

She plucked the knife off the counter and licked jam off the blade.

'Be careful,' he said.

She put the knife on the table. 'I'm done with it,' she said, and left the kitchen again.

It wasn't until Pulpy put on his boots that he remembered he'd left his coat at work, and on top of that he had to stand on the bus. He gripped a pole with one hand and cradled his pastry, which he'd wrapped in wax paper, with the other. People shoved past him on their way on and off and he had to keep shifting his weight to balance himself. Spearmint gum and strong perfume and various other up-close smells surrounded him, and he was cold without his coat.

When his stop was coming up, Pulpy tried to make eye contact with the passengers who could reach the dinger, but nobody looked back at him. 'Ma'am?' he said to a lady sitting near him who was wearing a parka.

The lady fluffed up her hood and turned away.

He saw his stop getting closer and reached out with his pastry to tap her on the shoulder.

She flinched and glared at him. 'Please don't touch me with your bread.'

'It's puff pastry,' he said. 'Could you please pull the dinger?'

She made a disapproving sound and gave the dinger a yank, but the bus kept going.

Pulpy frowned and leaned in to pull the dinger again.

The bus driver went on the intercom. 'Please stop playing with the bell. This is not a contest. You're not going into the bonus room.'

'But that was my stop,' said Pulpy.

The bus pulled over at the next stop and Pulpy stood on the step to get off. The doors didn't open. He pushed on the yellow bar.

'You have to push on the yellow bar,' said the driver over the PA. 'The one that says "Push."'

'I am pushing,' said Pulpy.

'On the yellow bar.'

The woman in the parka glared at him again.

'GET OFF THE BUS!' another passenger yelled.

'The bar isn't working,' said Pulpy. He shoved the puff pastry under one arm and leaned his shoulder against the bar. It wouldn't budge. Then a green light blinked on overhead and the doors gave all at once. Pulpy tripped down the steps and lost his footing on the icy sidewalk. The bus pulled away as he fell backward and landed on his potluck contribution.

When Pulpy stumbled, shivering, into the welcome area, the receptionist was bent over, stacking files in the small space between her desk and the photocopier. She looked over her shoulder at him. 'Why aren't you wearing a coat?'

'I left it upstairs,' he said. 'Where's Beatrice?'

'She's not here, so I'm blocking off her pathway.' She dropped a telephone book on the pile. 'She comes through this opening to sneak up on me, and I don't like her creeping around my workspace like that. When she comes back in she'll have to go around the regular way like everybody else.'

He rocked back on his heels. 'The potluck's today. She'll probably be here for the potluck.'

'Do you know what he said to her the other day, in front of me? He said, "You'll be inheriting this documentation." Meaning *my* documentation. Like I was dead. Like I'd even put her in my will if I was dead.' She sat in her chair and crossed her legs. 'And now with the filing she keeps asking me,

"What's the FN number? Tell me the FN number." Even though "FN" stands for "File Number." I want to scream at her, "You're saying what's the file number number! Just say F number, or FN or file number. Don't say FN number." It's repetitive and it's unnecessary. I can't stand it.'

'Did you get the email I sent, about the potluck?' said Pulpy.

'I already told you I can't go to the stupid potluck.'

'But did you get it? I sent it last night.'

She reached for her mouse and squinted at her screen. 'Yeah, I got it. Hey, did you get my email, then?'

Pulpy nodded and swallowed. 'I did.'

She grinned. 'Wasn't it funny? Did you see the answers? They were at the bottom, if you scrolled down.'

'They were?' He shook his head. 'I didn't see them. But what I was going to say was, maybe it's not a good idea to send me those types of emails.'

She pulled in her chin. 'What do you mean?'

'It's just that, well, I'm flattered, but –' He took a deep breath. 'I'm in love with my wife.'

'Yeah, you told me that already.' The receptionist frowned at her screen and clicked her mouse a few times, hard.

Pulpy felt the back of his neck heat up. 'Well, anyway, it's probably not a good idea to send those types of emails at work. Because Dan could see them – they're all on the company server.'

She looked back at her computer. 'I don't really care.'

He cleared his throat and headed for the stairs. 'I can bring you something from the potluck if you want.'

She didn't answer him.

'Pulpy!' said Dan when Pulpy walked by his office. 'Come in here and keep me company!'

Pulpy stepped over the threshold and stood there.

'Take a seat anywhere.'

Pulpy sat in one of the cushiony chairs.

'Actually,' said Dan, and pointed to the two hard-backed chairs in front of his desk, 'I said anywhere but I'd prefer you to sit in one of these seats here.'

Pulpy moved.

Dan laced his fingers together. 'What's going on with you, Pulpy? And by that I mean what's going on with this potluck? You sent the email last night. How are people supposed to bring anything when they only found out about the potluck this morning?' He shook his head. 'I thought we discussed this.'

Pulpy pinched the crease down the front of his pants. He was wearing the black ones. 'They could bring their lunches to share.'

'I do not think *lunches* are a viable option.'

He took a breath. 'The email was just a reminder. People have known about the potluck for a week now, since I posted the sign-up sheet.' He saw that Dan's big 'Back off – it's early' mug was on his desk, next to the receptionist's smaller duck mug.

'Yes, well.' His boss frowned. 'What did you bring, anyway?'

'Puff pastry with jam.'

'That sounds pretty good.' Dan nodded. 'I brought Jamaican patties. Spicy ones. They need to be nuked.'

'What did Beatrice bring?'

Dan coughed into his fist. 'Beatrice couldn't make it today. The Jamaican patties are from both of us. She had some appointments.' And then he grabbed both mugs by their handles and banged them together with a crack, dislodging a small chip of red porcelain from 'Back off – it's early.'

Pulpy put his hand over his mouth and looked away.

'Dammit!' Dan shuffled some papers on his desk. 'So. Back to work.'

'Okay.' Pulpy stood up. 'Um, so when and where is the potluck, exactly?'

'One o'clock in the boardroom. I thought I told you that already.'

'No, I don't think so.'

'Well, now you know.'

'I'll send a follow-up email.'

'Yeah, you do that.'

'All right.' Pulpy started to leave.

'Wait just one minute,' said Dan.

Pulpy stopped.

'Now, that right there was my work face. This right here –' Dan smiled ' – is the Dan you know and love. So, tell me. Is there anything you need, Pulpy?'

Pulpy stood in front of Dan's desk with one foot placed slightly behind the other. 'I'm not sure what you mean, Dan.'

'Is there anything I can do for you, to make your job easier? I want you to be happy.'

'Hmm.' He pointed his back foot and tapped that shoe on the floor, then blinked at his now-grinning boss. 'I guess my keyboard tray is slightly too low.'

Dan stood up and walked around his desk. 'Then let's go fix it.'

The two of them marched to Pulpy's cubicle and stood there together with their arms crossed.

'Show me what's wrong,' said Dan.

'Okay.' Pulpy sat down at his desk and pulled out his keyboard tray. 'See there? How it hits my legs like that? I asked Building Maintenance to fix it and they tried, but they didn't get it right.'

'That Building Maintenance man is no good,' said Dan. 'Let me in there.'

Pulpy wheeled his chair out of the way, and his boss dropped to his hands and knees and crawled under his desk.

Eduardo leaned around the partition. 'What's going on?'

Pulpy pointed to Dan's rear end wiggling at them.

Eduardo's eyes widened.

Pulpy coughed.

Dan started banging on the underside of Pulpy's keyboard tray. 'Is this what the Building Maintenance guy did?'

'Sort of,' said Pulpy. 'He wasn't quite so loud, though.'

Dan banged some more. 'Ow!'

Pulpy watched Eduardo grin and reach for his phone.

Dan emerged, sucking on his knuckles. 'I don't know what's going on down there.'

'That's okay. You tried.'

Dan stood up and frowned at Eduardo, who was laughing into his receiver. 'Well, back to work.'

'Back to it,' said Pulpy, and watched Dan walk away.

Eduardo put down his phone and rolled his chair around to Pulpy's side of the partition. 'He's an idiot,' he said.

Pulpy shrugged and jiggled his keyboard tray.

Eduardo frowned. 'Why's your coat on the back of your chair?'

He looked sideways at his co-worker and felt the soft bulk of his coat pressing against his back. 'I was cold so I brought it up with me.'

The other man wheeled closer to him, and lowered his voice. 'What did you see last night, Pulpy?'

'Nothing,' he said quickly. 'I sent the potluck email and I left.'

'Have it your way, then.' Eduardo crossed his arms. 'Just so long as you don't go having a heart-to-heart with your pal Dan.'

'He's not my pal.'

'That's good to hear, Pulpy.' Eduardo slid back around his corner. 'Have fun at your potluck.'

At one o'clock, Pulpy, Dan, Cheryl from Active Recovery and Roy from Customer Service sat around the boardroom table with four dishes of food between them.

Dan bit into one of his Jamaican patties. 'The team spirit in this place is embarrassing.'

'Good sticky rice, Cheryl,' said Pulpy, serving himself a second helping.

His co-worker ducked her head. 'Thank you. My husband made it.'

'Your husband, eh?' said Roy with a wink. 'I think that's cheating, Cheryl. I went and purchased my shortbread cookies all by myself!'

'At least it's homemade.' Dan licked his lips at Cheryl approvingly. 'Anything homemade is delicious.'

Roy lifted the box the Jamaican patties had been in and peered at Dan through the plastic window. 'I guess you whipped these up *and* made the packaging too. Or was Beatrice the chef? Where is Beatrice, anyway?'

Dan took his eyes off Cheryl, who looked flustered, and said to Roy in a low voice, 'My *wife* had some appointments to attend.'

Roy put the box down and shrugged. 'More for us.'

'We should've thought to bring drinks,' said Pulpy. 'We have food but no drinks.'

'A complete lack of interest.' Dan brushed some crumbs off his sleeve. 'That's what we're dealing with here. Total employee apathy.' He turned back to Cheryl. 'Except for our intrepid and, might I add, quite lovely Active Recovery specialist over here.'

Cheryl squirmed under his gaze. 'Like I said, my husband deserves all the credit.'

'I'll bet he does,' said Dan.

'Al didn't do this sort of thing,' said Roy. 'He pretty much just let us go about our day. Sometimes he'd suggest a spontaneous get-together, like a bunch of us would take a longer lunch at a pub or whatever.'

'Those were good times,' said Cheryl.

'Well, Al isn't in charge anymore, is he?' said Dan, raising his voice. 'Isn't that right, Pulpy?'

Pulpy ate some sticky rice and swallowed, hard. 'Right,' he mumbled.

Dan broke a shortbread cookie into tiny pieces and then crushed them into powder. 'How does sitting around in a pub foster team-building? You tell me, because I can't figure it out.'

'It was fun,' said Roy.

'It was,' said Cheryl.

Pulpy nodded, but when he saw Dan glaring at him he looked around quickly at the Crock-Pot of sticky rice and the paper plates of Jamaican patties, shortbread cookies and his flattened jam-filled puff pastry. 'But this is fun too. Look at all this food.'

Dan shook his big head. 'Something needs to be done about this.'

'Pulpy, could you pass me some more of your pastry?' said Roy.

'Me too,' said Cheryl.

'I'm glad you like it,' he said. 'It's not supposed to be squashed like that.'

'I propose,' said Dan, 'that we do something about this.'

Nobody said anything. The sound of chewing filled the room.

Dan brought his fist down on his plate, flattening what remained of his lunch. 'This potluck is a piece of crap!'

Pulpy, Roy and Cheryl looked at each other, and Dan stood up and walked out of the room.

When he'd finished eating, Pulpy brought a plate of food to the receptionist.

'Thanks.' She scratched her cheek. 'What is this, strudel?'

'It's puff pastry. It's supposed to be puffier. It's got jam inside.'

'Huh. Why's this rice so sticky?'

'It's sticky rice.'

She picked up the plastic fork he'd given her and dangled it above the plate. 'Wait, what did *he* bring?'

'The Jamaican patty's his.'

She lifted the patty by the edges with her thumb and forefinger and pitched it into the garbage. 'There. That's better.' She looked at him. 'Nobody in this office cares whether I live or die, except for you. You're the only one.'

He focused on the pearly grains of rice on her plate, clumped into a small peak. 'That's not true. Nobody wants you to die.'

'Pulpy!' Dan yelled from the top of the stairs. 'In my office, please. Emergency Social Committee meeting. I've got Beatrice on speakerphone.'

'Coming!' he called back, and then shrugged at her. 'I'd better get up there.'

The receptionist gave his pastry a jab. 'Duty calls.'

'Beatrice, I've got Pulpy here,' Dan said to his phone.

'Pulpy!' Beatrice said, loud enough to distort the speaker.

'Hi, Beatrice.' Pulpy waited for Dan to tell him where to sit.

'How's Midge?' she said.

'She's fine.'

'That's good. We miss her!'

'Enough chit-chat,' said Dan. 'We've got a situation here.'

'What's the situation?' said Pulpy.

Dan rolled his eyes. 'Were you not there at one o'clock?'

'Was it fun?' said Beatrice. 'I'm sorry I didn't make it. I just didn't feel like leaving the house today.'

'It was nice,' said Pulpy.

'Oh, good. Did everyone like the Jamaican patties?'

'*Everyone,*' said Dan, 'was four people.'

'Only four?' she said.

'It could've been five,' Dan muttered.

'What was that, dear?'

'Never mind. What we're here to talk about is staff morale, of which we are sorely low on. Of which we, in fact, have none.'

'Maybe people just weren't very hungry,' said Pulpy.

'Or maybe they didn't know about the event,' said Dan.

Pulpy's arms dangled at his sides. 'I sent the emails.'

'You sent them too late.'

'I posted the sign-up sheet early.'

'I saw your sign-up sheet. It was very well done,' said Beatrice. 'I liked the font you used.'

'Thank you.'

Dan slapped his palm down on his desk. 'We are not operating on optimum drive at this office! We're operating on something more like non-optimum drive.'

'What does Pulpy think we should do?' said Beatrice.

Pulpy tugged on the lanyard around his neck. 'I think things are fine the way they are.'

'Well, you're wrong,' said Dan. 'In the ideal state of affairs, things would be the way they should be, but they aren't. This is not an ideal state of affairs.'

'You should make a policy, honey,' said his wife. 'You make really good policies.'

'Thanks.' Dan trailed a finger along the side of his handset. 'Maybe I should.' He looked at Pulpy. 'What are you and Midge up to tonight?'

'Tonight? Oh. Well –'

'Great. Tonight it is. We'll all make a policy together.'

'I'm not sure if I can make it,' said Beatrice. 'I'll see how I feel.'

Dan shot an angry look at his speaker. 'I'll call you later,' he said, and hung up on her. 'I've made reservations for the four of us at our new favourite restaurant, Pulpy. You and Midge can meet us there at seven.'

'I'll have to call her,' said Pulpy. 'I think she might have plans.'

Dan stared at him. 'Seven o'clock.'

He nodded. 'Seven will be fine.'

Pulpy sat down at his desk and dialled home.

Midge picked up after a few rings, sounding out of breath. 'Hello?'

'Hi, Midge.'

'Oh, hi.'

He heard someone's voice in the background and then Midge muffled the receiver and said, 'It's Pulpy.'

'Who's that?' he said.

'Jean's over here with me.'

'Oh, that's right. You're having coffee with her.'

Midge laughed. 'Actually, we started with coffee but then we switched to wine! I wanted to make mojitos again but Dan and I finished all the rum that night. Want to hear something disgusting?'

He heard Jean laughing too. 'Okay.'

'Jean told me about a rude email she got from her husband today, a quiz. Somebody sent it to everybody in his office and he sent it to her.'

'What kind of quiz?' Pulpy pressed the receiver against his ear.

'It had really rude questions, but that was a trick, because the first thing you'd think to answer would be ... a rude thing, but really the answer would be something not rude at all.'

'Give me an example.'

'I don't know if I could.'

He pushed his chair in further, knocking his thighs on his keyboard. 'Try.'

'All right.' She paused, and giggled. 'Like ... "I go in your mouth hard and I come out soft. What am I?" Hmm. But I don't remember what that one was for. There was another one, though. Something about a shaft ... then "discharging my load" ... what was it? Oh, I know. "Guys and gals both go down on me. What am I?"'

Pulpy's ear was hurting but he didn't loosen his grasp on the receiver. 'I don't know.'

'An elevator!' said Midge, and a high, excited hoot blew out of her. 'See, the answers were innocent like that, but the questions weren't innocent at all! Jean says her husband told her the email's going around the Internet, so everybody's getting it. If somebody sends it to you, you should print it out. Then we can read the riddles to each other!'

'I'll keep an eye out.'

She went quiet. 'Why don't you sound excited? I'm telling you about something sexy.'

Jean said something else and Midge snickered, then shushed her.

He jiggled his knees against his keyboard tray. 'I don't know how I'm supposed to feel anymore.'

'Well, maybe you should figure that out.'

'You're right, I should.' He cleared his throat. 'So, um, Dan wants us to meet him and Beatrice for dinner tonight. He wants to discuss the potluck.'

'I thought the potluck was over.'

'It is. It didn't go very well.'

'I'll have to see, Pulpy. Right now I'm here with Jean.'

'Yes, right, of course. But he doesn't want to meet until seven, so maybe you could meet us at the restaurant? It's the hotel surf-and-turf where I wanted to take you when I thought I was getting the promotion. Which is still a possibility, I think, maybe. I just really think I should probably go if he wants me to go.'

'You know I don't eat fish, Pulpy.'

'I know, but you could eat something from the turf part.'

She sighed. 'Fine, I'll meet you there at seven, then.'

'Do you mind, really? Because you know what? I'll go back to him and say we can't make it. I'll go back and reschedule.'

'I don't mind,' she said.

His shoulders went up to his ears and then fell again. 'Thank you, Midge.'

'Pulpy?'

'Yes?'

'We can't ever take each other for granted.'

His hand slipped a little on the receiver. 'We won't.'

She hung up, and he held the phone against his ear a little longer.

After work, Pulpy stood at the top of the stairs with his coat on and looked down at the receptionist's desk. The receptionist was under it, yanking at the wires that linked her to the Winter Flute.

'Be careful with that,' he said. 'You might get a shock.'

'I already did.' She didn't look up. 'I already got a big one.'

He hurried down the last few steps. 'Are you all right?'

She straightened, still kneeling, and shook a plug at him. 'Not from this. Not from these –' She ducked back behind her desk and surfaced with an armload of cables. 'From *him*, when he told me I couldn't go to "Be An Exceptional Receptionist" tomorrow.' She tossed the cables over the side.

'When did he say that?'

'Just now.' She sat down heavily on her chair. 'When I asked him. He said I should've asked sooner, but I know it wouldn't have made a difference.'

He put his hands in his pockets. 'I guess it is kind of last-minute, though. To wait so long to mention it.'

'No, he never would've let me do it.' She slapped the flyer on her desk. 'I just faxed in my registration, though, and I've got the confirmation report so I know it went through.' She patted another piece of paper next to the flyer.

'I'm not sure that's such a good idea, if he told you you're not supposed to go.'

'Oh yeah?' Her diamond eyes glittered behind her glasses. 'Whose side are you on, anyway? Oh wait, that's right, I forgot. You're his buddy.'

'I'm not his buddy,' he said quietly.

'You think he would've said yes if I'd asked him sooner? I got everything done. I set everything up for tomorrow, so all *she* has to do is sit here. I did extra work so I'd be free and clear. And he still said no.' She collapsed backward, looking exhausted. 'They're in on it together, you know. They want me out of here.'

'But you're doing a good job.'

'You're the only one who seems to think so.' She took a shaky breath, and her eyes watered.

'Oh no,' he said. 'Don't cry.'

A tear spilled down her cheek and she swiped at it. 'I'm not crying.'

He felt around in his coat to see if he had any tissues, but all he found was a used napkin in his breast pocket, with mustard on it. He held it out to her.

'No thanks,' she said, and smiled a little. 'You're the best thing about this place, you know that?'

Pulpy stood a little taller. 'I am?'

She sniffed and nodded. 'Would you do something for me?'

'Sure, anything.'

'I'm going to the Poacher's Oar and I could use some company. You want to come and have a drink with me?'

'Hmm,' he said. 'What about your boyfriend?'

'I said company, not misery.'

He coughed. 'I have to be somewhere at seven.'

'But the Oar's just around the corner from here. Come on, just one drink.'

'The place I'm going is just around the corner too.' He nodded. 'All right, if it'll make you feel better, then why not.'

'Why not?' She smiled at him. 'Exactly.'

'I don't know about you,' said the receptionist, 'but I'm getting a rusty nail.'

'What's in that?' said Pulpy.

'It's got Scotch and Drambuie, with a lemon twist.'

'That sounds pretty good. Two rusty nails, please,' he said to the bartender.

The Poacher's Oar was dark and cavernous with nets, anchors and wire snares hung on the walls.

'I like the idea of a rusty nail,' she said. 'Because it's sharp and it's dirty, and you drink it.'

He held on to the coat hooks under the bar. 'So, do you like coming here? I mean, is this a place you go to – have you been here before?'

She grinned. 'Do I come here often?'

'Oh, ha. Ha, ha. No, I didn't mean – I wasn't trying to say that.'

'Yeah, I come here a lot,' she said. 'Lester and I come here. They do a tuna-and-ribs special on Thursdays.'

'What day is it today?'

'Not Thursday.'

'Right. Ha, ha.'

The bartender watched them, grinning, while he poured the Drambuie.

'What about you?' she said.

Pulpy shook his head. 'Midge and I don't like to eat fish.'

'No, I mean, have you been here before?'

'This place?' He looked around. 'No.'

She snorted. 'You're funny sometimes.'

'I am?'

The bartender set their drinks down. 'That'll be twelve dollars.'

The receptionist looked at Pulpy. 'You want to get the first round?'

'Oh, sure. Yes.' He reached for his wallet and smiled at the bartender. 'Round number one is on me.' On their way to a couple of chairs he said to her, 'I thought you said just one drink.'

She rolled her eyes. 'I'll reimburse you.'

'No, no, it's not that. It's just I have to meet Midge at the Rod and Rifle at seven.'

'Then you're in luck, because we're right next door.'

He blinked at her. 'We are?'

'That's the hotel restaurant and this is the hotel bar. Look, you can even see the tables from here.' She patted the chairs they were standing beside. 'So there you go. We'll have time for round number two after all.'

He saw the restaurant seating at the other end then, slightly less dimly lit and decorated with fishing tackle and large steel traps. He swallowed and pointed across the room. 'Let's sit over there.'

'Don't you want to be closer to the restaurant?' She arched an eyebrow at him. 'Oh, I get it. You don't want your wife to see us together, right?'

'She wouldn't mind.' He looked down at his rusty nail. 'We're just having a friendly drink.'

'Exactly. You have a life, don't you? I bet she does things you don't know about. Like right now – you don't know what she's doing right at this minute, do you?'

He tinkled his ice, which had barely started to melt. 'She's with her candle friend.'

'Well, then that's an exception.' She led him across the room to two other chairs. 'How's that candle thing going for her, anyway?'

'Pretty well, I guess.'

'Good.' She took a drink. 'That's good.'

He looked at his watch.

'We just got here,' she said. 'Relax. Have a seat.'

'Okay.' He sat. 'Ha, ha.'

'I'll tell you what. When she gets here you can introduce us, and that way she's got nothing to worry about. There's no mystery, you're not trying to hide anything, and I'm just the receptionist. Problem solved.'

'There's no problem,' he said.

'That's what I'm saying.' She downed her drink and set the empty glass on the table.

'I guess I'll –' He finished his drink too. 'I'll go and get the next round, then.' He stood up.

'Make my next one a double,' she said. 'It's been a long day.'

By seven o'clock they were onto round number five.

Pulpy leaned against the bar and nodded at the bartender. He didn't have to specify their drink anymore – the man made up two double rusty nails and Pulpy paid him, focusing hard as he counted out the bills.

Then he heard Midge's laugh, and at the sound of her voice his hands locked with the money fanned between his fingers. She laughed again, and he ducked.

'You all right, buddy?' The bartender peered at him over the railing.

Pulpy looked up from his position between two stools. 'It's my wife!'

'You mean that's not your wife over there having drinks with you?' The bartender was smiling.

He shook his head. 'She's the receptionist.'

'Right.' The bartender laughed. 'Of course she is.'

'Could you please do me a favour?'

'Sure, buddy. What'll it be?'

'Could you check – that laughing woman with the beautiful hair is my wife. Is she looking over here?'

'Hold on –' The bartender squinted across the room to the restaurant. 'Nope, she's talking to another couple, looks like.'

'Good. Thank you.' Pulpy wiped his forehead. 'I'm not – I'm not here doing anything wrong, if that's what you're thinking. I love my wife. The receptionist and I are just having a friendly drink together.'

'Hey, so long as you pay me for this round of friendly drinks I just poured and tip me generously, I don't judge.' The bartender looked in Midge's direction again. 'The coast is clear, if you want to make a run for it.'

'Thanks.' Pulpy handed up all of the money he was holding and then headed back to the receptionist's table in a low crouch. 'Midge is here,' he whispered.

'She is?' The receptionist stood up unsteadily. 'Where is she? Let's go say hi.' Her voice was loose and loud. 'What are you doing on the floor?'

'No,' he said. 'She's with – people. Never mind. I thought she'd be alone, so now you don't need to do anything. Don't even look over there, maybe.'

She scowled across the room. 'Why are *they* with her?'

'We're having dinner with Dan and Beatrice.' He sighed and sank down onto his knees. 'I didn't want to mention that part in case it might upset you.'

'Oh, I see.' She reached for her coat.

'We're not friends with them,' he said quickly. 'It's just a work thing.'

Midge's laugh bounced across the room again.

'It doesn't *sound* like a work thing,' she said.

He peered up at the underside of their table and saw that someone had carved a heart with two sets of initials into the wood. He thought that must've been a hard thing to do, carving upside down like that. Half of the heart was covered by a big wad of gum. 'So, um, do you want to come over and introduce yourself to Midge?'

'Are you kidding me? With them there?' The receptionist grabbed her purse. 'I don't like to talk to them when I'm in the office, let alone on my own time. I'll see you later.'

'Then could you just –' He looked down at his hands. 'Could you please leave quietly, then?'

She glared across the room. 'It's too late. They've seen me.'

Pulpy slumped sideways and pulled his knees up to his chest. 'Oh, no.'

'Don't worry about it. Just stay down there until I leave. Then you can crawl over and pretend we never did this.'

'I think I'm drunk,' he said.

'Well, that's your problem, isn't it?' And she walked away.

Pulpy sat there on the floor until he saw the door swing shut behind her, and then he looked at the bartender and jerked his head toward the restaurant.

The bartender gave him the thumbs-up.

He reached up to yank his coat off his chair, and then crab-walked over to the bar and eased himself onto a stool. Only then did he turn his bleary gaze to the low-lit depths of the restaurant.

The three of them were sitting together talking and not looking in his direction. Pulpy took a deep breath and called out, 'Midge! Over here!'

They all turned their heads, and Midge smiled and waved.

He got off the stool and teetered, but steadied himself on the bar. Then he tottered across the room. 'Hi, Midge. Hi, Dan. Hi, Beatrice.'

'Hi Pulpy!' Midge's cheeks were bright pink. 'Are you all right? You look a bit ... not yourself.'

'I got here early and had a few drinks at the bar,' he said. 'I guess they caught up with me on an empty stomach, ha, ha!'

'We just saw the secretary from our office,' said Beatrice. 'She was in the bar too, did you know that?'

'She was? Huh. Maybe I saw her. I can't remember.'

Midge giggled. 'Her hair is so *bushy*, Pulpy!'

Beatrice gave Midge's upper arm a tweak. 'Midge says you gave her the secretary's hairdresser's card!'

'Oh, well, I –' Pulpy blinked. 'That was just ...'

'We like Midge's hair just fine the way it is,' said Beatrice.

He reached for the edge of the table and held on. 'So do I.'

'Rolled right up to the canteen after work, eh?' said Dan. 'That's my boy!'

'It's not something I usually do,' said Pulpy in a fast voice. 'But Midge was with her friend at our place, so I thought I'd leave them to it and get here early.'

'We were drinking wine!' said Midge. 'So I'm feeling a little bit not myself, myself!' She giggled some more.

Dan and Beatrice looked at each other across the table, and Dan grinned. 'The drunker the merrier, I say. Looks like Beatrice and I are going to have to play catch-up!'

'We didn't see you sitting at the bar earlier, Pulpy,' said Beatrice. She was wearing an outfit that stretched and glinted.

'The stool I was sitting on was very low, maybe that's why.' He took his linen napkin out of his waterglass and placed it on his lap. It covered his thighs and draped over his knees, so that all he could see when he looked down was an expanse of white. Midge could skate on his lap, he thought.

'And you didn't see the secretary.' Beatrice smoothed down her bangs. 'Isn't that strange?'

'Very strange indeed!' Dan laced his thick fingers together under his chin.

Midge frowned and picked up her menu, which had velvety tassels on it.

Pulpy stiffened and looked quickly between his boss and his wife. 'So, Dan,' he said. 'I've been giving this potluck issue some thought, and –'

Dan held up a hand. 'There's plenty of time for that. But first, we are men of action, and men of action must eat!'

'What about the women of action?' said Beatrice, and she winked at Midge.

Midge smiled. 'I meant to tell you, Beatrice, if you ever want more wax information, or hostessing tips, or if you want a Candle-Brations order form, please let me know.'

Beatrice pursed her lips. 'I just might do that,' she said. 'Maybe Pulpy could let me flip through that catalogue you gave him for the office.'

'He hasn't shown it to you yet?' Midge frowned at him.

He shook his head. 'I've been meaning to, Midge, really. But the potluck –'

'Potluck, botluck,' she said.

Dan lifted his napkin and waved it at a pinched-looking young man in a bow tie, who hurried over to their table.

'Good evening,' said the waiter. 'How may I help you?'

'It is,' said Dan. 'It *is* a good evening. Could you please, if you would be so kind, provide our table with a bottle of your house wine, which would be on par with the goodness of the evening?'

'Will that be red or white, sir?'

'"Red or white," he says.' Dan looked at Pulpy. 'Pulpy? What do you say?'

'Red?' Pulpy looked at Midge, who was staring at the table-cloth. 'Or white. They're both nice.'

Dan nodded. 'You're right. You could not be righter. Bring us two bottles of each.'

'Excellent choice, sir.' The waiter left.

'This is nice, the presentation.' Midge took a bun from the bowl on the table. 'Usually you see buns in baskets. Putting them in a bowl – they're still only buns but they look like nicer buns.'

'Ho-ho, nicer buns are the way to go!' said Dan.

Beatrice did a little hop in her seat and grabbed Midge's wrist. 'Don't you love this place?'

Midge flinched. 'I've never been here before.'

Pulpy had the feeling he should say something. 'We both like fish.'

'They do an excellent red snapper here,' said Dan. 'It's got lemon pepper. Lemon and pepper – together at last!'

'No, he means live fish,' said Midge.

Pulpy looked across the table and smiled at her, then said to Dan, 'But cooked fish can be nice too.'

Dan nodded and gave the cuffs of his blue blazer a tug. 'I'm glad the secretary got rid of that fish she had on her desk. It was starting to stink up the office.'

Midge looked at him. 'What fish?'

'She had a fish,' Pulpy said quickly. 'He died.'

'She never asked permission to keep a fish there, either,' said Beatrice.

'Where did she get her fish?' said Midge.

'Her boyfriend.' Pulpy took a bun and ripped it in half. 'He won him for her at the winter fair.'

'That was nice of him,' said Beatrice. She looked hard at Dan. 'You never won *me* anything at any fair.'

'Giving someone a sick fish,' he said. 'I don't call that nice in my books.'

'He wasn't sick at first,' said Pulpy. 'He was healthy in the beginning.' He plucked some crumbs off his side plate when he saw they were all looking at him. 'She just never changed the water.'

'What kind of a person doesn't change a fish's water?' said Dan. 'She abused that fish.'

'I think maybe it was because she never gets a chance to leave her desk,' said Pulpy. 'She says she gets dehydrated.'

'Then why bring the fish in the first place?' Dan straightened in his chair. 'She should have kept it at home where she has easy access to a tap.'

'Maybe she was trying to prove a point,' said Pulpy, and his eyes widened when he said it. He saw that Midge was looking back and forth between them, chewing. 'Anyway, I was changing the water for her.'

'Wait a minute now,' said Beatrice. 'Didn't you tell me that was *your* fish, Pulpy?'

'Pardon?' He coughed, and Midge handed him her ice water.

'When I saw you in the hallway after it died.' Beatrice nodded, and pointed at him. 'You were carrying it and I said was that the secretary's fish, and you said no it was yours.'

'Pulpy keeps his fish on his desk,' said Midge. 'Don't you, Pulpy?'

'Really? I've never seen a fish on his desk. Maybe he keeps it in his drawer!' Beatrice licked butter from the corner of her mouth. 'I think I'm going to order that snapper. All this fish talk is making me hungry.'

The waiter came back with their wine and positioned his corkscrew over the first bottle.

Pulpy cleared his throat. 'Maybe you should ask Eduardo about my fish,' he said to Beatrice. 'He sits next to me, and our desks are also very close to Dan's office.'

The cork on the first bottle popped, and the waiter started on the second.

'So that was *you!*' she said, and turned to Dan. 'See, I told you we heard somebody.'

Pulpy blinked at the gold buckles that joined Beatrice's sleeves to the neck of her elasticized top. 'You and *Eduardo* heard somebody.'

'Right.' Dan reached for the open bottle and poured himself a glass of red. 'Her and Eduardo.' He took a swig and grinned at Pulpy. 'I guess you figured I don't know what she gets up to, huh?'

Pop! The waiter jammed the corkscrew into the top of the third bottle. *Pop!*

Beatrice reached for the open bottle of white and tilted it over her glass.

'Pulpy,' said Midge, 'what are they talking about?'

'Have a drink with us, darling,' Beatrice said to her. 'We'll all feel better.'

Pulpy reached for the second bottle of white and filled Midge's glass, then his. Then he took a gulp. 'Midge, the receptionist wanted my fish so I gave it to her. Because I felt sorry for her, because she's all by herself out there. And I was here with her earlier too, but just for a friendly drink. Because she needed to be cheered up so I kept her company. She was going to introduce herself to you so there'd be no mystery, but then she saw Dan and Beatrice and she left.' He picked up his glass again with shaky hands.

Midge went pale and fumbled with her cutlery.

Pop! The waiter stepped back and looked at the four full glasses. 'So, is everyone all right here?'

Dan winked at him. 'Give us five minutes.'

The waiter went away.

'She needed to be cheered up because you won't let her go to her seminar,' Pulpy said to Dan. 'All she wants to do is improve herself.'

Midge let out a small, sad sound and stood up.

'Midge,' said Pulpy, 'please don't be upset. It really wasn't anything.'

'If it wasn't anything then why didn't you tell her in the first place?' said Beatrice.

'Yes,' said Midge. 'Why didn't you say that before?' She pulled her coat over her shoulders and pushed her chair back.

Pulpy saw that she was wearing her new clamdiggers. 'I didn't want to hurt your feelings.'

'Well, too late. And anyway, Dan and I had our *own* friendly drink, didn't we, Dan? We had our own friendly mojitos last Friday, after you went to bed.'

Pulpy pressed his rubbery-feeling hands together under the table. 'You said you didn't remember anything.'

'I don't,' she said. 'But that doesn't mean nothing happened, now does it?'

Pulpy could hear his wife's boots, with her lovely bare calves overtop, make two small stomps as she moved away from the table. He looked away from her to the crumbs left in the bread bowl.

Midge started to cry. 'You don't care about me and you don't care about my candles!'

'How can you say that?' said Pulpy. 'Of course I care!'

'Then why didn't you show anyone the catalogue?'

'Yes,' said Beatrice. 'Why didn't you?'

'It got wet.' He sighed a miserable sigh. 'I dropped it on the bus and it got wet.'

'That is *it*!' Midge was wailing now. 'I'm going home!'

'I'll go with you,' said Beatrice. 'You shouldn't be alone right now.' She gathered up her coat and took Midge's arm.

Pulpy stood up but Midge waved him back down. 'Stay here and have your *Social Committee* meeting. I don't want to interrupt any more of your important business!' And she ran out of the restaurant with Beatrice following close behind.

Dan dragged his chair closer to Pulpy's. 'I guess it's just you and me and the rest of this wine, Pulpy. Boys' night!'

Pulpy tugged on the edge of the tablecloth. 'What was Midge saying, Dan, about the mojitos?'

'We had a few more drinks after you hit the hay, that's all. And we talked about candles – you know that. I told you that already.' Dan poured red into Pulpy's half-empty glass of white. 'Oops, looks like you're drinking rosé now, ho-ho! Go ahead and finish that and we'll pour you a proper glass of red. That's a man's colour, none of this white for us, no sir! Until we finish the red that is, ha!'

Pulpy drank it down and felt woozy. 'What did you mean about knowing ... what Beatrice is up to?'

Dan leaned back. 'It works for us.'

The waiter appeared again and looked at the two empty chairs.

'It's just us boys now,' said Dan. 'The hens have flown home to the coop. Bring us a couple of steaks, will you? Rare. And another bottle of house red.'

'Actually, Dan,' said Pulpy, 'I take my steak medium-well.'

'Don't listen to him,' Dan said to the waiter. 'I'm his boss, and he'll eat rare and like it.' He elbowed Pulpy. 'Trust me on this one.'

'Very good, sir.' The waiter left them.

'So, like I was saying,' said Dan, 'I let Beatrice have her own fun on the side because it turns her crank, and when her crank is turned she's a lot more agreeable, if you get my drift.' He refilled both of their glasses. 'The thing is, it's not cheating if the other person knows about it.'

'Oh,' said Pulpy. 'I guess I've never heard of that kind of thing before.'

'Stick with me, Pulpy. I'll show you the world.'

'Well,' he said, 'I'm not really sure that world is for us.'

'You just haven't tried it yet. Once you try it, you'll be hooked. Believe me.'

'Hmm.' Pulpy took another drink.

'Listen, I'll tell you what. You and Midge talk it over, and if it sounds like something you might want to sample, Beatrice and I'll be there for you.'

Pulpy choked and coughed and dribbled red wine onto his lap napkin. 'Pardon?'

'If you want to give it a go we can help ease you into things. We play safe too, so there's nothing to worry about there.'

Pulpy wiped his mouth and stared at his boss.

'And if you don't like it, nobody ever has to be the wiser. We all go home and never speak of it again. If you *do* like it, though, then the sky's the limit. I'm telling you, Pulpy, this will change your life. And it'll change your relationship too, for the better.'

Pulpy finished his glass and poured himself another. He was having trouble sitting up straight now so he slumped sideways onto the arm of his chair. 'Midge is always on the lookout for new ways to improve our relationship.'

'I knew it!' Dan pointed at him. 'You see what I'm talking about? And right now Midge and Beatrice are having a chat just like this one, and Midge is probably saying the same things you're saying. You both want your relationship to succeed. You both cherish what you have, right?'

'Right.' Pulpy's mouth was dry so he moistened it with more wine. He was mildly surprised by what he said next, but that didn't stop the words from coming out. 'I'll have to talk to Midge about this.'

'Of course you will. No question. You two jaw it over and see what's what. And if you decide to give it a go, we'll be waiting.'

'Thank you, Dan, that's – that's very nice of you.'

'Nice, shmice. It's not like we're not getting something out of this, am I right? Ha!'

'Ha,' said Pulpy, and then he slid onto the carpet and blacked out.

'Pass me the swatter,' said Midge.

Pulpy squinted at her. The sun was right behind her head, framing the flicked-up edges of her hair. 'Is there one by you?'

'A big one,' she said. 'Hand that swatter over.'

'Let me get him.' He stood up from his lawn chair with the swatter held high.

The wasp flew past Midge and she squeezed her eyes shut. 'Don't let him sting me.'

'I won't.' He watched the wasp zoom back and forth, each time coming closer to the pink expanses of his wife's exposed skin. 'I've almost got him.'

The wasp was hovering over the soft crease at the top of Midge's forearm. Pulpy wound up, aiming to knock it out of the air before it struck.

The wasp dove and Pulpy.swung.

And missed.

'Owww!' Midge clapped a hand over her arm and opened her eyes. Then she looked right at Pulpy and slowly uncovered the red welt that had already started to form.

'Ho-ho!' said the wasp. 'Am I right?'

And it soared over to Pulpy, and Pulpy could see there was something about this wasp that he recognized. Something about the shape of its head, or the way it kept opening and closing its wings around nothing.

Pulpy awoke to a buzzing sound and he sat up with his arms flailing. 'Look out, Midge!' he shouted, but then realized she wasn't beside him.

He'd been dreaming about wasps and now he was alone, on a long, hard couch, wearing only his briefs. He ran his hand along the velvety fabric beneath him. Dan and Beatrice's divan. He blinked at the sunlight pouring in though the lacy drapes over the bay window. Dan and Beatrice's living room. And the buzzing was coming from down the hall.

Pulpy covered himself with the blanket that had fallen down to his waist and looked around for his clothes. He couldn't see them anywhere.

The buzzing stopped.

He heard heavy footsteps coming down the hall and he yanked the blanket up to his chin.

Dan appeared in the doorway wearing slippers and a yellow bathrobe. He put his hands on his hips and grinned at Pulpy. 'I just ground some beans for the best cup of joe you will ever have in your life. Do you take sugar? I know you're a cream man.'

Pulpy nodded, then shook his head. 'Why am I in your house?'

'Why do you think?' Dan's shins were thick with dark hair, and his slippers were open-toed.

'Um.' Pulpy shivered. 'I don't know.'

'Look at me, the host with the least.' Dan shook his big head. 'There I go and strip you down and I give you one of the thinnest throws in the linen closet. Sit tight, I'll be right back.'

Pulpy watched Dan bound up his spiral staircase, his robe billowing, and took a few deep breaths. His recollection of the night before ended at the restaurant. There was nothing after that.

Dan came down the stairs with his slippers flapping. 'Ta-da!' he said, and tossed a blue robe similar to his own onto the divan. 'Prepare to be toasty!'

Pulpy's eyes rested on the soft pile of terry cloth at his feet. 'Where are my clothes, Dan?'

'Ho-ho! You really don't remember anything, do you?'

'Not really.' His head pounded.

'Well, put that on and I'll fill you in over that coffee I was telling you about.'

'I should call Midge.' He sat up further and felt dizzy. 'She must be wondering where I am.'

'You know, I'd advise against that.'

Pulpy looked down at his bare thighs. He had goosebumps. 'Why is that, Dan?'

'I talked to Beatrice a little while ago and she said that lovely wife of yours is still living it up in Dream Land. What's good for the goose, huh? I wish! Working men like you and me are needed elsewhere, unfortunately. AKA the office. Ha!'

'Where's Beatrice?'

'She's already there, holding down the fort. Lucky for us we have flex hours, but then we can only stretch those so far before people start to talk. Am I right?'

'No ... I mean, Beatrice stayed over at our house?'

'You got it.'

Pulpy rubbed his eyes. 'What time is it?'

'I'll tell you what. Put that robe on, follow me to the kitchen, and all your questions shall be answered.'

'All right.' Pulpy sat there, still clutching the blanket to his chest. 'Could you please, um, just ...'

'The man wants his privacy. I can respect that. I've seen it all in this life but I can certainly respect that.' Dan started whistling and turned to stroll back down the hall.

Pulpy let out a long breath. His hands shook slightly as he pulled on the oversized robe and tied the belt in a double knot. He folded the blanket and laid it on the divan, then slowly made his way over the cold floor in the direction his boss had taken.

'There he is!' said Dan when Pulpy shuffled into the big, bright kitchen. 'Now go ahead and pick a mug and I'll fill you all the way up.'

There was an array of large mugs in the style of Dan's 'Back off – it's early' one lined up along the counter. Pulpy stepped forward and selected the only one without a phrase on it. 'I take sugar,' he said.

'Ho-ho, you may want to look inside there and see what else you take!'

Pulpy peered into his plain white mug. On the bottom was a perfectly curled miniature turd. His stomach lurched and he set the mug back down with a clatter.

'It's fake, don't worry. That's my gag mug. Isn't it great? Ha, ha!'

'Yes. Great.'

'Oh, it's good to laugh.' Dan pointed the coffee pot at him. 'Grab yourself another one. Unless you like that kind of thing, ha!'

'Ha.' Pulpy picked up one of the mugs with the sayings on them. This one read 'Go ahead – make my morning' and had a cartoon of a piece of toast wearing a cowboy hat.

Dan poured coffee into it and then filled a mug for himself; his had a picture of a moose with what appeared to be dirty laundry hanging from its antlers and the caption 'Moose-t Be Monday.'

Pulpy watched Dan's shoulders bunch under his robe as he replaced the coffee pot on its burner, and then looked down at the pale triangle of his own concave chest. Half of one nipple was visible, and when he raised his head he saw Dan looking there too.

'What's that line you've got there?' his boss said. 'Some kind of scar?'

'Sorry?' Pulpy put his mug on the counter and covered himself with the robe, then cinched the belt tighter.

'That line down your chest. I saw it last night when I took off your shirt.'

Pulpy peered out one of Dan and Beatrice's tall windows, at the shiny crust of snow that had hardened over their backyard. Then he noticed something green outside and took a few steps closer to see what it was.

He heard the fridge opening and closing behind him. 'Cream and sugar,' said Dan. 'Come and get 'em!'

It was the plant that he and Midge had bought, just sitting there in the cold. There was a layer of frost all over it, like icing, and the spiky leaves had curled in on themselves.

'Chow time!' said Dan in a loud voice. 'Who's hungry?'

Pulpy turned to face him. 'It's a love connection line,' he said. 'Whenever Midge and I are apart I can just touch it and think about us.'

Dan's grin went lopsided for a second and he seemed to sway a little. Then he said, 'Huh,' and opened the fridge again. He pulled out a brown paper bag with dark stains on the bottom and dropped it onto the counter with a thud. 'Sounds like voodoo to me.'

Pulpy frowned and darted a hand inside the front of his robe when Dan turned his back to open a drawer. His fingers grazed the line Midge had made. 'You said you were going to tell me what happened last night.'

'I did say that, didn't I?' Dan picked up the bag and held it upside down, and two thick slabs of grey-edged red meat thumped onto the counter. 'What happened is, we didn't get to eat these steaks we ordered! Ha! So belly up, compadre. We are going to right that horrible wrong before we mosey on back to the ranch.'

Pulpy went pale. 'I don't really feel like eating, Dan. I think I'd just like to get dressed.'

Dan had already started cutting. He paused with a hunk of beef at his lips. 'Just wait until I'm done here and then I'll get an outfit together for you.'

'I was thinking more about wearing my own clothes, actually.'

Dan's jaw muscles flexed as he chewed. 'Be my guest,' he said with his mouth full, 'but Beatrice might hose you down with that citrus spray of hers if you walk in there smelling like puke.'

'What are you talking about?'

Dan grinned, showing off a piece of sinew stuck between his large front teeth. 'You mean you really don't remember throwing up all over yourself last night?'

Pulpy grimaced. 'No.'

'Huh. I guess you did black out, but still.' He sliced a strip of fat off the edge of his steak and shoved it in his mouth. 'I figured it would come back to you.'

'Well, it hasn't,' said Pulpy. 'It hasn't and I want to get dressed and go to work.'

'All right, all right. If you're going to get all bent out of shape.' Dan thrust a finger into his mouth and dug around, then swallowed what he'd dislodged and wiped his finger on his robe. 'Wait here. I'll get you one of my suits.'

Pulpy watched Dan stride out of the kitchen, and then walked over to the window and looked down at the frozen plant again.

His mug of coffee sat steaming on the counter behind him.

When Pulpy and Dan walked into the office, the receptionist wasn't there, and Beatrice was bent over the desk aiming a small can with a long nozzle at the receptionist's keyboard.

'Mmm,' said Dan to his wife's rump, on prominent display and encased in pants that Pulpy thought looked familiar.

At the sound of the door closing, Beatrice turned and flashed her teeth at them. 'Good morning, boys.' She pointed the spray can at them and squeezed the trigger. 'Did you sleep well?'

'Did we ever!' said Dan.

Pulpy realized he was staring and switched his gaze to the wall behind Beatrice, but not before Dan gave him a wink and elbowed him in the ribs.

'These air dusters are lifesavers.' She arched forward and blasted the can at the receptionist's keys. 'You would think that a person who eats at their desk would have the common sense not to eat over the keyboard. Fortunately there are tools like this for people like myself, who prefer things crumb-free. You have to get the kind with the slip-on extender, though. Otherwise the penetration just isn't deep enough.'

'Are those Midge's clamdiggers?' said Pulpy.

'Well. Aren't *you* the observant one?' She traced a long red fingernail along her waist to her hip, and then fitted that hand into a back pocket. 'I hope she doesn't mind. I would've asked her but she was sleeping.'

'But why are you wearing them?'

'Our Pulpy isn't quite himself today,' said Dan. 'We drove in together and he didn't talk to me once. Not a word the whole trip. How's that for gratitude? He even stiffed me on his half of the bill last night! Lucky for him I've been feeling generous lately.'

Beatrice ignored him and smirked at Pulpy. 'Would you rather I take these clamdiggers *off*, then?'

'I just don't understand why you needed to borrow my wife's clothes, that's all.'

'Because if I came to work in the same outfit as yesterday, people might have something to say about that.' She smiled and fluttered her eyelashes at him. 'That's how rumours get started.'

Dan snorted and hung his coat up in the closet. 'Where's the secretary?'

Beatrice stopped smiling. 'She called in *sick* this morning.'

'Is that right?' Dan frowned.

'Is she okay?' said Pulpy.

'Well, I would hope not, or else she'd be here, wouldn't she? What you should be asking is, is the *desk* okay?' Beatrice flicked her hair. 'It is, but only because I'm here. She's just lucky I was able to cover for her.'

'But she told me she got everything ready ahead of time –' Pulpy closed his mouth.

Dan and Beatrice looked at him and then at each other.

'I mean, she told me she always does that,' he said quickly. 'Just in case.'

'Uh huh,' said Beatrice. 'Well, anyway, I'm managing.'

'I think she's lying,' said Dan. 'I don't think she's sick at all.'

Beatrice took a step toward them, her eyes bright. 'You don't?'

He shook his head. 'I think she's gone to that seminar on how to be a better secretary.'

'Receptionist,' said Pulpy. 'She likes "receptionist" better than "secretary," remember?'

Beatrice's nostrils flared and she picked up the receptionist's nameplate between her thumb and forefinger. '*This* says "Secretary."'

'Yes, but she'd really like that to be changed.'

'Pulpy,' said Dan. 'Can I see you in my office, please?'

'In a minute,' he said. 'I have to put my coat away first.'

Dan raised an eyebrow at him. 'Fine.' He started for the stairs but then stopped. 'Hold on. What happened to the Winter Flute?'

'That's another thing,' said Beatrice. 'I think she disconnected it.'

Dan's fingers constricted on the railing. 'She *what?*'

'I came in this morning and it wasn't playing. She must've done it before she left last night. Listen.'

They all stood there and listened.

Pulpy tilted his head. 'You're right. I don't hear it.'

Dan stomped up the stairs to his office and slammed his door behind him.

'Isn't he such a baby?' said Beatrice, and resumed her keyboard cleaning. She kept her eyes on Pulpy, though, letting the spray can dangle from one hand.

He coughed. 'I guess I'd better get up there too.'

'I bet you're wondering what Midge and I talked about last night, aren't you?' She brought the air-duster nozzle to her pink lips. 'I bet you'd really like to know.'

'Not really.' He moved past her to the closet, feeling too aware of his body contours and her eyes on them.

'She's a fascinating woman, your little wife. So many insights.'

He reached up to unzip his coat, and she positioned herself on a corner of the desk to watch him take it off. 'She has fantastic ideas,' he said.

'She certainly does. And I'll bet you and Dan had a good talk too. I'll bet the two of you had *lots* to talk about.'

In one movement Pulpy removed his coat and held it in front of him, like a shield. 'I don't really remember much of our conversation, Beatrice. I think I was a little drunk.'

'Oh, drunk, shmunk!' She giggled. 'I think you remember *exactly* what you and my husband chatted about.'

He peered into the closet. 'Hmm,' he said, and then his heart skipped a beat. There was one unused hanger, gleaming on the rack like a beacon.

'I gave this duster to the secretary with her ergonomic package but she said she didn't need it,' said Beatrice. 'That woman doesn't know *what* she needs.'

Pulpy glanced over to see Beatrice drape herself across the desk, stretching out her arms and scissoring her legs and pressing one hip against the glossy slab of wood. 'But I do,' she said.

He looked away quickly, back to the single unused hanger tangled in the nest of the ones attached to coats. He tried to separate it from the others but they were all stuck together. Out of the corner of his eye he saw Beatrice put down the spray can and start blowing on the keyboard, puckering her lips and focusing her breath on the gaps between the keys.

Pulpy yanked on the wire hanger. He yanked until it came loose and rattled onto the floor, but not without taking a few coats down with it. He lost his grip on his own coat and it fell.

She pointed one of her red nails at him. 'Now you've done it.'

He felt heat spread up the back of his neck and across his shoulders, and he knelt down to clean up his mess.

'Have you been working out?' said Beatrice. 'That suit is just hanging off you.'

'It's Dan's,' he said without looking at her. The suit was several sizes too big for him.

'You mean I'm wearing your wife's clothes and you're wearing my husband's?' She threw open her mouth and laughed. 'We should swap like this more often!'

Pulpy replaced the last hanger and its accompanying jacket on the rack and stepped back, almost tripping over his coat. He frowned at it on the floor. Where had the extra hanger gone?

'The best thing about swapping is you get a whole new wardrobe!' Beatrice stretched her arms over her head. 'I like new clothes *a lot.*'

He made a decision then, and picked up his coat. Hidden by the half-open door, he took Dan's coat off its hanger and tossed it into the back of the closet, and hung up his own coat. Then he closed the closet door and turned to face Beatrice, who had started massaging her temples. 'Duty calls,' he said, and headed for the stairs.

'I'll miss you!' she called after him, and he quickened his pace to the top.

Pulpy sat down at his desk and turned on his computer, and his phone rang. He grabbed the receiver. 'Hello, Midge?'

'No, it's me. The receptionist.'

'Oh.' He looked left and right and whispered, 'Where are you?'

'I'm at the seminar. It's the break right now.'

He huddled in closer to the phone. 'Beatrice said you called in sick.'

'It was easier that way.' Her voice lightened. 'I had a good time last night. Until *they* showed up, anyway. Did you have a good time?'

'It was nice,' he said, 'but I probably shouldn't do it again.'

'Why not?'

'Because of my wife.'

'Oh yeah?' Her voice lost its lilt. 'Why are you so concerned about *her* all of a sudden?'

'What do you mean?' he said. 'She's my wife.'

She was quiet for a moment. 'But didn't we have a good time?'

'Sure we did. It was a nice friendly drink.'

'Is that all it was?'

He twirled the phone cord around his wrist. 'Well, yes.'

'But you gave me your *fish*,' she said.

'What are you talking about? You wouldn't let me take him upstairs.'

'Fine. Have it your way, then.'

He felt the weight of the keyboard tray on his legs and lowered his voice again. 'Dan doesn't believe you're really sick. Did you cover your tracks about the seminar?' He cupped a hand around the receiver. 'What about the fax confirmation?'

'It's around there somewhere.'

'You mean you left it on your desk? What if they find it?'

'Then I guess they'll know I wasn't sick.'

'How about I get it for you,' he said. 'So they don't see it.'

'Whatever. I don't care.' She sighed. 'I have to go. They're calling us back to tell us the seven greeting principles.'

As soon as he heard her hang up, Pulpy dialled zero.

'Hello, Reception,' said Beatrice.

'Hi, Beatrice, it's Pulpy.'

'Hi, Pulpy! You missed me too. I knew it!'

He ran a finger around the edge of his computer screen. 'Um, I think Dan wants to see you.'

'My husband wants to see me. How come he can't call me himself?'

'I think –' he said. 'Hmm. I'm not sure, exactly.'

'Well, I don't know what his problem is,' she said. 'Whatever. Tell him I'll be up in a minute.'

'Okay.' He hung up and sat there until he saw Beatrice reach the top of the stairs, scowl and head for Dan's office. Then he hurried over to the steps and down to the welcome area.

He searched the receptionist's in- and out-trays first but couldn't find the confirmation page anywhere. He tried her big desk drawer but it was locked, so he went through the filing cabinet next. When he didn't see it there he looked at the shredder, but the bin underneath it was empty.

'What are you doing down here, Pulpy?' said Beatrice.

He tensed, and turned to see her watching him from the stairs. 'Nothing. I was just, um, looking for a file.' He pointed to the stack of files next to the printer, then laced his fingers on top of his head in a casual way and took a step back.

She came down the steps, frowning. 'Dan didn't want to see me. He looked at me like I was crazy when I told him you said that.'

'Hmm,' he said. 'Then I must have heard him wrong.'

'You must have.' She shrugged and sat in the receptionist's chair. 'But that's okay because I didn't want to see him, either.'

Pulpy squinted out the window at all the white and said, 'So.' He brushed his hands on his pants and started for the steps. 'See you later, then.'

'Wait,' she said, 'what about your file?'

He stopped. 'Right. My file.'

'Which one is it? I'll get it for you. You know, I like doing reception. It's a breeze!' She half-stood, poised by the file stack.

'Actually, never mind,' he said. 'I remembered I don't need it after all.'

'Okay.' She sat back down and crossed her legs.

He looked at her. 'Isn't that bad for your back, crossing your legs? I mean, ergonomically?'

Beatrice slowly lifted her top leg off her bottom one, and arranged them side by side on the receptionist's chair. 'There, is that better?'

'I should get upstairs,' he said, and headed for the steps. 'I have work to do.'

She considered him. 'You know what Dan said just now? He said if he finds proof the secretary went to that class, she's gone. Because he told her she couldn't go. So if she went, that means she disobeyed a direct order from a superior and that's cause for dismissal.'

'I need to get back to work now.' He took the stairs up two at a time.

'Hey, Pulpy, I heard you got a ride in with the big boss this morning.'

The voice had come from over his shoulder. Pulpy swivelled on his chair to see Eduardo poking his head around their partition. 'So what if I did?'

'Ooh, touchy.' Eduardo noticed Pulpy's ill-fitting outfit. 'What's up with your clothes? Are you shrinking or something?'

Pulpy pushed out his chest, trying to fill Dan's baggy suit jacket. 'Maybe I've been working out.'

'That's a good one,' said Eduardo. 'But seriously.'

'It's none of your business.'

'Oh no? Well, I think it is.' Eduardo's fingers slipped over the partition edge and he dragged himself around to Pulpy's side. 'I think if you're cozying up to Mr. Big Man then it's definitely my business.'

Pulpy stiffened. 'Who said anything about cozying up?'

'It's all over you,' said Eduardo. 'Everybody knows.'

'Everybody knows what?'

His co-worker's face tightened, his lips thinning across his teeth. 'That you're *friends*.'

Pulpy jolted as an itch ran a lightning course from his scalp to his nape. 'I told you,' he said. 'We're not friends. He's my boss.'

'Are you sure about that? Because you wouldn't catch me staying the night at my boss's house.'

'No,' said Pulpy. 'You'd be in his office instead.'

Eduardo's eyes flamed and he wheeled himself closer. 'Don't you even threaten me,' he said in a hoarse whisper. 'Don't you fucking dare threaten me like that.'

'Ooh.' Pulpy's heart was thudding hard and he felt a bead of sweat squeeze out behind one ear and slide down his neck. 'Touchy.'

His co-worker stomped one foot, and the sole of his loafer slapped the plastic floor mat that demarcated their cubicles. Then he shoved himself backward to his own side. 'Just don't even,' he said, and disappeared around the corner.

Beatrice wasn't there when Pulpy went downstairs on his way to lunch.

He stood in the empty welcome area and peered down the hallway. There was nobody around. He hurried over to the receptionist's desk and did another quick search, peeking into some file folders he hadn't tried last time. Nothing. Then he heard voices in the hallway. He scurried around to the other side of the desk just as Beatrice appeared with Davis, the Building Maintenance man.

'Uh-oh, looks like you caught me!' she said.

Pulpy felt a blush mounting his cheeks as he moved toward the closet. 'I was just on my way out.'

The man from Building Maintenance manoeuvred his bulk around her and nodded at Pulpy before lumbering down the steps to the basement.

'Leaving the desk unattended.' Beatrice curled herself into the receptionist's chair and ran a hand through her tousled bangs. 'Whatever must you think of me?'

Pulpy retrieved his coat and bundled up. 'I'll see you after lunch,' he said, and jerked open the front door.

'Tell Midge I say hello!' she called, and then he was in the middle of a snowstorm and the wind slammed the door shut behind him.

Pulpy stood in front of the pay phone with snowflakes in his hair. The storm had come out of nowhere, whipping up around him and following him all the way to the mall, and then it just quit.

He was contemplating a waxy pink bubblegum wrapper on top of the phone. It looked kind of nice and he wished Midge could see it too.

Pulpy took a deep breath and dialled home. No answer. He focused on the gum wrapper, half-afraid Midge wouldn't pick up and half-afraid she would.

She answered after a few more rings. 'Hello?'

'Midge, it's me. Pulpy.'

'I know who it is.'

'I just wanted to call.' He took two tiny steps forward and two tiny steps back. 'Did anything neat happen on your route today?'

'I was sleeping,' she said. 'You woke me up.'

'But it's lunchtime.'

'So? I make my own schedule around here, in case you didn't know.'

Neither of them spoke for a moment, and then Midge said, 'How's the *receptionist*?'

The food court was bustling behind Pulpy but he tuned it out. He felt like the two of them were in a cocoon. He reached out a fingertip and pushed the gum wrapper to the edge. 'She's not in today.'

'Well, la-di-da for her, then.'

'I think Dan and Beatrice are going to fire her.'

'Why are you telling me this?' she said. 'You think I care about her?'

He shuffled his feet. 'Did you talk to anybody else this morning?'

'What do you mean? I told you I just woke up.'

'I slept at Dan's last night. I slept at Dan's and I don't know what happened.' Pulpy loosened the unfamiliar tie around his neck. 'He wanted me to eat steak for breakfast.'

'I think Beatrice stayed over at our place.' She made a sniffing noise. 'It smells like her in here.'

'She did stay over.' He gave the wrapper the tiniest nudge and it fell off the side and floated to the floor. 'Everything's all mixed up.'

Midge let out a sob. 'You went drinking with the receptionist!'

'*Friendly* drinking!'

'That's the worst part!'

'Shh,' he said. 'Midge, it's okay.'

'It's *not* okay!' She hiccupped and then made rummaging sounds. 'I can't find my clamdiggers!'

He cleared his throat. 'That's because Beatrice is wearing them.'

There was silence on the other line.

'But I'm wearing Dan's clothes,' he said, 'so we're even.'

'What is going *on* here?' she shouted.

'I don't know. But I'll be home soon.'

'Meet me at the mall after work,' said Midge. 'I have to buy some new shoes.'

When Pulpy came back from lunch, Dan was sitting on the receptionist's desk. 'I'm glad you're back, Pulpy,' he said. 'There's been a development.'

Beatrice was making photocopies. 'We're assembling an official record.'

'What are you talking about?' said Pulpy.

'We know where she went today,' said Dan.

'"Don't look for easy answers to hard questions,"' said Beatrice. 'Sound familiar? And she left the evidence in the recycling bin, in case you were wondering.'

'Beatrice says you were snooping around her desk earlier today,' said Dan. 'Why were you doing that, Pulpy?'

'I needed a file.'

'Are you sure about that?'

Pulpy's hands opened and closed. 'And it's not Beatrice's desk.'

'Isn't it, now?' said Dan. 'I think it is. Because first thing tomorrow, when the *receptionist* walks in here with all her new performance-improvement knowledge, she's going to find out she doesn't have anywhere to sit in this office anymore.'

'Meaning she won't have a job,' said Beatrice.

Pulpy looked between them. 'Can't you give her another chance?'

'She *lied*, Pulpy,' said Dan.

'What kind of an eager envoy behaves that way?' said Beatrice.

Dan shook his rectangular head. 'So much for the "Samaritan pretense."'

Pulpy moved past them and climbed the first step. 'I have to get back to work.'

Beatrice snickered and sat down at the desk. 'You have a soft spot for that secretary, don't you?'

'I don't.' He stood there with one foot in the air. 'I don't have any spot for her.'

The three of them were quiet for a moment, and then Dan jogged over and slung an arm around Pulpy's shoulders. 'Leave the man alone, will you?' he said to Beatrice, and gave Pulpy a squeeze. 'Why don't we switch gears and go have a talk, you and me? Just give me a minute here, and you go on up to my office and grab yourself a piece of that soft hide you like so much.'

Beatrice smirked. 'He means the loungers.'

'I know what he means.' Pulpy climbed the rest of the stairs and then hurried into Dan's office.

He folded himself into one of the deep leather chairs and crossed his legs. Then he uncrossed them and put his hands on his knees. He looked at the receptionist's duck mug sitting on Dan's mouse pad, which had a cartoon of a lion wearing a business suit with a word bubble that said, 'I'd rather be at the watering hole!'

Pulpy missed the old boss and his quiet nature statuettes. He wished he'd rescued them – especially the camel – from the garbage when Dan threw them out, but he'd missed his chance and now they were all long gone. He hoped at least that they were still together, keeping each other company.

He glanced toward the door then and reached out quickly to grab the receptionist's mug by the handle. He stuck it under Dan's big shirt and whispered, 'Not another crisis – you're safe with me, duck.' He checked to see if the small bulge was noticeable but he couldn't be sure, so he hunched over a little.

Dan bounded into his office then and launched himself backward into his chair. He looked at his mouse pad for a second, then shrugged and smiled at Pulpy. 'I told Beatrice to lay off. Sometimes my wife gets a little hyperactive.'

'Oh no, that's ... she's fine.'

Dan's grin widened. 'I'm glad you noticed.' Then he frowned. 'Please don't abuse our trust, Pulpy.'

He felt the cool ceramic heating up against his skin. 'Sorry?'

'Trust is all we have. Once it's gone, you might as well forget it.'

Pulpy felt the mug roll across his stomach. He stiffened and grabbed it through the shirt.

'You all right over there?' said Dan.

'Yes. Ow. I had a pain. But it's gone now.'

'Good stuff, good stuff.' Dan crossed his arms and nodded. 'Oh, the joy of it, eh, Pulpy?'

He tried to sit as naturally as he could without exposing the mug. 'Um, the joy of what, exactly?'

'Of this! Of me and you, here. Doing work. Doing *our jobs*. If it wasn't for men like us, being in offices, accomplishing things, then where would we be?'

'I guess nowhere.'

'Nowhere is right! Nowhere is absolutely – Hold on one minute.' Dan picked up his phone and punched zero. 'Beatrice? Can you come up here, please?' He listened. 'Forget about the front desk. The front desk can wait.' He hung up and fixed his gaze on Pulpy. 'And that is terrifying, isn't it? Being nowhere. Not belonging, when it comes down to it. Not having a community to call your own.'

'I suppose that might be scary, yes,' said Pulpy, 'but I'd have Midge, so it wouldn't be so bad.'

Dan scowled for a second, and then beamed at his doorway. 'There she is!'

Pulpy turned to see Beatrice leaning against the doorframe.

'Hello again, gents,' she said.

'Now, Pulpy,' said Dan. 'Al told me before he left that you're in line for a promotion, is that right?'

Pulpy straightened in the chair, struggling against the softness, and swallowed. 'Yes?'

'Don't say, "Yes?" like that, like a question. Say it like you mean it!'

'Yes!'

Beatrice stepped into the office and closed the door behind her.

'You've been doing good work around here, Pulpy.' Dan put his arms in the air and stretched. 'But not quite good enough. You were late again today, for example.'

Pulpy pushed his neck back against the slick leather behind him. 'But I came in with you. And you gave me flex hours.'

'The flex hours only come into effect if you get all your work done. And I don't see you organizing the company Frisbee tournament, now do I?'

'Frisbee?'

Dan crossed his big arms over his massive chest. 'Do I?'

'Well no, I suppose not. But I didn't – What Frisbee tournament?'

'For the company. How are you at Frisbee, Pulpy?'

'I bet he's a whiz!' said Beatrice.

Pulpy's eyes widened. 'Well, I think I've played it once or twice, when I was younger.'

'I'll bet you have,' said Dan. 'And you've got the physique for it too.'

'You really do!' said Beatrice, and sat down on the arm of his chair.

Pulpy reddened and quickly looked down at himself. Only the tips of his fingers were visible outside the voluminous sleeves of Dan's suit jacket. 'I don't know. I've never heard that before.'

'But people have *thought* it before,' said Dan. 'And that's why you're the team captain.'

He looked from Dan to Beatrice and back to Dan again. 'But it's winter.'

'It's never too early to be prepared. We'll round everybody up in the boardroom tomorrow so you can choose the teams. Now go ahead, Pulpy.' Dan leaned forward. 'You can tell us. Who's your first pick?'

'I – I don't know.'

Beatrice rested a hand on the top of his head. 'How about me?'

Pulpy felt the warmth of her palm through his hair to his scalp. 'Well, sure. Okay.'

Dan clapped his hands together, once, and the *crack* they made filled the room. 'Sleep on it,' he said. 'You've got some big decisions to make.'

'I'm looking for something open-toed,' Midge told the shoe clerk. She already had her boots off. 'But they have to be wide, and they can't show *too* much toe. Just a hint.'

'Just a hint of toe.' The clerk was wearing a jaunty cardigan. He fingered one of the large, colourful buttons that ran down the front and appraised Midge's pantyhosed feet.

'But it's the winter,' said Pulpy loudly. 'Your toes will be cold in shoes like that.'

She gave him a look that was as close to a sneer as Midge got. 'The summer's coming.'

'I suppose it is.' He watched the clerk kneel down with a measuring device and guide Midge's foot into the metal hollow.

'Eight.' The clerk smiled. 'That's a good size.'

Midge bowed her head. 'Thank you.'

Pulpy poked at a pair of loafers on display. They were burgundy and canoe-shaped, with a jagged ridge on the sole.

The clerk swivelled his efficient oval head. 'Did you want to try those on?'

'No.' He shoved his hands into his coat pockets, and in the left one he felt the reassuring shape of the receptionist's duck mug.

'I need to make sure my heel is tightly held in,' said Midge. 'I need a snug fit.'

'We have a full range of strappies.' The clerk motioned her to a rack where several pairs of brownish open-toed shoes were lined up next to a high price tag. 'They're leatherette.'

'Ooh!' she said. 'I'd like to try on a pair of those.'

'I'll be right back.' The shoe clerk disappeared into the rear storage space.

'I'll be right here,' she said, and sat on the cushioned bench next to the foot mirror.

Pulpy rested a hand on her shoulder.

Midge flicked a glance his way and dislodged him with a hard shrug. 'It's a beautiful strappy. I hope it fits me.'

'I'll have to see it on you. It's a lot of money for not very much shoe.' He stood back and looked at her feet with their delicate ribbons of blue veins showing through her nude hose. She was pointing and unpointing her toes while she waited.

The clerk reappeared with an open white box and handed Midge a shoe from inside. 'There was only one size eight left,' he said. 'Looks like fate to me.'

Midge reddened and wedged her foot into the proffered sandal.

'They're perfect,' said the clerk.

'Hmm,' said Pulpy. 'Your skin is sort of sticking out of the holes.'

'It's supposed to do that,' she said in a mean voice, and then blinked up at the clerk. 'Isn't it?'

'Oh yes,' he said.

'I don't know,' said Pulpy.

'They're very supportive, with the straps.' Midge pushed her finger against the three small triangles of her soft, white flesh that bulged out between the thin strips of leather.

Then the clerk reached out and touched them too.

'All right,' said Pulpy. 'That's it.'

'Excuse me?' said the other man, his stubby finger still on Midge's skin.

Pulpy felt acutely aware of every corner of the room. The shelves and racks of shoes and boots stood at attention all around him. 'Get your hands off my wife. Right now.'

'Pulpy!' Midge's mouth was a perfect circle.

The clerk retracted his hand in a rush, almost falling backward with the effort, and pocketed it in his cardigan. 'I'm sorry,' he said, 'I didn't mean –'

'Come on, Midge,' said Pulpy. 'We're leaving.'

She stared at him and for a moment she just sat there. But then she said, 'Okay,' and pulled on her boots. She moistened her lips and hopped to her feet and they left the store together.

'Oh, Pulpy!' said Midge.

'Oh, Midge!' said Pulpy, but it came out more like 'Mmft, Mmdge!' with her ear filling his mouth. He was frantic for her.

Midge had wide, downy ears that Pulpy liked to pretend to eat. He liked her to feel him humming around those ears.

She pressed her fingertips against his neck and he felt all five of them – small, circular points of even pressure, cool at first but then warming.

They were half on, half off the loveseat, both delighted that they hadn't made it to the bedroom.

'The way you talked to him,' said Midge. 'I loved the way you talked to him!'

He released her ear with a slurp. 'I loved it too!'

She tugged at Dan's belt, which Pulpy had buckled to the tightest hole.

His head filled with an urgent beeping and a tremor shot through him.

'What's that?' said Midge.

He fit his palm against her wide brow. 'What's what?'

'That beeping.' She sat still, listening, then pointed to his groin. 'It's coming from your pants.'

His pocket was throbbing. He reached in and his hand closed around something small and rectangular, and then he started to sweat.

'What is it?' she said.

The pager. 'It's nothing.' He groped for the Off switch.

'Let me see.' She was panting a little, her brown eyes fixed on him.

His wrist was going numb from the vibrations. 'Just kiss me,' he said.

She started to slide Dan's belt out of the loops. 'Show me what you've got first.'

'Ha!' He tried crushing the pager against his thigh to silence it. 'Ow!'

Midge's hands wilted on his waist. 'What is it, Pulpy?' She moved away slightly.

He sighed, and pulled out the pager. It was still going off.

Her bottom lip sagged. 'Well,' she said.

'Midge, I tried to tell him not to page me here. I really tried to tell him.'

She stood up and tucked her blouse back in. 'Answer it.'

'Midge –'

She picked up their coats, which they had tossed on the floor in their rush to the loveseat.

He looked at the numbers on the pager's display. The small piece of plastic felt hot and far too heavy for its size. He heaved himself into a standing position, walked slowly to the phone and dialled.

'Why did you bring a mug home?' said Midge.

'That's the receptionist's –' His eyes widened.

'Hello there!' said Dan on the other line.

Midge was scowling at the cartoon duck, looking ready to smash it.

'Hello?' said Dan.

'You paged me,' said Pulpy, his eyes on his angry wife.

'That's right, ten minutes ago. Where were you?'

'Tell me why you brought this home!' Midge raised the mug over her head.

'We need to work on your response time, Pulpy. Lucky for you this was just a test.'

'Dan, I'm in the middle of something here. Can we talk about this tomorrow?' Then to Midge, 'Please don't. Please let me explain.'

'You're in the middle of something, eh?' Dan made a wet, squeaking sound.

Pulpy moved the phone away from his ear and mouthed, 'I love you,' to Midge.

She lowered her arm and let the mug fall.

'No!' he said.

Her face went white. The mug landed on the rug, rolled a little and then came to rest, intact. She made a move to kick it, but didn't. 'Tell Dan I say hello,' she said, and darted across the living room, through the kitchen and down the hall to their bedroom.

'What's going on over there?' said Dan. 'Sounds like hijinks to me.'

Pulpy heard a door slam. 'I can't talk now,' he said. 'I'll talk to you tomorrow.'

'Don't forget about the Frisbee teams. We're counting on you, Pulpy.'

'Uh huh.'

'Have a good night,' said Dan. 'I'd tell you not to do anything I wouldn't do, but then you wouldn't be left with much, ho-ho!' His boss hung up.

Pulpy stood there listening to the dial tone and then his ear filled with the bleeps of numbers being pressed on the other phone. 'Hello?' he said. 'Midge? Who are you calling?'

'Hang up, Pulpy!' she yelled.

He replaced the phone in its cradle and sat down on the rumpled loveseat.

A few minutes later Midge reappeared with the fishbowl in her arms. 'Mr. Fins and I will be staying at Jean's tonight,' she said.

He stood up. 'Midge, please, if this is about the mug –'

'It's not about the *mug*,' she said. 'You went out for drinks with her. And you gave her our fish!'

'But I already told you, she was lonely. And Dan and Beatrice are being so hard on her. I just did those things to cheer her up.'

'You're such a good person, Pulpy. Nice through and through.'

He looked at the duck mug on the floor. 'She's going through a rough time.'

Her mouth crumpled. 'Well, so am I.'

'Midge,' he said, 'don't think anything bad.'

'I don't know what to think.' Her wide-set brown eyes were shiny. 'I don't know what to think, I don't know what to think.'

'Please don't think anything bad.'

'I'm trying, Pulpy. But it's really hard.' A tear spilled over her bottom lashes and slid down her cheek to her chin, where it hung for a second before dripping into the fishbowl.

'You're going to get Mr. Fins all salty,' he said.

A horn honked outside, and he jumped.

Midge swiped at her eyes with the back of her hand. 'I have to go.'

'Please stay.' He reached for her but she moved out of his grasp. 'Midge, really, there's nothing – there isn't anything.'

The horn honked again.

'That's Jean.' She opened the front door. 'I'm going.'

He looked at the fishbowl nestled in her arms, at Mr. Fins blowing angry bubbles at him. 'What about clothes?' he said. 'Did you pack an overnight bag?'

She stood there hugging the bowl, making little waves on the water's surface.

'I'll get you something to wear. You can't wear dirty clothes around on your route tomorrow. That's how rumours get started.'

She lifted one foot off the floor and then put it down. 'I –'

'Stay right there.' Pulpy ran to the bedroom and yanked open her dresser. He stared for a second at her underwear, the shiny kind with the lacy elastic, and then shook his head and grabbed a pair and some pantyhose. He opened another drawer and found her skirt with the palm fronds on it, and went to the closet for her favourite blouse. Then he heard the front door close.

'Midge!' He sprinted back to the living room and over to the door, her clothes held tight in his hands. He opened it to see her getting into Jean's car. 'Midge!' He flailed his arms and the two women watched him, and he realized he was waving his wife's underwear like a flag.

The car sped away, and Pulpy stood there feeling the soft weight of Midge's empty clothes. And then she was gone.

'*H*old on, Midge,' said Pulpy.
  '*I am holding on.*'
  '*Tighter. There you go. You're doing it!*'

The first time Pulpy and Midge attended Couples Ice Dance Expression, they shuffled around the outside of the community-centre ice rink while the rest of the class learned and practised forward and backward crossovers in the middle with the instructor.

Midge was panting a little as she inched her skates along. Her ski pants made a vvvrrtt when they rubbed together. 'Okay, that's enough.' She squeezed Pulpy's arm as they watched the twirling figures of their peers.

'You just let me know when you're ready to get in there,' he said. 'Whenever you're ready.'

'I wish I had your confidence.' Midge dug in her toe pick. 'I just want to jab in my pick and ruin all this beautiful ice, just hack at it in little kicks. But that would be a shame, or else it would take too long. Either way I wouldn't really do it.'

Pulpy leaned in to kiss her forehead. 'We don't have to do this.'

'Pulpy, this is one of my goals.'

He slid one of his blades forward and back. 'I know.'

'For a relationship to be fulfilling, both partners need to help each other achieve their goals. One of my goals is I want to skate. I want to be graceful.'

'Here comes the dip!' shouted the instructor. 'I hope you're all paying attention!'

'Ohh, the dip,' said Midge.

'You are graceful,' said Pulpy. 'You're full of grace.'

'No, I'm not,' she said. But she smiled.

FOUR

Pulpy woke up on the loveseat with Dan's belt coiled around him and Midge's underwear tucked under one arm. His neck was sore and his knees ached from being bent all night. The loveseat wasn't meant for sleeping.

He turned his head sideways and looked across the empty room. There was a small puddle on the carpet runner, from Midge's boots or Mr. Fins' bowl. He eased himself off the cushions, walked over and soaked up the water with his socks.

Pulpy stood there with wet feet. He couldn't think of anything to do except get ready for work, so he showered and dressed like usual. Then he went to grab money for the food court but stopped, and headed to the kitchen instead. He needed a new routine. There was a loaf of bread on the counter and he put that in a bag. He opened the fridge and found the jar of Peach Delight and put that in the bag with the bread, squishing the first few slices.

Then he headed back to the living room. He put the bag of bread and jam on the loveseat and sat down next to it to put on his boots. And then he noticed the black-and-white grin of their keyboard poking out from under the coffee table.

He leaned forward and pulled it out. Parts of it gleamed and other parts were smudged with Midge's fingerprints. A tiny light lit up when he turned on the power.

He went for the pre-programmed songs first. With the jab of a button he unleashed a Motown hit, a power ballad, the dirge Midge had played for him before. He played the dirge twice and then he laced his long fingers together and cracked his knuckles.

The receptionist's mug was still lying on its side on the rug next to him. He picked it up and righted it so the poor, stressed-out duck was facing him. That yellow beak, those crooked glasses. Those white wings.

'Here goes nothing, duck,' he said, and started to play. After a few uncertain minutes his wrists relaxed into it, channelling the melodies he kept remembering. He swayed a little to the music he was making.

He was going to be late.

When Pulpy got in, the receptionist was packing her belongings into a cardboard box on her desk. 'What are you doing?' he said.

She didn't look up. 'What does it look like?'

He had her mug in his coat pocket and he fit a few knuckles into the smooth ceramic hollow it made. 'Oh.'

She paused with her hole punch halfway into the box. 'They said I disobeyed a direct order. They said that's cause for immediate dismissal.'

'But that's not fair to you. You're good at your job. They shouldn't let you go over this.'

'If it wasn't this it would've been something else. They don't want me here.' She continued her packing. 'Anyway, Lester said he can pick up a couple of extra shifts at work until I get another job.'

'Who's Lester?'

She made a face at him. 'My boyfriend.'

'Oh.' He puffed out his cheeks. 'Les?'

'What, you know him?'

'No. I just wondered if you called him that. Les.'

'Oh.' She gave her hole punch a quick polish on her blouse before putting it in the box. 'No, I don't. I call him Lester.'

'Right. So, are you on your way out, or –' He slid his fingers around the handle of her mug.

'Well, *she's* not here, so he asked *me* to cover the desk. To cover my own desk! I should just walk out.' She sighed. 'But I don't think I will.'

'That's good. I mean, it's good you're not going right away.' He took his hand out of his pocket, leaving the mug in there for now. 'Why did you just leave the registration stuff in the recycling bin like that?'

'I didn't need it anymore.'

'I guess that's reason enough.' He looked at her half-full box. There was some old tape stuck to one corner. 'So how was the rest of the seminar?'

She held her eraser dish up to the fluorescents and examined its underside. 'It wasn't really what I expected. I thought it would be more in-depth.' She dropped her arm and put the dish into the box. 'But it was worth it.'

'I'm glad.' He headed for the hallway.

'Aren't you going to take off your coat?'

'I will later.' He walked into the kitchen and put his sack of bread and jam in the fridge.

The empty fishbowl was sitting on the table, and he pressed his hand against the glass and craned his neck so he could observe the pink smear of his palm from the other side. Then he returned to the welcome area, smiled at the receptionist and went upstairs.

When he reached the top he saw Dan standing near his desk, talking to Eduardo. The two of them watched him approach.

'Pulpy!' said Dan. 'I was just asking your cube-mate here if he'd seen my mug.'

'What mug?' Pulpy hung his coat, with the mug still inside, over the back of his chair.

'You know –' Dan raised his elbows and flapped them up and down.

Eduardo narrowed his eyes when he noticed the way one of Pulpy's coat pockets was hanging lower than the other.

'I'm not really sure which mug you mean, Dan,' said Pulpy.

'Brrr,' said Eduardo. 'It's cold up here, isn't it? I wish I'd brought *my* jacket to my desk.'

Pulpy frowned at him.

'You know –' Dan rapped the top of Pulpy's monitor. '"My schedule's full"?'

Pulpy chewed on his upper lip. 'Oh, you mean the receptionist's mug.'

Dan stared at him. 'Could I see you in my office, please?'

Eduardo smirked.

Pulpy watched him over his shoulder as he followed his boss down the hall.

Dan sat at his desk and turned to his computer screen. He gave the Return key a couple of light taps and said, 'I'm onto you, Pulpy.'

Pulpy squirmed in the leather lounger. 'What do you mean?'

'You've got a thing for that secretary and it's tearing you apart. It's tearing your marriage apart.'

Pulpy blinked at him. 'No, I don't.'

Dan increased his pressure on the Return key. His tone was low and measured. 'Then why do you care if she's leaving?'

'Because she didn't do anything wrong. I just feel bad for her.'

'Did you hear anything when you came in this morning? That's right, you didn't. You didn't hear the Winter Flute, that's for sure, because she disconnected the wires. What kind of a person doesn't like the Winter Flute? I've tried to hook it back up but I can't, so now I need to get the guy back in. But until then, no music. She stopped the music for everyone.'

'I think she was worried about electrocution.'

'Then what was she doing messing with the wires? She's a menace, that woman, and I'm glad she's going. She's been poisoning our work environment, Pulpy – she is a toxic employee. You can't approach her. You can't ask her to do anything. And you'd better not touch her duck mug, because if you do you're in big trouble. You are in *big* trouble.'

'But *you* touched it,' said Pulpy. 'You took it.'

'So what?' Dan's phone rang but he ignored it. 'So what if I did?'

Pulpy focused on Dan's mouse pad, with the lion who would rather be at the watering hole. The big cat was smiling with sharp, sharp teeth. 'Why do you hate her so much?'

Dan picked up his phone. 'Hello? Oh, hi.' He frowned. 'Yeah, he's here. Why? Yeah, hold on.' He activated the speakerphone. 'It's Beatrice,' he said to Pulpy. 'For you.'

'Pulpy!' said Beatrice. 'I'm at Passionate Bath!'

Pulpy leaned closer to the phone. 'Where?'

'Listen, I need your advice. I'm buying a parting gift for the secretary.'

'You're buying her a *what*?' said Dan.

'Why are you asking me?' said Pulpy.

'You're friends with her, aren't you?'

'Ah,' he said, and sat up a bit straighter. 'Well, I guess I am, yes. We're friends.' He thought about the receptionist's rude forward, which he still hadn't deleted.

'So what kind of bath products do you think she likes to use?'

He considered that for a second. 'Do they have any Tropical Mist?'

'What the hell does she need a parting gift for?' said Dan. 'We're talking immediate dismissal. We're talking walking papers. We're talking termination here, for – We are not talking about anything that involves a *gift*.' He furrowed his brow at his red-and-white mug.

'She took that course to better herself,' said Pulpy.

'I told her not to go,' Dan said slowly, 'and she didn't listen to me.'

'Well, anyway, I think Beatrice has the right idea.'

'Thank you, Pulpy,' said Beatrice. 'I was actually thinking about buying her some spray lotion.'

'We'll just see about that,' said Dan. 'We will just see what *I* have to say about *that*.'

'Is that possible?' said Pulpy. 'Can you spray a lotion?'

'There's three kinds here,' said Beatrice. 'Vanilla, peach and Brazil nut.'

'Get the peach.'

'You think the peach? I was more thinking the Brazil nut. Brazil nut is big now, especially the butter – they lathered it all over me at the spa. But I did ask your opinion, so I'll get the peach. I'll get the medium size because the large is too expensive.'

'The large would be a nice gesture,' said Pulpy. 'And you should probably pick up a cake.'

'No cake,' she said. 'She doesn't deserve a cake.'

Dan bounced his fist off his desk. 'Now, that is more like it!'

'I'll be there in an hour or so,' she said.

'We're doing the Frisbee picks in twenty minutes,' said Dan. 'I need you here sooner.'

'Then do the Frisbee picks *later*,' said Beatrice.

'I said twenty minutes!'

Pulpy stood up. 'I'd better get working on that sign-up sheet.'

'An hour at the *least*,' she said.

Pulpy stood next to Dan at the front of the boardroom with the rest of the workers ringed around them in a horseshoe formation.

Roy from Customer Service was beside Cheryl from Active Recovery and Carmelita from the Parts Department, and all of them were giving Pulpy sympathetic looks. Eduardo stood with his arms crossed, sneering.

Dan cleared his throat. 'There are a few issues I plan on raising at this meeting. I know that may sound obvious, but these are things that are on my mind and in order to clear it I have to raise them.'

One of the fluorescent ceiling tiles was flickering, casting shadows over the faces of Pulpy's co-workers. He looked away from all the down-turned mouths and toed the thin carpet.

'I mean, you really have to wonder about people who don't care about their place of work,' said Dan. 'Don't you have to wonder? I said to Pulpy, "This is unacceptable, and we need to take action." "What kind of action?" he said to me. "Serious action," I told him.'

Pulpy could feel everyone's eyes on him and he turned to his boss. 'I don't really remember that conversation, Dan.'

'You were probably drunk.' Dan addressed the assembled employees. 'Pulpy and I go drinking together, did you all know that? This man here has the inside track on pretty much the whole shebang. I confide in him and he confides in me.'

Eduardo started to sneeze into his hand but, to Pulpy's horror, the word 'blow job' came out instead.

'Now, see?' Dan pointed at him. 'That's your problem right there, that kind of ignorance. Just because two men get together for a few stiff shots does not imply anything more than that.'

Eduardo guffawed loudly and a few other employees, including Jim from Packaging, tittered.

Pulpy scuffed his feet on the carpet some more and felt a static charge building up in him. The air ducts made rushing and rattling sounds overhead.

'But you know what? That kind of acting out doesn't faze men like me and Pulpy. Because the only way to get by in this world is to keep your sense of humour. And the way to accomplish *that* is –' Dan reached over and put his arm around Pulpy's shoulders. 'Pulpy?'

'To play Frisbee,' said Pulpy in a very small voice.

'That's right!' Dan punched the air. 'And now I'm going to turn the floor over to our Frisbee team captain so he can sort out the teams.'

'In case you didn't notice,' said Eduardo, 'it's snowing outside.'

More laughter.

'Oh, I noticed,' said Dan. 'And it's comments like *that* that separate the clowns from the ringmasters.'

Eduardo furrowed his brow. 'What does that mean?'

Pulpy noticed something red in a far corner of the boardroom, and realized it was one of Al's retirement balloons. It still had quite a bit of air left in it, and it bobbed with the slight breeze of so many shuffling feet.

'The earlier we choose our teams, the earlier we rally our team spirit. Which is exactly what we need around here. An injection of oomph.'

'I'll give you an injection of oomph,' Eduardo muttered.

Dan tilted his rectangular head so that one side of his neck was stretched taut. 'Haven't you already been doing that to someone else, Eduardo?'

A ripple of murmurs passed around the semicircle.

Eduardo reddened and aimed a glare at Pulpy.

Then the boardroom door flew open and Beatrice sashayed in with an armload of shopping bags. 'Sorry I'm late, everyone. Whose team am I on?'

'You're on Eduardo's team,' said Pulpy.

She jutted her hip out sideways. 'Am I now?'

Eduardo growled and walked out of the room.

Pulpy looked at Dan, but he was looking at his wife and smiling.

'I didn't think you'd make it,' he said.

Beatrice rolled her eyes. 'Don't go getting all grateful on me. I'm not here because of *you*.' She blew a kiss at Pulpy. 'I came to support our captain!'

The smile died on Dan's face as quickly as it had sprouted there.

'Okay!' Pulpy clapped his hands together. 'Let's get back to picking those teams!'

After the picking was over, Pulpy sat at his desk and pulled out his keyboard tray. It clacked and rattled and banged onto his knees and he said, 'This is ridiculous.' He got off his chair and crawled under the desk and flipped onto his back. He squinted up at the underside of the tray, where it fit into the docking device. 'It's not level,' he said, and reached up and moved the tray along and off the track and then into the proper position, higher up. He checked to see that the grooves were aligned on both sides, then crawled back out, brushed himself off and sat down in his chair to test his work. The tray slid out smoothly and noiselessly and there was now a good inch between it and his knees. He slid his keyboard tray in and out, enjoying the easy motion.

Then he thought about the receptionist leaving, and he thought about going downstairs and saying goodbye. He would give her the mug back and that would make her so happy. 'Could I ask you something?' he would say.

She'd look at him. 'What is it?'

'Your name,' he'd say. 'You told me once but I forgot it.'

'Oh,' she'd say, and smile. 'It's –' And she would tell him her name.

'That's a nice name,' he would tell the receptionist.

'Thank you,' she'd say. 'Thank you, Pulpy.'

'What did you think you were trying to pull in there?' said a low voice behind him.

Pulpy turned quickly to see Eduardo sneering around the partition. 'Nothing,' he said. 'I don't know what you're talking about.'

'Didn't I tell you not to mess with me? What goes on between yours truly and the boss's wife is *private*.'

Pulpy's palms went cold and he pressed them against the fabric of his chair. 'Are you sure about that?'

Eduardo wheeled closer, his shoes smacking out a staccato on the plastic floor mat. 'What the hell are you playing at, Pulpy?'

'Dan *knows*, Eduardo. And not because I told him.' He was sweating now, an icy sweat that felt like it could freeze his collar to his neck.

Eduardo blinked. 'How would he know if you didn't tell him?'

'They have an *arrangement*.' Pulpy formed his mouth around the shape of the word. 'And if you want to know something else, you're not the only one.'

His co-worker's flashlight eyes dimmed. 'What?'

'Why don't you give Building Maintenance a call? Tell them you need something fixed.' Pulpy reached into his coat and took out the mug. 'See you later, Eduardo.' He pushed back his chair and stood up.

'Yeah.' Eduardo was staring across the room toward Dan's office, his hands clasped together in his lap. 'See you.'

'I would've thought they'd do a cake,' said the receptionist.

She was sitting in her chair with her coat on. Her now-full cardboard box was on the floor by her feet.

'Don't forget your international garden calendar,' he said.

'It can stay.' She waved a hand at February's flowers, all lined up with their faces pointed toward the sun. 'I was using it to count down the days before I was out of here, so I guess I don't need it anymore. I took everything else.' Her desk was empty now except for her computer, her phone and a red bag with crinkly silver paper poking out the top.

Pulpy pointed to it. 'What's in there?' His other hand was behind his back.

She sneered. 'My parting gift. It's peach spray. She hands it to me and says, "Here you go." She just hands it to me like that – no ceremony or anything. I would've thought a cake, at least.'

'She gave you the peach spray,' he said. 'Everybody likes peach.'

'It's peach spray *lotion*.' She made a face. 'Who ever heard of lotion you spray on? I'm leaving it here. I don't want it in my house because it stinks. It stinks and it's cheap and it would give me hives.'

'It's peach.'

'Exactly. And I didn't even get a card. Everybody else gets a card when they leave.' She put her hands on her desk and pushed the bag aside. 'I thought at least they'd do a cake for me.'

Pulpy stood there feeling sad for her. 'People are talking about you leaving. I heard someone say they'd miss the way you did things.'

'Really?' She looked a bit happier. 'Who said that?'

'I just heard it,' he said. 'I didn't see who it came from.'

'I hate this place,' she said.

He crossed one foot over the other. 'I got you something.'

'You did?'

'I found it, actually.' And he brought his hand around and gave her the duck mug.

She put both hands around the mug and pressed it down hard on her desk. 'Where?'

He cleared his throat carefully. 'Dan had it.'

She nodded. 'He takes my mug and she gives me hives.' The receptionist lifted her mug again and stuck her nose in. 'Smells like coffee.'

'I think he drank coffee out of it.'

'Only tea.' She held the cartoon duck level with her eyes. 'There's only ever been tea in here. Are you all right, duck?' And she tapped it on the bill.

'Quack,' said Pulpy softly.

'What?'

'Nothing. I should probably get back upstairs.' He stuck his hands in his pockets. 'Well, so long.'

She stood up. 'Hold on a minute.'

'Yes?' He waited with his ears wide open.

'Here.' She thrust the mug at him. 'You keep it. I don't need anything reminding me of this stupid job.'

'Really?' He removed his hands from his pockets and took it from her. 'Are you sure?'

She hoisted the cardboard box onto her hip. 'It's from the staff cupboard, anyway.'

Pulpy smiled. 'I'm glad you went to that seminar, even if it wasn't as good as you thought it would be.'

'Me too,' she said.

He made an awkward writing motion with his free hand. 'Should I maybe get your –'

She shook her head. 'You wouldn't call it, anyway.'

'No. I guess I wouldn't.'

'Besides –' She headed for the door. 'I'm going to forget you as soon as I walk out of here.'

'I wanted to get you a cake,' said Pulpy.

The receptionist turned to smile at him. 'I know,' she said. And then she was gone.

Pulpy stood there looking at the space she'd occupied, and then he heard clapping, and Dan's voice behind him.

'Well, now, wasn't that touching?'

He turned around slowly to see Dan and Beatrice perched at the top of the stairs, grinning down at him.

'I'm not sure Midge would feel the same way, though, do you?' said Beatrice.

'How long have you been sitting there?' said Pulpy.

'Long enough,' said Dan. 'And now if you and the duck don't mind, I'd like to see you both in my office.'

Beatrice came down the steps, pointing her pointy shoes ahead of her, and slid past Pulpy into the receptionist's chair. 'What an ungrateful bitch,' she said, frowning at the gift bag.

'First things first,' said Dan when Pulpy reached the top of the stairs, and he grabbed the receptionist's mug out of Pulpy's hand.

'Hey!' he said, and saw Beatrice scurry under the desk as Dan tossed the mug over the railing into the welcome area below. It hit the tile floor and exploded. 'Why did you do that?'

Dan dusted off his palms. 'Because I can.'

Beatrice reappeared and put her hands on her hips. 'I'll call Building Maintenance to clean this up.'

'I bet you will,' Dan said, and ushered Pulpy into his office. 'Sit down, Pulpy. In front of my desk here.'

Pulpy lowered himself into one of the hard-backed chairs, every rigid contour conspiring to make him uncomfortable.

Dan sat in his leather recliner and leaned forward. 'Things are not looking good for you right now. You stole that mug from my desk.'

'But it belonged to the receptionist first.'

'Don't give me excuses, give me results!' Dan was yelling now. 'You're a thief, Pulpy! And you knew she went to that seminar. You demonstrated a wilful and reckless disregard for the front desk. That kind of behaviour will not be tolerated.'

'All she wanted was to improve herself. And she had everything prepared.' Pulpy's hands were shaking all the way up to his forearms. 'Besides, Al told her she could go to the seminar.'

'Al, Al, *Al*! Al this, Al that.' Dan's voice was mock whiny. 'I've had it with hearing about Al's way of doing things. Al retired, Pulpy, and he's not coming back. He doesn't care about this office and he doesn't care about you. He abandoned ship to get old and grow vegetables, and in case you didn't notice, *I* took over when he left!' Dan slammed his elbows down on his desk. 'You are in some kind of serious shit here – this is your *job*! Forget about that promotion we were discussing yesterday. Right here and right now we are talking about the very polar opposite of a promotion.'

Pulpy shrank back against the chair.

'You were a regular Bonnie and Clyde outfit, you and that *secretary*.' Dan made the last word sound like the worst word in the world.

'I don't know what you're talking about,' Pulpy whispered.

'We saw that dirty little email she sent you.'

He blinked. 'How did you –'

'We bought software, Pulpy. We've been monitoring things.'

'But ... it was just a forward.'

'Is that all it was? Then why didn't you delete it?'

'I was going to. I just hadn't gotten around to it yet.'

Dan rocked his big head back and forth, and his voice went soft. 'Poor Midge.'

'I love my wife,' said Pulpy. 'I love my wife more than anything.'

'I wish I could believe you.'

'But there's nothing to believe. I love Midge.'

'Have you talked to her today?'

'She stayed over at a friend's house last night.' He looked at his lap and his upturned palms resting there, the fingers rubbery and useless. 'But that doesn't mean anything.'

'Oh dear.' Dan leaned back and crossed his arms. 'I hate to say it, Pulpy, but in my experience that means a lot.'

'We'll get through it.'

'Will you? Because this is big. This is big, big marital badness.'

Pulpy's mouth wasn't working properly. His tongue was too heavy and his jaw was too tight. 'So what should I do?'

'Let me help you. Let Beatrice help you.' Dan's gentle baritone lapped Pulpy's ears. 'Give Midge a call. Tell her you want to put the spark back with some mutual adventure. Tell her a vote for mutual adventure is a vote for your future together.'

He shook his head. 'She'd never go for it.'

'Then just get her over to our place and we'll take care of the rest. Tell her it's just for dinner.'

Pulpy rubbed his chin. 'I really don't know about this.'

'Your job and your marriage are on the line here, and you're hesitating?' Dan made a sad face. 'I'm not sure you're the man I thought you were, Pulpy.'

'I'm not hesitating. I don't know if this is the best thing for us, that's all.'

'Just get Midge over. We'll have a nice dinner. Then we'll see what the best thing is for all concerned. And no pressure – just good times with good company.'

Pulpy felt Dan's quality wood pressing against his back. His arms went limp and he let them dangle. 'If that's all it is, then I guess I could give her a call.'

'Yes!' Dan made two shooting guns with his hands, twirled them in the air and holstered them at his sides. 'Now there's the Pulpy I know and love!'

'Just dinner, right?'

'We'll take it slow.' Dan winked at him. 'Trust me on this.'

Beatrice wasn't in the welcome area when Pulpy went downstairs for lunch.

A broom and dustpan were leaning against the desk, and the broken pieces of duck mug had been swept into a little pile in front of the garbage can.

He peered down the hallway. It was empty. He headed for the kitchen, glancing at the men's room door as he passed.

The kitchen was empty too. He opened the fridge and a large Tupperware container full of something dark and wet fell out and hit the floor. The contents sloshed as Pulpy tried to shove it back in, but there were no empty spots. The shelves were crammed full with plastic tubs and Thermoses and colourful fabric lunch cozies, climbing on top of each other all the way to the very back.

He crouched and groped for his plastic bag, nearly toppling milk cartons and juice boxes and a pyramid of yogurt cups. He finally located the spongy cushion of his white loaf and the hard cylinder of his jam jar in the right-hand crisper, which wasn't where he'd left it, and forced the Tupperware container into its place.

He put two slices in the toaster and took a knife from the cutlery drawer, and waited.

'Smells good!'

Pulpy jumped, but relaxed when he saw Roy in the doorway. 'It's only toast.'

Roy looked pale and his smile was set at an odd angle. 'Smells better than toast.'

'Toast is like that sometimes.'

'I guess you have a point there.' Roy walked over to the bulletin board with his hands in his pockets and began to read the postings.

Pulpy moved the toast-colour indicator from yellow to light brown. 'Are you all right?'

Roy didn't say anything for a moment. Then he turned around and said, 'You're a family man, aren't you, Pulpy?'

The elements heating his bread glowed bright orange. 'I guess I am, yes.'

'You have a wife, don't you, and an apartment together?'

Pulpy nodded, watching a tendril of smoke curl up past the coiled wires.

'See, there you go. You're all set up. Guys like me envy guys like you.'

'Really?' His toast popped up, only slightly burned.

'What do you mean, really? You have a woman at home who *loves* you. Shit, Pulpy.'

He tried to open the jam jar but the lid was stuck, so he tried harder.

'Your wife had that bird that died, didn't she?'

'That's right,' he said. 'Mrs. Wings.'

'Man, that sucks. That sucks that had to happen.' Roy shook his head. 'But, you know, you should tell her what a great party everybody thought that was. We all still talk about it.'

'Thanks.' The lid came off with a sucking sound. 'That's nice.'

Roy heaved a sigh. 'The chick I'm doing it with is doing it with somebody else. I just found out.'

'Oh,' said Pulpy. 'I'm sorry to hear that.'

'The guy's got a tool belt. He *fixes* things. How am I supposed to compete with that?'

Pulpy paused with the knife in the jar, sunk down into the sweetness, and turned to look at the empty fishbowl on the staff break table. He remembered Roy's hand on his shoulder in the men's room, after the fish died. The knock on the door. And Beatrice in the hallway.

'Pulpy? You okay?' said Roy. 'Hey, buck up. I'm the one telling his tale of woe here.'

'Sure.' Pulpy turned back to his co-worker. 'I was just thinking that you're probably better off without her.'

'Yeah, well.' Roy shrugged and turned back to the postings. 'Did you do this Frisbee sign-up sheet here?'

Pulpy started spreading Peach Delight on his toast. 'Yes.'

'Why did you do a sign-up sheet if the teams have already been decided? There's nothing to sign up for.'

'You're right,' said Pulpy. 'I guess it's more of a team allocation sheet, then. I should change the title and print it out again.'

'No, you shouldn't. Frisbee is stupid. Who wants to play Frisbee at work?'

'Not me, that's for sure.'

Roy grinned at him. 'I always knew you were all right, Pulpy.'

'Really?' Pulpy focused on evening out the layer of jam.

'That potluck you organized, that was pretty good.'

He stopped spreading, his hand gummy with Peach Delight. 'Thank you, Roy.'

'You're welcome. I'll see you later, Pulpy.' Roy smiled again. 'And take care of that wife of yours.'

'I will, thanks.' He watched the other man leave, and then looked in dismay at the crumby, sticky mess he'd made of everything.

He hadn't even used a plate, for heaven's sake.

Midge had given him a list of emergency contacts for his wallet, printed in multicoloured ink on a recipe card. He pulled it out and flicked it against the pay phone, then held it in front of his face and let the quarters drop into the slot. This was definitely an emergency, he thought, and dialled Jean's number.

'Hello?' said Jean.

'Hi, Jean, it's me, Pulpy.'

She made a disapproving noise. 'She doesn't want to talk to you.'

'Please, Jean, it's really important.'

'I can give her a message, that's the best I can do.'

Pulpy saw the teenage conference caller then, standing around the rib place with some of his friends. He was wearing the suspenders again. 'Sometimes we have to wait,' he said quietly.

'Wait for what?' said Jean.

'Nothing, sorry. I saw someone I know. Some teenager.'

'Who do you know that's a teenager?' She made a disgusted sound. 'First it's secretaries and now it's people half your age? You're not the man I thought you were, Pulpy.'

'Put Midge on the phone, Jean,' he said. 'This is about my job.'

'Your job? What about your job?'

'Just put her on.'

Jean let out a half-grumble, half-sigh. 'Okay, Pulpy. But she really doesn't want to speak with you.'

Pulpy turned back to the food court and blinked. The conference caller was walking toward him, chomping on a rack of short ribs.

Midge came on the line. 'I can't talk long,' she said. 'Jean's teaching me how lustre crystals can make a candle glossier.'

'Midge!' said Pulpy. 'How are you?'

'I'm fine.'

'Midge, I love you. And nothing happened between me and the receptionist, you have to believe me. I love you more than anything.'

The kid stopped in front of him. He had a rib sticking out between his teeth like a cigar. 'I need the phone,' he said.

'Well, I'm on it,' said Pulpy.

'What?' said Midge.

The kid took the rib out of his mouth and dropped it on the floor. 'I said, I need that phone.'

'Tough.' Pulpy turned his back to him.

'Who are you talking to? Hello, Pulpy? I'm going to hang up.'

'No! Midge, please don't. This is really important.'

The kid tapped him on the shoulder, leaving a sticky red fingerprint behind. 'Hurry up!'

Pulpy looked down at the stain on his coat. 'Now you've done it,' he said.

'What is going on there?'

'Excuse me, Midge,' said Pulpy. He faced the kid. 'I am talking to my wife. When you get a wife, then you can have the phone.'

The kid poked out his tongue to lick at some barbecue sauce in the corners of his mouth.

'Sorry, Midge,' said Pulpy. 'So, like I was saying –'

'I don't know what's happening with you anymore.' Her voice was shrill.

He watched the kid hitch up his suspenders and make his way back to the food court. 'My job is on the line, Midge. But if you just come with me to Dan and Beatrice's tonight, for dinner, I think everything will be okay.'

'What do you mean your job is on the line? And how will me having dinner with them make things okay?'

'I don't know. It just will. We can all sit down and discuss the situation in a non-work setting.'

'Why can't you go by yourself?'

'Because they want you too, Midge.' His palm was damp and the receiver almost slipped from it. 'They like your company. You're part of the non-work equation.'

'This all sounds very strange to me. Exactly what kind of job trouble are you in, Pulpy?'

'Desperate. Desperate job trouble.'

'And you said just dinner.'

'Yes, just dinner. That's right.'

'Well, okay then. But only because it's desperate.'

'Thank you.' He switched the phone to his other hand and wiped his palm on his pants. 'Thank you, Midge.'

'So should I just meet you at their place?'

'No!' he said. 'No. I'll meet you at home first. This is going to be good for both of us, you'll see.'

'Well, like you said, if it's your job at stake. Without your job, we wouldn't be able to buy a house.'

He pressed the receiver to his ear. 'You still want to buy a house with me?'

She went quiet. 'Of course I do.'

'Oh, Midge.'

'I have to go now,' she said. 'The crystals.'

'Sure. I'll see you tonight, then. I'll come straight home after work.'

'What should I wear?'

'Anything,' he said. 'Wear anything you like.'

'Okay. Goodbye, Pulpy.'

'Goodbye, Midge.'

She hung up.

Pulpy hung up too, and stared at the phone on its cradle. He thought about taking Midge out for dinner to celebrate when this was all over. Just the two of them, eating. That's all they had to do.

The welcome area was vacant again when Pulpy walked in after lunch. The empty fishbowl was sitting on the receptionist's desk. A sticky note posted on the glass read 'Drop In Your Business Card To Enter Our Raffle!!'

He stood there and listened for someone coming, but the only noise he heard was the hum of the receptionist's computer. He walked around and sat in her chair, and then he saw the seminar flyer in the recycling bin. He retrieved it and smoothed it out on her desk. 'Defeat the Office Downers!' said the flyer. 'Take a chuckle break!'

Pulpy nodded and read on. 'Hostile co-workers are hostile because ... it *works* for them!'

It sounded like a good seminar. He folded the flyer into a neat square and slipped it into his coat pocket. Then he let his hand stray to the handle of her big drawer and tug.

It opened easily, laying its contents bare for him: Styrofoam plates, boxes of plastic knives and forks, Styrofoam cups, napkins and boxes and boxes of colourful mini-candles. The cake drawer. He nodded and closed it gently.

'Hi, Pulpy. What are you doing?'

He looked up to see Beatrice striding toward him with her fingers curled around a glass of water.

'Oh, hi, Beatrice. I was just –' He pushed himself away from the desk. 'I was just admiring what you've done with the fishbowl. What's this raffle all about?'

'Isn't it great? It's something I'm implementing. Visitors to the office can put their business cards in the bowl, and then we enter them in our contest!' She was standing beside him now and she pressed her mouth against the waterglass, fogging it up and squishing her lips into an obscene pink mess.

He stood up and backed away from her, banging his thigh on the corner of the desk. 'What's the contest?'

She shrugged. 'I'm still working on that part. Anyway, it's a proven contact generator.' She took a long drink and her throat bulged with her swallowing.

He rocked back on his heels and looked past her to the receptionist's garden calendar, still brightening the wall behind her desk like a promise of better days to come. 'It sounds like you've got a lot going on.'

'Oh, I know how to stay on top of things, darling.' She ran her gaze over him, and then her eyes widened. 'Oh, no! What happened to your coat?' She dipped one of her sleeves in the water and rushed at him.

'It's nothing,' he said. 'It'll come out.'

'Not if you let it set, it won't. Come here.' She dabbed at the rib sauce on his shoulder, pressing harder and harder each time. 'Your beautiful, beautiful coat,' she murmured, and slid her hands under his collar.

He pulled away from her but she was stuck to him. 'If you don't mind, Beatrice –'

'Ho-ho! What's going on down *here*?' Dan came down the steps, squeezing the railing. His grin was massive.

Pulpy jerked forward and Beatrice's hands snagged on his coat, choking him. He started to cough and she let him go, but not before giving him one last, lingering knead.

'Pulpy had a stain,' said Beatrice. 'But I blotted it.'

Pulpy shucked off his coat and went to the closet.

'How was your lunch?' said Dan. 'Did you get a hold of Midge?'

'Ooh, did you?' said Beatrice.

'I talked to her,' he said with his back to them.

'And?' said Dan.

'And?' said Beatrice.

He let his coat drop, then kicked it toward the back and closed the closet door. 'She said okay.'

'She did!' Beatrice clapped her hands.

'To dinner.' He turned around. 'She said okay to dinner.'

'Oh, we'll have dinner,' said Dan. 'And then we'll see if we can coax her to stay for dessert.'

'Everybody likes dessert, mmm!' Beatrice licked her lips. 'Especially the way I make it.'

'I know what you mean when you say that,' said Pulpy. 'Don't think I don't know what you mean.'

'What are you talking about?' She pouted. 'I make a baked Alaska that is out of this world. The meringue, Pulpy –' She skimmed her thumb along the curve of her waist and down her lower back, stopping just over her behind. 'It's fluffier than a cloud.'

When Pulpy got home, Midge wasn't there.

'Midge!' he called. 'Midge!' He walked through the whole apartment to the bedroom with his boots still on. Midge wasn't there and neither was Mr. Fins.

Her Candle-Brations catalogue was sitting on her bedside table, and he flipped through the glossy pages. The book was filled with photos of candles – fat ones, skinny ones, square ones, oblong ones – in so many different colours and with so many imaginative names. Pulpy closed his eyes and pictured a flickering row of Lemongrass Toddies on the mantel of the fireplace he and Midge would have in the house they would buy someday.

Then he heard the key in the front door. He put the catalogue down and rushed back through the living room, and tripped over the keyboard. Something crunched under his foot and he knelt down. 'No!' he yelled, caressing the black and white keys. He flicked on the power switch and waited.

The green light came on just as Midge walked inside.

'It's okay,' he said. 'It's not broken.'

'Well, that's a good thing.' She took off her coat. 'I have to get changed.'

'You look really nice.'

'Thank you. But I still have to put on something different. I'm wearing the same outfit from yesterday.'

'Right.' He nodded. 'Well, I'll wait here for you.'

She moved past him.

'Where's Mr. Fins?' he said.

She stopped and crossed her arms. 'I left him at Jean's. I'm still not sure where I'm staying tonight.'

'Oh.' He pulled the keyboard onto his lap, bumping it over his boots and balancing it across his knees. 'Okay.'

'This is a favour, Pulpy. I'm doing you a favour going back there.'

'I know.' He ran a hand along the length of the keyboard. 'Maybe –'

She uncrossed her arms, and he saw that her clothes were wrinkled and her eyes were sad. 'Maybe what?'

'Maybe we could stay home instead.' Then his pager beeped.

'There's your answer.' The corners of Midge's mouth sagged. 'I'm going to change.'

Pulpy watched her leave the room and then he punched Dan and Beatrice's number into their phone.

Dan picked up on the first ring. 'She's coming, right?'

Pulpy frowned. 'I already told you she was.'

'Yes! That's the answer I was waiting for.'

Pulpy arched his index finger and brought it down on one of the keyboard keys. *Plink.*

'What was that?' said Dan.

Plink, plink. 'I don't know, Dan.'

'What's that plinking sound? Is that coming from your end?'

Pulpy zipped the same finger along the row of keys, and the cascading *doo-doo-doo-doo-doo* made him feel like there was possibility in every corner of the room.

'Okay, come on,' said Dan. 'That was definitely something.'

'I don't know what you're talking about, Dan, but if you don't mind, we're in the middle of getting ready here.'

'Ho-ho, don't go to too much trouble on our account!'

'We won't. It's just dinner, after all.' He turned off the keyboard and slid it gently under the coffee table. 'So did you have something you wanted to tell me, or –'

'Nah. I just called to see if you needed any, you know, encouragement.'

'No thanks, we're fine.' Pulpy inspected the soles of his boots and noticed a brown leaf stuck to the bottom of one of them.

'So we'll see you soon?'

He took the leaf and plastered it onto the back of his hand. 'We'll be there.' Then he hung up and smiled at Midge, who was standing in the kitchen wearing a squiggly-patterned top and a fresh pair of slacks. 'You look beautiful. Are you ready?'

'I guess so.' She shrugged. 'What's that on your hand?'

'It's a leaf. The snow must be melting.' He peeled it off. 'I'll throw it out.'

'Don't,' she said. 'You should take it back outside.'

He nodded and offered his elbow to her. 'Shall we go?'

Midge took his arm and held on tight. 'Let's get this over with.'

Beatrice answered the door in a kimono.

Pulpy watched Midge take in the shimmery blue silk and the embroidered dragon that stretched along one side, with an impossibly long tongue snaking down Beatrice's leg. 'Isn't that a nightgown?' she said.

'Oh, Midge.' Beatrice tinkled out a laugh. 'You slay me!'

'Well, isn't it?'

'It's Japanese.' Beatrice gave them a little bow.

'I know *that*,' said Midge.

Pulpy handed Beatrice a plastic bag. 'These are Dan's clothes and belt from the other night. Plus some wine.'

'Aren't you just the thoughtful-est!' Beatrice stepped back and the kimono swooshed around her bare legs. 'Why don't you two come in and take off your boots? And let me take your coats. You must be sweltering.'

'It *is* warm in here,' said Midge. 'It's warmer than it was before.'

'Do you think so?' said Beatrice. The heated air rushing out from behind her was thick with the smell of cooking meat.

Pulpy gently removed his wife's coat and handed it to Beatrice, and then gave her his own. He stepped out of his boots and Midge stepped out of hers, and his heart thumped at the sight of her round toes lined up under the wide brown band of her pantyhose.

Beatrice swished off down the hall with the armload of heavy fabric slung over one shoulder, then stopped and looked back at them. 'Coming?'

Pulpy nodded and put a hand on the small of Midge's back. 'We'll just have dinner,' he whispered.

She glanced at him and proceeded slowly ahead. The meat smell intensified.

'Well, look who it is!' Dan was stirring a pot on the stove. 'It's Pulpy and Midge!'

'And they brought us libations!' Beatrice rattled the plastic bag. 'As well as your, ahem, *clothes* from the other night.'

'Ho-ho!' said Dan. 'You sure you don't want to keep those as a souvenir, Pulpy?'

Pulpy shook his head and frowned. 'I'm fine, thanks.'

Dan was wearing a long, black garment that looked like a skirt, and Midge did a double take. 'Is that a dress?' she said.

'It's a kurta,' said Dan. 'From India. Some people like to wear pants with it but I'm flaunting tradition. And I don't know if you noticed but it is *hot* in here!'

'Tonight is ethnic night.' Beatrice twirled around in her kimono. 'We added some jerk seasoning to the pot roast.'

Pulpy noticed his and Midge's coats heaped on the floor in a far corner of the room.

Dan left his spoon in the pot and opened his arms wide. 'Midge, you're a vision! You're a vision in paisley.'

'Thank you, Dan.' Midge looked at the two big hands clenching and unclenching over the black tunic, which hovered over Dan's bare knees.

'And I'm making my special peas again, because I remembered how much you liked them last time.'

'Oh, you should've heard him earlier, going on about the peas,' said Beatrice. 'Personally, I think they're vile. But nothing's too good for our Midge!'

Dan sneered at his wife and resumed his stirring.

'Mmm, is that a baked Alaska?' Midge pointed to a huge white mound on the kitchen table, oozing sweetness onto its shiny platter.

'You bet it is!' said Dan.

'It's my secret recipe. You're going to love it!' said Beatrice. 'Now, who wants a drink?'

Midge was fanning herself. 'Could I please have something cool?'

'I've got just the thing.' Beatrice opened the fridge and pulled out a tray of small paper cups filled to the brim with red, orange and green. 'I made Jell-O shooters!'

Midge looked at Pulpy. 'I was thinking a glass of water might be nice.'

'Oh, but you have to try one!' Beatrice took four cups off the tray. 'Here, we'll all do it.'

'Clinky-clink!' Dan hoisted his shot. 'To us!'

'Clinky-clink.' Pulpy watched Midge squeeze her eyes shut as she swallowed her shooter. Then he squished his own cup between his thumb and forefinger and filled his mouth with the cold, slippery contents.

'Mmm,' said Midge. 'That was good.'

'Have another!' said Beatrice.

Midge selected a green one and held it to her lips. 'Is everybody else doing more?'

'Green means go!' Dan said, and sucked one back.

Pulpy slurped up another orange shooter. They all tasted the same, sweet and ripe and slick.

Dan pointed at him. 'I knew you'd like the orange ones! I said to Beatrice, "Just watch Pulpy. He'll pick orange every time."'

'Here, Midge.' Beatrice filled a very small glass with tap water and handed it to her.

'Thank you.' She sipped at it.

Pulpy cleared his throat. 'So I told Midge we're here to discuss my job,' he said in a loud voice.

'Yes, your job.' Dan nodded. 'Your job indeed.'

'Indeed *indeed*!' said Beatrice, and giggled.

'What's so funny?' Midge finished her water and set the glass down on the counter. It made a resounding *thut* in the now-quiet kitchen.

'Work is funny!' Dan cranked up the heat under his peas. 'Life is funny! Hot damn, you want to talk about *comedy*?'

'What *my* husband is trying to say,' said Beatrice, 'is that *your* husband's career is in fantastic shape. Just super.'

Midge's brow creased. 'But I thought you told me your job was on the line,' she said to Pulpy.

'And it is!' Dan said quickly, scowling at Beatrice. 'It is absolutely on the line. Now, who wants to eat?'

'I do!' Beatrice raised her hand and the sleeve of her kimono slid down to expose her long arm.

'Are you hungry, Midge?' said Pulpy.

'I guess a little,' she said.

'What you need is another aperitif!' said Dan.

'I'd better not,' said Midge. 'I'm feeling a bit lightheaded.'

'Are you kidding me? A light head is what you want! Who wants a heavy, fat old head?'

'Not me, that's for sure!' said Beatrice, and inhaled another Jell-O shooter.

'You don't have to if you don't want to, Midge,' said Pulpy.

'No, no, I do want to.' Midge plucked a red cup off the tray. 'Just as long as I keep drinking water, then I suppose there's no harm.'

'Listen to that!' said Beatrice. 'She's a regular Buddha, our Midge!'

'And might I add a gorgeous Buddha,' said Dan, 'without all that pudge he's got. But still with the curves – she's got those in spades!'

Midge blushed.

'And Buddha's Chinese, which fits with our international theme!' said Beatrice.

'Speaking of which, wait until you see the dining room,' said Dan.

'I'll escort them in,' said Beatrice. 'You take care of the pork.'

Pulpy and Midge followed her into the dining room, which was dark. Beatrice produced a book of matches from the folds of her kimono and lit several candles and an incense pyramid on the liquor cabinet. In the resulting glow they could see a number of afghans tacked to the wall, and four small woven mats arranged around one larger mat in the centre of the floor.

'Where's the table?' said Midge.

'That's the exciting part,' said Beatrice. 'There is no table! Well, we moved it into the garage. Don't you think it's like Arabian nights in here? Now all we need is a belly dancer. And if I have enough to drink you might even get one!' Beatrice flung her arms into the air and undulated in a circle for them. 'Now make yourselves comfortable and we'll join you momentarily.'

Pulpy and Midge eased themselves onto their knees and watched Beatrice shimmy out of the room.

'How are you doing, Midge?' said Pulpy.

'I feel flushed.' She pressed her hands to her cheeks. 'Am I flushed?'

He peered at her. 'I can't tell in this light.'

She shrugged. 'It's not a bad feeling. It's kind of nice, actually.'

He rested a hand on the hem of her slacks, which had hiked up to expose her pantyhose-clad calves. 'Just let me know if the feeling stops being nice, okay?'

She cocked her head at him, and then their hosts bustled in with steaming dishes and the shooter tray.

Dan distributed the plates in a crouch, and Midge averted her eyes as his kurta rode up to a precarious level just below his groin. 'Something wrong, Midge?' He grinned at her. 'You're not fooling me.'

'What are you talking about, Dan?' said Pulpy.

'I've seen this woman put away a pitcher of mojitos like a frat boy. There's no way she's drunk off two shots!'

Beatrice thrust the Jell-O shooters at Midge and Pulpy. 'Then let's have more!'

Midge took one and said, 'Those are nice candles, Beatrice.'

'They are, aren't they?' Beatrice gave her a wide smile. 'But from now on, you're my candle supplier, missy!'

'Burn it and earn it!' Midge said, and downed her shooter.

Dan waggled his eyebrows, and Pulpy pointedly avoided the orange cups and went for a green one.

'Ooh, my employee's feeling feisty!' said Dan.

Pulpy frowned and swallowed hard, forcing the last of the sweet slime down his throat.

When Dan and Beatrice had arranged themselves on the other two mats and everyone had food in front of them, Midge smiled politely and said, 'I think I'm missing my cutlery.'

'We all are!' said Dan.

'That's another exciting thing,' said Beatrice. 'We're going to eat with our hands! What do you think about *that*?'

'Hmm,' said Midge.

'It's easy – watch me!' Dan balanced some peas on a slice of pot roast and fit everything into his mouth.

'Oops, I forgot something!' Beatrice stood up, her kimono parting slightly.

This time it was Pulpy's turn to avert his eyes, but the vodka in his system had slowed his reaction time. He looked away a beat too late and the white flash of their hostess's upper thighs nearly blinded him.

Dan winked and Pulpy glanced at Midge, but she was using her thumb to mash a red shooter into a green one.

'Do you think if I mix red and green together I'll get grape?' She giggled.

'Ho-ho, that's the spirit, Midge!' said Dan.

She furrowed her brow at the two colours. 'Or is that red and blue?'

'So, Dan,' said Pulpy. 'About my job.'

'Yes!' Dan's expression went grave. 'Yes.'

Midge downed the thick, swampy mess she'd made and looked between them. The air swirled with incense smoke.

'The bottom line,' said Dan, 'is that you've got productivity, and then you've got the opposite of productivity.'

Pulpy rested his hands on his folded knees. 'Are you saying I'm not productive?'

'Whoa, whoa. Not quite.' Dan held up a gravy-speckled hand. 'I'm not speaking in absolutes here.'

The three of them sat there, their faces shadowy with candlelight, and then the thumping of tribal drums filled the room.

'I'm back!' Beatrice swooped in and sat down with another plate, its contents obscured by a cloth napkin. 'I can't believe I almost forgot this *and* the rest of the ambience!'

'Is that a world-music compilation you put on?' said Pulpy.

'It certainly is. My, don't *you* have an ear!' Beatrice closed her eyes and swayed to the beat.

'Pulpy knows his music.' Midge said, and smiled at him.

Pulpy smiled back.

'I like this.' Midge rocked a little from side to side. 'It's rhythmic.'

'It's no Winter Flute,' said Dan.

Beatrice opened her eyes and scowled at him. 'You and your woodwinds.'

He scowled back and made a flapping-mouth motion with one hand.

'Anyway.' Beatrice took a deep breath and smiled at Pulpy and Midge. 'So Dan and I went to an Ethiopian restaurant once, and –'

'The food sucked,' said Dan.

She glared at him briefly, and went on. 'The food itself was awful, completely inedible. Honestly, I don't know how those people live. But they had this one thing – they used this pancake-type bread to scoop everything up. So *I* thought, why don't we try that at home? But I couldn't find the recipe, so I got the next-best thing.' She whisked off the napkin to reveal a stack of pale waffles underneath. 'Besides, I bet if they had frozen waffles in Ethiopia they'd use them instead. All you have to do is pop them in the toaster!'

'It's certainly creative,' said Midge.

'Do you think so? I tell Dan all the time that I have a creative streak but he doesn't believe me. The problem is I just don't have enough avenues. That's why I'm doing the front-desk makeover.'

Midge smirked a little. 'And what does the *receptionist* think of that?'

'Nothing.' Beatrice shrugged. 'She's gone. You mean Pulpy didn't tell you?'

The two women stared at him, and he squirmed. 'I thought I told her.'

'Well, you didn't,' said Midge.

Pulpy looked down at his feet in their thin brown socks, the pair that always left a pattern on his skin.

'What happened?' said Midge. 'Why did she leave?'

'She didn't leave,' said Beatrice. 'She was dismissed.'

Midge's eyes widened. 'Why?'

'Inappropriate emails,' said Dan. 'Among other things.'

Pulpy jerked his head up.

Midge picked up a waffle. 'I can't say I'm surprised.'

'Nobody was,' said Beatrice. 'She was a very shoddy secretary.'

Midge washed down a large bite of waffle-supported pot roast with another Jell-O shooter. 'This is like a picnic!' she said.

'It's not a *picnic*, Midge,' said Beatrice. 'It's Persian.'

'Ladies!' said Dan. 'Why don't we all just take our plates into the living room? I'm cramping up down here, anyway.'

'I'm easy,' said Midge, and hiccupped.

'Ho-ho! Let's get out there, then!' Dan stood and offered Midge his hand. She took it, and he hauled her to her feet.

Pulpy stood up on his own and almost lost his balance.

'Head rush!' Beatrice laughed, and grabbed him before he fell over.

The two pairs made their unsteady way into the living room, and then Beatrice sat next to Pulpy on the sectional and Dan sat next to Midge on the divan.

'My, aren't we a merry bunch!' Beatrice reached over and set the shooter tray on the coffee table.

Midge was looking around the room. 'Did you find a home for that plant we gave you?'

Pulpy looked at Dan.

'You know, I'm not exactly sure where I put it,' said Beatrice. 'But I can tell you it's thriving, wherever it is.'

'Oh, good.' Midge nodded. 'I'm glad.'

'Does anyone else find it dry in here?' Beatrice stood up. 'My skin feels as tight as these jungle drums!'

'That reminds me,' said Midge. 'I should probably have some more water.'

'In the desert they just eat lots of salt,' said Dan.

'Then maybe I should have some of that too!' said Midge.

'Ha!' Dan pointed at Pulpy. 'Didn't I say she's a firecracker?'

Pulpy chased some peas around with his waffle. The tiny green spheres rolled across his plate and bumped into each other. 'You did.'

Beatrice wobbled toward the doorway. 'I'll be right back.'

'Watch this, Midge!' Dan aimed the remote at the fireplace and the hearth flared to life.

Midge pressed her hands against her cheeks. 'I like your fire a lot, Dan.'

'It's not as nice as ours,' said Pulpy quietly.

'What was that, Pulpy?' said Dan.

'I said it's not as nice as ours. Our fire at home.'

'I didn't think you had one.'

'We don't,' said Midge. 'It's a video fire.'

Pulpy's shoulders sagged. 'I thought you said we weren't supposed to call it that.'

'Oops!' She covered her mouth.

'A fire on TV is no match for real flames!' said Dan, wielding the remote. 'Ho-ho, get it? *Match*? Speaking of which ...'

'Here I am!' Beatrice floated back in, brandishing a bottle of lotion. 'Oh, Midge, I forgot your water. Why don't you just have another Jell-O shooter instead?'

'Okay.' Midge took one. The shiny red contents jiggled, and she tossed her head back and swallowed the entire thing whole. 'These are really good.'

'You too, Pulpy.' Beatrice sat next to him again. 'We can't have you falling behind, now, can we?'

Pulpy took a green one and held it in front of his nose. The gelatin quivered.

'Go ahead.' Beatrice squeezed his knee. 'Put your tongue right in.'

The alcohol smell was strong. He held his breath and did the shot. He felt the cool mouthful slide down his throat, and the room wavered.

'Now, here's something I wanted to show Midge.' Beatrice held up the lotion bottle and depressed the nozzle, and a wad of golden goop shot out and landed in her open palm. 'It's peach spray lotion!' She massaged it into the skin of her arm with languorous circles.

'How can you spray a lotion?' Midge snorted, and then she was laughing. Laughing away on the divan next to Pulpy's boss. 'Can you make the fire bigger, Dan?'

'You bet!' Dan punched a button and the flames shot up with a *whoosh*.

Pulpy was sweating. He leaned forward and moisture slithered down his back.

'Come on, Pulpy.' Beatrice slid her glistening arm under his nose. 'Take a whiff.'

Undigested waffle and peas and jerk pot roast sloshed around in his stomach, and he set his dish down on the floor.

'Ooh, you nearly cleaned your plate!' she said. 'I hope you saved room for my baked Alaska!'

'Hooo! Are we in the Sahara here? Because I am h-o-t!' Dan flapped his hem up and down to make a breeze, then leaned toward Midge. 'But this lady here is an oasis. Look at you – I just want to dive right in.'

Beatrice shook her head and in a low voice said, 'Dan.'

'Midge, if you think that fire over there is nice, wait until you see *this*!' With a jump Dan propelled himself off the couch and turned so he was facing her.

Pulpy opened his mouth but no sound came out. The already thick air seemed to congeal around him and he sunk further into the deep suede of the sectional.

And then Dan undid his kurta.

'Dan!' shouted Beatrice.

Dan let the tunic fall and the rich fabric slid down, down, down, and then he wasn't wearing anything at all.

Pulpy sat looking at his boss's broad naked back and bulbous naked rump, and there, curling around and over him, was a long lick of red and orange and yellow burning across his bare skin. 'I'm on fire, Midge,' said his boss. 'Put me out!'

Nobody moved. Nobody said another word. And then Midge reached a tentative, drunken hand toward the tattoo and pulled it back again, and she looked away and looked back, and Pulpy was so very far from her, acres of hardwood away and now Beatrice's right breast was in front of him, slicing out from the folds of her kimono. 'Touch it,' she said. 'It's yours to touch.' Her fly-away strands of hair writhed.

And now Dan was reaching for the buttons of Midge's paisley top, those funny swirling shapes all over her, and now Beatrice's kimono was wide open and there was all of her underneath, gleaming at Pulpy, and now Midge was staring straight ahead with big, big unfocused eyes.

She pushed herself back against the couch, away from Dan, and Pulpy nudged Beatrice aside. He hadn't even realized his shirt was gaping open, exposing his concave chest with Midge's love line, which was starting to grow back now, and he stood up and then he was across the room already, in fewer steps than he thought it would take. He laid a hand on his boss's pink shoulder – there were a few dark hairs on it, and the skin was warm – and said in a loud, clear voice, 'That's enough, Dan.'

The large shoulder muscles bunched under his smallish palm. 'What did you say?'

'I said we're leaving. Come on, Midge. Let's get out of here.'

Midge stood up and blinked, and took a deep breath like she was coming up for air.

Behind him, Beatrice yelled at Dan, 'Idiot! What did I say? We didn't even get to dessert! I told you you were moving too fast!'

'And another thing.' Pulpy reached into his pocket and groped for the pager. He took out the small, black rectangle and tossed it onto the coffee table. 'I don't want this anymore.'

Midge rubbed her face and walked over to him, pausing in front of Beatrice on the way. 'I'm going to need my clamdiggers back,' she said.

'Sure.' Beatrice lay on the sectional with the overripe peach smell coming off her in waves. 'I'll bring them into the office.'

With his back still facing them, Dan shook his huge head slowly from side to side. 'You're making a big mistake here, Pulpy.'

Pulpy opened Dan and Beatrice's front door, and smiled a little. 'I don't think I am, actually.'

Dan breathed a long, loud breath out of his nose.

'Pulpy,' said Midge, 'what about our coats?'

'We'll get them tomorrow,' he said. 'Dan can bring them into the office for us.'

'Yeah, sure.' Dan snorted. 'But I think you're forgetting it's winter outside.'

'Well, it'll be spring soon.' Pulpy put his arm around Midge, and smiled wider when he saw that her scallops were starting to grow back. She put her arm around him too, and on their way out the door Pulpy said, 'I'll see you tomorrow, Dan.'

'Uh huh.' His boss stood there with his thick arms at his sides. 'See you tomorrow.'

'*I*'*m getting sleepy,*' *Midge had said near the end of their first date.*

They were in Pulpy's apartment, sitting on his bedroom floor with music playing in the background.

The Fancy Guppy he'd bought her earlier that day was doing laps in Pulpy's favourite mug, from college.

'*Listen to this chord,*' *said Pulpy.* '*It's a really good chord.*'

'*You music people,*' *she said.* '*All chords and trebles and clefs.*' *She pointed to a pen and the notebook he used for song ideas, sitting nearby.* '*Would you please hand me that paper and pen there?*'

He gave them to her.

'*Thank you.*' *She balanced the notepad on her knee and took the pen in her right hand. She flipped to an empty page and wrote* '*Pulpy*' *in a careful, looping script. Then she switched to her left.*

He watched her write his name the same way with her other hand, and when she was finished he held up the paper with the two '*Pulpy*'*s on it and admired the way she had put equal flourishes on both sets of P's. Then he said,* '*If you're tired, I have a bed you could sleep in.*'

She patted his mattress. '*I saw it.*'

'*It's pretty comfortable. I can sleep on the couch.*'

'*You don't have to. It's your bed. We could sleep in it together.*'

'*Well, all right, then,*' *he said.*

'*Do you have anything I could wear? For sleeping?*'

'*Yes, I think so.*' *He opened a dresser drawer and pulled out a sweater.*

'*No, I think that might be too hot.*'

'*Oh. How about a big T-shirt, then?*'

'*A big T-shirt would be perfect.*'

He opened a different dresser drawer and pulled out his favourite T-shirt, with the empty music staff on it. He handed it to her and stood up. '*So I'll just let you –*'

She smiled, and he backed out of the room and closed the door.

'*Do you like candles?*' *she called to him through the wood.*

'*I love them,*' *he said.*

'*I'm glad to hear that! Candles are my passion.*'

He laid a hand on his door. 'I'm applying for a new job tomorrow. Cross your fingers for me, because I think this might be the career break I've been waiting for.'

'They're crossed!' she called. 'Now come back in.'

'Oh,' he said when he saw her. 'My T-shirt looks nice on you.'

'Thank you. I like all the horizontal stripes.'

'Thank you. Well, I should –' He went back to his drawer and pulled out another T-shirt and a pair of boxer shorts. 'I'll be right back.'

'I'll be here,' she said.

'That's good.'

And she was.

ACKNOWLEDGEMENTS

Many thanks to my family (especially Mom, Dad, Cameron, Marcella, Grandma 'Matriarch' Westhead and Kate) and my friends for all of their love and encouragement, always.

Thanks to Mike Stokes for magic and plastic cockroaches.

Thank you to Jim Munroe and the Hoity Toities, as well as the Humber Gals, Lit Crit and Critty for inspirational workshop action, and many thanks to Toronto's wonderfully nurturing small-press community. Thanks also to Fred Stenson and the Banff Wired Writing Program for giving me a huge boost when I needed it most.

Thanks to Lynn Coady for her incredible insight and Pulpster pep talks.

Thanks to Sam Hiyate for having faith in this story and in me.

Thank you to Sarah Selecky, literary light, for endless support and understanding.

Thanks to the Ontario Arts Council for generously helping to fund this project.

I'm grateful to everyone who read *Pulpy and Midge* at various stages and gave me their invaluable feedback: Ryan Bigge, Eva Blank, Beckie Calder, Jeff Chapman, Dad, Gary Flanagan, Jasmine Macaulay, Laura McCurdy, Jim Munroe, Jen Noble, Renee North, Aaron Peck, Susan Purtell, Emily Rossini, Carol Sakamoto, Steve Sakamoto, Sarah Selecky, Gene Shannon, Dana Snell, Ken Sparling, Craig Taylor and Sherwin Tjia (thanks also to Sherwin for his lovely drawings).

Thank you to Alana Wilcox for knowing what made Pulpy tick right from the start, and for taking such good care of him and Midge with her fantastic edits. I'm also grateful for Stuart Ross's keen proofreading eyes. Thanks to Evan Munday, Christina Palassio and the rest of the Coach House folks for all of their hard work and their excitement about this book.

And, most of all, thank you to my husband, Derek Wuenschirs, for (among so many other good things) listening.

Jessica Westhead is a Toronto writer who has published stories in litmags such as the *Antigonish Review*, *Matrix*, *THIS Magazine*, *Geist*, *Taddle Creek*, *Forget* magazine, *Word* and *Kiss Machine*. Her fiction was also included in the anthology *Desire, Doom & Vice: A Canadian Collection*, and her short-story chapbook, *Those Girls*, was published by Greenboathouse Books in summer 2006. *Pulpy and Midge* is her first novel.

Typeset in Legacy, American Typewriter and Linoscript
Printed and bound at the Coach House on bpNichol Lane

Edited and designed by Alana Wilcox
Drawings by Sherwin Tjia
Goldfish photo by Derek Wuenschirs
Author photo by Derek Wuenschirs

Coach House Books
401 Huron Street on bpNichol Lane
Toronto, Ontario M5S 2G5

416 979 2217
800 367 6360

mail@chbooks.com
www.chbooks.com